STORM OF MAGIC

SHADOWS OF CHAOS
BOOK 1

CASSIE GREUTMAN

Printed in the United States of America, March 2024

Published by Fully Invested Publishing

eBook ISBN 978-1-964185-00-2

Paperback ISBN: 978-1-964185-01-9

DEDICATION

To Anya. Thank you for all of your enthusiasm for my work over the years. You are greatly missed.

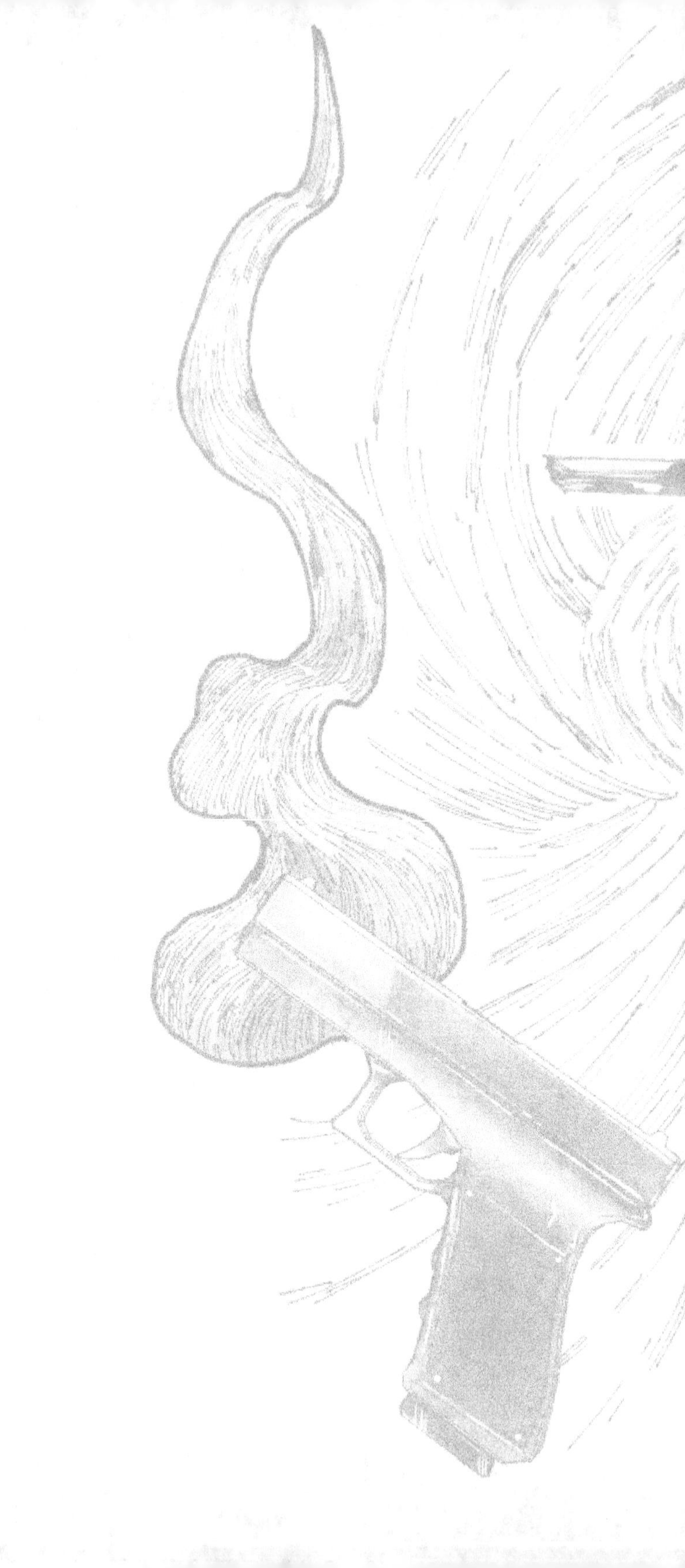

CHAPTER ONE

If I'd thought all the crazy surrounding the fae revealing themselves to the world this week was the worst that would happen, I was about to be proved wrong. Very wrong.

The eggs were cold, but they'd come out that way. I shoved them around on my plate, not really listening to anything my partner Grayson was going on about. A news story about the fae played on the TV over his shoulder, giving me something to look at that wouldn't make him suspicious and figure out that I didn't really care about what he was saying.

The waitress, Tanya, came by and refilled our mugs, filling the air with the smell of coffee and covering up the greasy aroma the place usually reeked of. She treated us better than most of the other waitresses in the area. Grayson's generous tips didn't hurt.

"Jayla. Come on, what do you think?"

I jerked my gaze away from the TV anchor sharing yet another video of the wild things happening in Indiana to look my partner in the face. He gave me a frustrated scowl and looked over his shoulder to see what had my attention.

"Ah. That mess. They should keep it off the air until there's more information. They're just scaring people now."

"People have a right to know what's going on." I gripped my coffee mug in both hands, letting the warmth seep into my muscles. The a/c blew hard enough that I wouldn't have minded a jacket even though it was eighty degrees outside.

"Yeah. But they aren't telling us anything new." Grayson turned back from the TV to his plate. "Just rehashing the same videos a thousand times. That same one was playing when we walked in."

An enormous monster made of rock tossed something at a dragon on-screen. A dragon. Insane. None of this seemed real, but apparently it was, or the department wouldn't be shoving us through the grinder of special training on how to handle the fae.

Like they knew. It was just to make the public feel better. I was under no delusion that my sidearm would do anything against an ogre.

"They should just shove the fae back through their portal and destroy the thing," Grayson said, sloshing his coffee around and grimacing. It was extra burned today. "But you know they won't."

Tanya, who was wiping down the table next to ours, leaned in. "I don't know what they want with Earth, but it can't be good." She nodded at the TV. "Not if that's how they introduced themselves."

I couldn't argue. Every time the story flashed back across the screen, my stomach churned. Protect and serve. How were we supposed to protect against *that*?

The table went quiet for a moment while Grayson shoved his biscuits and gravy into his mouth. Not a normal dish in LA, but he'd been a transplant from the Midwest years ago and that was something he hadn't given up. I couldn't hold comfort food against him with the line of work we were in. The bell behind the counter dinged for an order up. Gizzards. The smell was enough to make me want to head for the car.

"You got Kenzie this weekend?" Grayson asked.

"No," I answered. Keeping it short gave him less to pry into. Besides, if he pushed too much, I might snap back something I'd regret.

"Didn't he have her last weekend too?"

"It was a holiday. One of his holidays."

Grayson grunted. "You should take him to court again. You'll regret missing out on your little girl's life. She'll be going to college before long and not even know her mama."

"She's only three," I said. His words stung. As if I didn't feel like a bad mom already. "I don't want to talk about this." Talking about it only made me question everything in my life. If I didn't have my daughter, at least I had my work. I stood and stretched, body aching from the old cracked booth, and dropped money on the table. The waitress hadn't brought the bill yet, but it would be exactly the same amount as yesterday and the day before.

Not in any hurry, Grayson continued eating.

My radio crackled. "Domestic in progress at a warehouse near Ninth and Hawthorn. Any units in the vicinity, please respond."

"That's us," I told Grayson, then held down the talk button on my radio. "This is 705. Unit 618 responding. ETA, seven minutes." I kicked Grayson's boot. "Come on. Let's go."

"Copy, 705," the dispatcher answered. "Caller advised shouting coming from the warehouse, and screams."

Grayson shoveled another bite in his mouth, looked longingly at his half-full plate, and dropped a twenty on the table. "Let's go."

"Be careful," Tanya yelled after us as we left.

I waved. "Always are." The bell above the door went wild as I muscled through.

I was already getting in the squad car by the time Grayson reached the door. Per usual, he wasn't in any hurry. Saying something would probably just make that fact worse.

Once in the car, I started the engine and flipped on the lights, but waited until Grayson closed his door to start the sirens.

But I didn't wait for him to fumble with his seatbelt. Checking for traffic, I jerked the car out onto the street.

"Hey!" he said. "What's the rush?"

"Someone could be in trouble."

"Yeah, or much more likely, some couple got into it, they're mad and trying to kill each other. We'll get there and they'll have a common enemy and they'll try to kill us instead. You know how this goes."

"That could happen. That does happen. But we don't know that it will happen this time."

"True." He dropped his visor and checked his graying stubble for food, wiping off a bit of gravy. "But based on past experience, that *is* what's going to happen today. Ninety-nine times out of a hundred. You gotta learn when to throw your all in, and when to cool your jets a bit."

I glanced up from the road, forcing my hands to relax on the steering wheel. "Cool my jets? How would you feel if it was T.J. in that warehouse? We treat every person like they're our family."

"Oh, come on. Bringing my daughter into this is low. And treating everyone like they're family is a good way to get someone killed. Trust me, they don't see you as family. And it's only getting worse on the streets. I've been to this warehouse a hundred times in the years I've been on the force. Some homeless person stole some other guy's jacket. That's the kind of thing this call boils down to."

I gritted my teeth as I jerked the wheel to the right, dodging an idiot in a sports car who was too important to move over for the flashing lights, and then braking hard when a car in the other lane finally noticed us and swerved to get out of the way. LA streets. "Whatever, Grayson. If I ever get to the point I see things the way you do, I'm going to quit."

"No, you're not. For the same reason I never did, even when I got injured and could have left. You don't know what else to do with your life. Protect and serve, right?"

He had me there. With Travis taking custody over Kenzie when we'd split, I'd lost the only thing I'd cared about, until I'd gotten into the Academy. Helping people gave me purpose. A reason to be alive, other than the one that I only saw two days every other week.

There. The warehouse. I hit the brake and skidded to a stop, leaving the lights on but flipping the off switch for the sirens. In the background, Grayson called us in on scene.

Nothing looked out of place from here. I opened the door and swung my legs out, keeping the door between me and any potential danger out of instinct. LA was a treacherous place, if your beat covered certain sections of town.

And mine always did. I'd learned the hard way not to assume anything about any type of call. The most benign situation could turn deadly in less time than it took a person to snap their fingers.

Grayson got out of the other side of the car. He seemed less concerned than me, but he always did. He'd seen enough in his thirty years on the force to not get too excited unless something big was going down.

"Hear that?" Grayson asked.

He had much better hearing than I did. "No."

"Screaming, coming from inside." Grayson pulled his weapon and stalked toward the closest door into the warehouse. As much as he hemmed and hawed about things, he cared about people. Now that he knew there was actually a problem, he'd be all in.

I followed, my thick boots protecting my feet from the broken glass and needles that littered the broken asphalt of the parking lot.

We reached the door at the same time. I moved to go in first, but he gently shoved me out of the way. This had been a real fight when we'd first become partners, but he wasn't sexist. He just thought better him than me, and though I'd never admit it, I had a tough time arguing when I thought of Kenzie waiting on me to visit.

When the door opened, I could hear the screaming. This wasn't some regular domestic. The wails made my body go cold, their unearthly tones haunting. Something was wrong here. Truly, deeply wrong.

The first room was dimly lit. After the California sunshine, I had to let my eyes adjust for a second. I nearly bumped into Grayson, who'd stopped cold. I stepped to the side to see what had stopped him in his tracks.

Empty. The entire room was empty of people.

Normally, the entire space was filled, the homeless trying to escape the strong sunlight of a California spring. This early in the morning, there should have been at least twenty people.

But everyone was gone. Their stuff still arranged in different areas, left behind. Backpacks, folded tents, sacks that most likely held clothes. Stuff people didn't leave behind without a good reason.

"This ain't good," Grayson said.

I had to agree. "Should we call for backup?"

"And tell them what? We got a bad feeling about this? We don't have the manpower. They won't send anyone unless we give them a reason."

"Okay then. I guess we'd better clear the place, or find a reason."

The screaming stopped. We exchanged looks. It stopping abruptly probably meant something bad. We picked our way forward, through a tunnel connecting sections of warehouse and into another room filled with empty boxes and trash. Skylights above let light trickle through the dust and grime, but not enough to help much. The whole place smelled. Not even something I could place, just... dirty.

At least it didn't smell like a dead body.

Moving in slow circles, Grayson and I watched each other's backs. I'd been working with him a year, since my first day as a rookie, and it showed in how well we knew what the other was about to do.

We cleared two more rooms, similar to the first one. With each step, my pulse beat a little louder in my ears.

Something scuttled in the next room. I signaled Grayson and he nodded, honing in on the slivers of movement we could see through some old crates. People.

There were two of them, male, 30s, wearing strange clothes, beaten and bloodied. Though neither of them seemed to notice their injuries as they faced off, aggression in every movement.

No weapons. I let a breath out my nose. No dying today. At least probably not with this call.

The men were arguing quietly enough that I couldn't make out what they were saying.

After taking in the room for a moment, Grayson stepped out of the shadows. "Hands where I can see them." He held his handgun in a neutral position, giving the illusion of being relaxed, but could have it pointed in the right spot in less than a second. "We got a call that there was something going on here."

Neither of the men answered.

"Is something going on here?"

I circled around to the side, letting him take all of their attention while I checked the room for other threats. Something about the vibe the men were giving off made my anxiety about the situation tick up.

They looked so calm. So unworried. It was weird.

"Nothing you need to concern yourself with," one of the men said. He was tall, handsome. Dark hair, with dark eyes that bored into Grayson. Even though he never looked my way, I got the distinct feeling that he knew exactly where I was. "You can move on through."

The redhead didn't say a word, just watched us with a predatory gaze.

The feeling that something wasn't right ratcheted up a notch. My hands started to sweat. I'd been in a lot of dangerous situations. What about this one was bothering me so bad?

Either Grayson didn't feel it, or he was better at hiding it than I was.

"Might I ask what caused this altercation?" Grayson said.

"No," the other man answered. He had a strange accent, one I couldn't place.

I'd nearly cleared the room when something caught my eye. Clothing. No. A person, huddled in the corner, not moving.

"Grayson," I said. I didn't need to say any more. He circled between me and the men, giving me the barrier I needed to check the woman and see if she was still alive.

"Hello?" I said as I inched forward. Behind me, Grayson and the men were discussing something, but their tone of voice was still civil, so I concentrated on the woman.

She didn't move.

"Ma'am, is everything okay?"

She turned to face me and I almost stepped back. Her eyes were a brilliant pink, skin white almost to the point of illness. "Help me?" she asked.

Fae. She had to be fae. I took a real step back this time. *Innocent until proven guilty, even if she's fae. This woman needs you.* "You're safe now, ma'am. Are you injured?"

She slowly sat up, raising a trembling hand, and pointed at the men. "Help me."

"Yes, I'm going to help you. Are you hurt?"

"No. I am not hurt." Her voice sounded odd. Not her pronunciation exactly, more her tones.

"Jay!" Grayson shouted.

I jerked around to see what had freaked him out, just in time to see the redhead being lifted off the floor by some invisible force. He clutched at his throat, his feet kicking in the air as he moved higher and higher, easily five feet in the air by now.

The sight of a floating man was strange enough on its own. But he was dying silently. Gasping for air, no thrashing, just pulling at his neck.

I'd holstered my weapon to keep from scaring the fae woman, but I jerked it free now. I tore my gaze away from the man in the air, searching for the cause.

The first man stood perfectly still, a slight smile on his face as the other died above him.

"They're all fae!" Grayson shouted. He squeezed off a round at the man standing on the ground. Red bloomed across his shirt near his shoulder and he snarled, letting the other man go.

The man in the air dropped like a rock, falling fifteen feet to the warehouse floor. He didn't move.

The bleeding fae with the weird powers turned and ran.

"I got this one!" I shouted, taking off after the running fae. I couldn't tell if the other one was dead or unconscious, but Grayson would know what to do either way. He'd had a lot more first aid training than I had.

I dashed recklessly through one of the warehouse tunnels, afraid I'd lose the fae in this mess, before my mind caught up.

Full on speed without thinking would get me killed. Obviously, we needed to get this guy off the streets, but Kenzie needed her mom too, no matter what Travis said.

I slowed a little, my heartbeat in my ears.

The fae ahead of me rounded a corner, and I skidded up to the wall, stopping to look around without exposing myself to extra danger.

This guy had some kind of ability. I wasn't taking any extra chances. Grayson would have called for backup by now. I only had to keep the perp in sight until more people got here.

I peeked around the corner. There, on the far wall, a large ring glowed blue, at least six feet tall and four feet across. Hazy light leaked through a bone frame, making it impossible to see what was on the other side.

A portal. I'd seen one on the news enough times to draw the thing in my sleep. How in the world was there a portal here, and no one had ever found it? If the fae went through, could he come and go at will? If he returned to Earth and killed again...

Something clinked over to my left, and I moved around the corner, slipping behind some boxes, gun raised. "LAPD. Come out, hands where I can see them." Maybe staying quiet would have been the better plan, but instinct had won out.

The fae from the other room walked out from the shadows in the other corner. "No need for that. I could have gone straight through the portal, but I needed to grab a few items. Let me go."

His voice held authority. He was used to being obeyed.

"Not a chance. I just saw you seriously injure or kill someone." My voice stayed steady thanks to the last year of training for intense situations. But my heart? It was about to burst.

"Brave of you. Courageous even." His voice turned to a hiss. "But foolish. I gave you your chance at life. But you choose death."

I raised my gun in time to fire one shot. It nicked him in the ribcage. That shot should have been straight on, but had gone wide. Wide enough that he'd been hit, but hardly seemed to notice. He sneered at me, and something grabbed me around the chest. I tried to shove it free, but couldn't see anything causing it.

He forced the hand holding my gun down, and the next shot I got off in his direction ricocheted across the cement. My heels left the ground, and I dangled in the air with only my toes touching.

An invisible hand clamped across my mouth and nose, and I struggled, fighting to scream. Spots danced in front of my eyes as my brain burned through the oxygen I had left in my system.

Kenzie.

My body went limp, and my gun slipped from my hand.

My daughter's face played on the backs of my eyelids, and I passed out.

CHAPTER TWO

Thud.

Something hit me in the leg. I didn't have enough energy to open my eyes and figure out what. The scents of soil and grass filled the air. Soil? In an empty LA warehouse?

Thud.

I cracked one eye open. Grayson kicked me again, proving that it was him who'd been the culprit in the first place.

A wave of dizziness hit me, and I took a moment to be surprised I was still alive. And not panicking.

But then, I still wasn't with it enough to panic. I blinked a few times, and it helped with the dizziness. Chilled, I reached up to rub my arms and looked around me.

Wait.

This wasn't a warehouse. This wasn't even LA. At least it didn't look like anything I'd ever seen in or around LA. In the entire world, actually. I bit my lip, trying to focus. The cobwebs in my head weren't helping.

"Jay? Jayla?" Grayson sounded worried.

Heck, yeah, he should be worried. Why were we in a forest?

I leaned back and looked up, trees towering above us. Trees, but purplish instead of green. Why were they purple?

"Jay, you've got to get it together and get my hands free. We have to make it back through that portal before we're both dead."

Okay, dead was definitely a powerful motivator. I rolled my head to the side. There. My attacker. He wasn't paying attention to me at all, too busy arguing with the pink-eyed fae woman from back in the warehouse. My hands still tied, I felt around for my gun.

"They took them," Grayson said.

Watching them, I scooted across the cool grass, closer to Grayson.

"Jay?" he asked again.

"Yeah, yeah," I muttered. The world shifted, and I had to close my eyes for a second.

"Are you okay?" Grayson asked. Finally.

"Been better," I ground out. I fumbled around, trying to find his hands. Zap! As soon as I touched the rope binding them together, pain knifed through my fingers. "Ow!"

"What?" Grayson asked. "What happened?"

"It shocked me!" I paused. "Or something like a shock. I'm not sure what to call it."

"Focus, Jay." Grayson went quiet for a second. "Okay then. We're just going to have to leave it for now. Don't be obvious about it, but look behind you."

I dropped down on my back, not minding a second to breathe. Then I turned my head, the grass incredibly soft beneath my face, and blinked. The headache wasn't a nine out of ten anymore, but it was still bad enough to make me foggy.

More odd looking trees. The colors were weird, and the leaves were different shapes too. And there wasn't really any brush, which was weird for a forest, right?

Then I saw what Grayson probably wanted me to be paying attention to. The portal. Glowing on the other side of two angry looking fae. How were we supposed to get back there?

They argued in another language. Even though I couldn't understand a word spoken, the whole exchange felt really aggressive. Were they like Russians or Germans and just sounded that way? Were they talking about the weather?

Or discussing the best place to dump our bodies.

The woman with the pink eyes pulled a knife and stabbed the other fae in the shoulder, driving him to his knees. She leaned down close and said something to him before knocking him flat, her blade pulling free and dripping blood.

Red. Red blood. Strange that it was the same color as mine.

"Keep it together, Jay," Grayson said. "Now's the time, while she's distracted."

I flipped over on my stomach and inched to the left, worming my way to the side of the fae. The one she'd stabbed managed to get back onto his knees. Wow, he could take some serious damage. He'd been shot twice and knifed once in the last hour or so. He bowed his head to her, and seemed to be giving in to whatever it was she had demanded.

That was bad for us. As soon as this distraction went away, her full attention would swing back in our direction.

"What?" the pink-eyed fae asked, in perfect English. Almost a completely different person than the one in the warehouse, begging for help. "You think I don't know you're awake? You think I don't know you are getting ready to make a run for the portal?"

I froze, my mouth going dry. Could she read minds? The clips that played on TV proved that the fae could do things humans couldn't. What tricks did they have up their sleeves that we didn't know about?

She walked over and used the toe of her boot to flip me on my back. "So. The name of the little human who thought she could spoil my plans is J. Just a letter in your human alphabet? You aren't important enough for a full name?"

Were all fae this rude? And could all fae hear as well as this one could? That was a more optimistic assumption than she could read my mind.

Grayson struggled to his feet, hands still bound. "I'm Grayson. Her full name is Jayla. What's your name?"

Using the negotiating skills we'd all had to learn in a clinic a couple months ago. Smart when we were at such a disadvantage.

"You aren't worthy of knowing my name." She didn't even look in Grayson's direction, just squatted down to eye level with me. "You weren't much of an opponent."

"I was there to help," Grayson answered. "I didn't know we were opponents."

She snorted. "Ha. Everyone is an opponent. But you'll either figure that out yourself, or you'll die young." She stood and glared at Grayson. "Who told you that you could get up?"

Grayson stayed standing, somehow staring her down.

"Fine then." The woman whipped out her knife. She lunged at Grayson.

With no time to think, I just reacted. I jumped at her from a crouch, knocking into her at the knees. We hit the ground and rolled.

Or at least I did. Before I knew what happened, she was back on her feet, laughing. "Well! Maybe you do have some spunk in you after all." She yelled something to the male fae in the other language without looking away from me.

I slowly stood, fighting down the nausea my headache sent in waves down my throat.

The stabbed fae walked over and pulled his sword.

I didn't move. Showing weakness was death.

He swung and cut my hands free, flipped the sword over and handed it to me by the blade.

I took it without hesitation.

The woman gave a slight bow. "I am Ghira. And I have nothing to do while I wait for my husband to arrive. Provide me with enough entertainment, and I'll kill you quickly instead of leaving your fate to Faerie." She angled forward conspiratorially. "Faerie isn't kind. Trust me."

The other fae knocked Grayson back to the ground.

She reached behind her and a sword magically appeared in her hand. Not the shorter blades that she'd used until now, but a full-on sword.

This was not good.

I lifted the tip of my sword just a little. Police Academy had not covered sword fighting. If this woman knew anything at all, I was in deep, deep trouble.

Whack! The tip of her sword nicked my blade. The reverberation of the blow made me drop it.

She laughed.

"She isn't trained for this," Grayson said from the ground, still trying to protect me. "How is this amusing for you?"

Ghira turned and kicked him in the face, knocking him flat without his hands to catch him. Blood spilled from his nose, lost in his dark uniform.

"Hey!" I shouted. "How does that make you a good opponent? Striking a man with his hands tied?"

Ghira shrugged. "I never said I was a worthy opponent. Sportsmanship is a human thing." She stepped in closer to me, like she was sharing a secret. "All the fae care about is winning."

When she looked back over at Grayson, I jerked my head toward the portal. One of us had to make it back to let the Army or Chief of Police, someone, everyone, know that there was a portal with an insane fae on this side in the middle of LA

He didn't give me any kind of acknowledgement that he'd seen me, but I didn't expect one. She would notice.

"Take up the sword," Ghira purred, her voice gentle like she was about to teach me how to bake cookies or something.

"Why? You'll just knock it out of my hand again." I had to keep her distracted. Anger was the easiest way to do that. Unless I made her too mad and she just killed me. With the lack of effort it had taken to disarm me the first time, killing me would be absolutely no problem for her.

"Because I said so!" she shouted.

"Wow. Just like my mom." I crossed my arms in front of my chest. Antagonizing an angry fae. Brilliant.

Ghira screeched something in the other language and the male fae walked over. He bent down and picked up the sword from the ground, not looking me in the eye as he held it up.

"Take it." All humor was gone from her voice.

Getting myself killed by making her too angry wouldn't help

Grayson any. I reached out slowly and took the sword, letting it hang loosely in my hand. If only I'd taken fencing instead of gymnastics my entire childhood.

His eyes fixed on us, Grayson inched his way toward the portal.

He was doing what he had to. Without our guns, we didn't stand a chance against this woman. I feinted at Ghira, drawing her attention toward me.

Basically in slow motion, she knocked the sword out of my hand again and cackled.

"Why do you find this entertaining?" I asked. A calculated risk. Maybe it would keep her talking for another minute and I'd avoid being skewered longer. Or maybe I'd make her mad and seal my fate.

"Does it matter? You get to live a few more moments. Isn't that all humans truly have to look forward to?"

"If you have such a terrible view of humans, why were you on Earth?" I picked up the sword, keeping my eye on her. Grayson was only about fifteen feet from the portal now.

The male fae saw me look. No! If he followed my gaze…

I shuffled my feet, trying to get his attention back.

No such luck. He had to have seen Grayson. He didn't immediately raise the alarm though.

"I've been trying to get back to Faerie for many years. But things have changed. Let's just say that fae leadership has had a major shift, and my husband would have a rough go of things in Faerie. The way he lives his life makes him many enemies. But he'll enjoy Earth. Oh, the things I have to show him…"

Her tone didn't imply she wanted him to see the Chinese Theater.

"I haven't seen him in…" she put the point of her sword into the ground, leaning on the hilt as she tapped her chin with her finger. "Sixty-three years."

Sixty-three years? How old was this woman? She had to be in her seventies, unless the fae were pledged at birth or something weird like that.

"I've been trapped on Earth, looking for a way home to him for what seems like an eternity." She moved closer. "Trapped with humans like you. Useless. Foolish." She grinned. "And tasteless as well. If I had any mercy, I'd let you live long enough to try the bounties of Faerie before slaughtering you." She shrugged. "But I don't see any reason to do that."

Faster than I could even get a squeak out, she slashed a small cut across the side of my jaw.

"Now you'll have a scar to match the one on the other side. Or you would if you lived long enough for it to scar." She whipped around and slashed at me again, sliding the tip of her sword through the skin of my abdomen.

I grabbed at the wound. Blood seeped from between my fingers. I dropped to the ground, pain making me grit my teeth. I wouldn't give her the satisfaction of crying out. The wound wasn't terrible. Not life threatening. But it sure hurt like nothing I'd felt in awhile.

"My queen," the male fae interrupted.

"What?" Ghira snapped.

I took her moment of inattention to check on Grayson. He was within a foot of the portal. I snapped my attention back, pretending to only focus on the warm blood staining my fingers.

"Might it not be more fun to see how long she can survive in Faerie on her own?" the male fae asked.

The dirtied tip of her sword dropped again, and she studied me.

Faster. I urged Grayson on in my head. I wasn't quite ready to count the guy fae as an ally, but he knew what was going on and was stalling Ghira. How long would that last? Was he just toying with me too?

"It would be a far more painful way to die." Ghira continued to stare me down.

"What would be?" Hey, my voice stayed pretty steady. At least I could say that for myself. *Keep her talking. Keep her distracted.*

Ghira's eyes sparkled with laughter, making me sick. I'd never seen such glee on someone's face as they thought of another person's death.

"That would be part of what made the whole thing interesting. There are thousands of ways to die in Faerie. And only two I would consider somewhat pleasant."

Grayson slipped through the portal. A pang of abandonment went through me. I shoved it down. I bit my lip, fighting back tears at being left here, alone, to die. But Grayson was doing the right thing.

Was doing what I'd wanted him to, until this moment. People had to know.

"At least leave me with a sword," I said.

"I don't know, Wenslo." Ghira propped her sword up on her shoulder. "We won't be here to see the results. How will that be any fun? We should just kill her. I'm getting bored of this, and Kienthall should arrive at any moment."

"Of course. My queen will do as she sees best." The male fae, Wenslo apparently, bowed.

"Of course she will," Ghira snapped.

Now was my moment. With her ire directed at him, it might be the only iota of a chance I'd get.

Gripping the sword tightly, I tore off toward the portal, one hand gripping the sword, the other holding the wound on my abdomen together. Grayson had enough of a head start. If she found him gone and had time to catch up with him, that was on his head, not mine.

Behind me, Ghira screeched, kicking my legs into overdrive. A few more steps and she wouldn't be able to stop me from going through the portal.

I felt her before I heard her. She slammed me in the back, tackling me. We fell through the portal together, back into the gloomy warehouse in LA. My head bounced off the cement, sending the room whirling. The metallic taste of blood filled my mouth, but I kept it together enough to throw her off me.

Rolling over, I bashed Ghira in the gut with my elbow, stumbling away from her. I took a wild look, checking for help, but there was no sign of Grayson. I'd kept my grip on the sword, and lifted it as Ghira stood and Wenslo stepped calmly through the portal.

I dodged around Ghira and struck at the wall of the portal. Shrieking in anger, she shoved me with her shoulder, knocking me into a crate. I went twirling to the floor.

Ghira stalked toward me. "This has gone on long enough." She lifted her sword, and I scooted away from her until my back hit a wall.

Crack!

After a year on the gun range, the sound processed before the bullet pinged off of the brick behind me.

Grayson slid around another stack of crates and into view, squeezing off another round. I should have known he wouldn't leave me.

This bullet flew wild as well. Grayson was a much better shot than this. What was going on?

Ghira turned to face the threat, apparently not worried about me on the floor.

Big mistake.

I took another run at the portal. A well-placed hit with the sword, and the strange material giving it shape shot off blue sparks and then splintered, just a little.

Another two shots rang out, but I had a job to do. I ignored everything else in the room.

Another swing and the ring around the portal cracked loudly.

"No!" Ghira screamed from somewhere behind me. But she was too late. One more blow, and the portal blinked out of existence.

CHAPTER THREE

I swung around to face Ghira. She stared at the smoking space where the portal had just blinked out of existence with laser focus.

"What have you done," Ghira hissed loudly. Her tone sent a shiver through me. Even as a cop in LA, I'd never heard such hate in four words.

"You didn't leave me much of a choice," I answered. "Grayson, you okay?"

The sound of sirens came into hearing range. Far away, but backup would be here soon.

"On your left," Grayson said from slightly behind me. I didn't turn to look, trusting him to have my back. He must have called for help and then came back for me.

"I told you what this meant to me," Ghira spat out. She didn't seem at all concerned that Grayson had his gun pointed at her, and I had a sword between us. Not being concerned about the sword made sense. But I wouldn't be so calm if someone was threatening to shoot me. Maybe she didn't know what a gun could do.

"She's dangerous, Grayson," I said, like he hadn't seen everything in that other world.

"I know, Jay."

"Do you think we're going to be able to hold her?" I spotted my handgun on the floor, about ten feet past the destroyed portal, where it must have fallen when I'd been knocked unconscious earlier. Before the whole trip through the portal.

"I don't know," Grayson answered.

I eyed my gun, slowly circling around Ghira and making my way over to it.

"You think that thing will protect you?" Ghira snarled. "It's useless against the fae." Okay, she did know about guns. Maybe. She charged me, completely unconcerned.

A shot rang out, but somehow Grayson missed her, only feet away.

Ghira was on me, sword flashing. I barely got my own up in time to meet hers, sending it grating down the blade, sparks flying. She wasn't playing with me. This time, I would die, and fast.

A loud pop, and her body stiffened, teeth clenched.

It took me a second to figure out what had happened. But in that moment, Grayson didn't hold back with the Taser. He held the button until it ran out of juice, Ghira's body twitching and falling to the floor.

I'd reopened the wound on my side. I put pressure on it, trying to stop it bleeding through my uniform, and inched toward her. I bumped her with my boot, completely ready to jump away. She didn't move. "Ha. Not so powerful against a Taser, huh?" I bumped her again for good measure, but didn't even get a groan in return.

"At least this thing worked on her, even if the gun won't." Grayson nodded toward my wound. "How bad is it?"

I pulled my hand away, slick with blood. "Not deep. Just long."

"Go get the first aid kit and show the new lot where to go."

Just because she sprawled unconscious on the floor didn't mean I thought Ghira wouldn't find a way to be terrible. "I'm not leaving you alone with her until she's got cuffs on."

Grayson snorted. "Like you'd be any help if something went sideways. We'd need an army." He bent down to cuff Ghira, moving slowly.

She twitched and he jumped. I didn't say anything though. She made me jumpy too.

The right cuff snapped into place easily. But then Ghira opened her eyes.

"Grayson!" I scrambled for the Taser. Grayson jumped clear and I hit her with a second charge. Her body twitched, one cuffed hand clattering on the cement, then went still. Had it really affected her as much as I'd thought the first time, or had she just been playing a game?

"Crazy fae," Grayson muttered under his breath as he rolled her over and pulled her left arm behind her back, slapping the cuff on.

The sirens stopped outside. The cavalry had arrived.

I slumped back against a crate, taking a deep breath and instantly regretting it when my wound separated again, sending a fresh splash of pain across my abdomen.

Two officers piled through the door, guns drawn. Grayson walked over and started explaining the situation as more of our friends burst into the warehouse.

Let him do all of the talking. I didn't take my eyes off the woman on the floor. She was starting to move a bit again. If the first tase was a standard for how long she would be down, we really needed to get her locked up. Fast.

"Hey," I waved one of the guys over. "We need to get this woman behind bars ASAP."

"Fae?" The word burst out of one of the officers talking to Grayson and spread around the room.

"Didn't dispatch warn you?" Grayson asked.

I lost track of the conversation then. The room swirled a bit. The blood loss wasn't terrible, but my body had been through a lot in the last hour.

Grayson jogged over and leaned down close to me while everyone else concentrated on Ghira. "I've got EMTs here, they're just waiting on the all-clear call. You okay to wait a couple minutes? I'd hate for them to walk in and have that," he nodded toward Ghira, "wake up and go at them."

"I don't need medical care," I said. Yeah, I might be a tough cop, but that didn't mean I liked needles any more than the next girl.

Grayson raised an eyebrow. "You let me see that wound, and then I'll tell you if you need medical care instead of you telling me."

"I thought maybe you'd let this go," I grumbled as I tugged my shirt up. I hissed as the fabric stuck.

Behind Grayson, cops drug Ghira away, one officer under each arm. Though I didn't pray often, I shot up a quick request for them to get her back to the station safely.

"Guns don't work right around her," I called after the crowd of people surrounding the unconscious fae.

"I already told them all that." Grayson poked at my cut and I winced away from him. "That definitely needs stitches."

"Oh, come on, Grayson. It'll be fine."

He straightened and put his hands on his hips. "No, it's not going to be fine. It's going to break back open every time you move for a month." He jabbed his thumb over his shoulder toward the fleet of people leaving. "I don't want to have to pick up some other rookie I don't know. Too much training."

I rolled my eyes, but couldn't help a small grin. Things hadn't been easy for us in the beginning, but we'd worked it out. Now there wasn't any other cop in the city I'd have at my back.

"Compromise," Grayson lifted an eyebrow. "I'll let the EMTs tell you that you need stitches."

The warehouse somehow still had a ton of people in it, even with the whole group escorting the first fae in the city to lockup. A light flashed, making me jump. But it was only CSU taking pictures of the body that had dropped what seemed like forever ago.

Which reminded me.

"Hey, you seen that other fae? The guy?" I shoved off the crates I'd been leaning against and took a second to get my balance.

"No," Grayson answered. "Should I have?"

I checked around us, uneasy. "I don't know. He came through. Before I destroyed the portal."

"Are you sure? I didn't see anything." He walked beside me, heading outside. While he carefully avoided actively helping me, he kept a close eye.

Was I sure? Not really. I hadn't been too concerned with him in that moment. I shrugged. "Everyone should be on the lookout, either way. He gave me the willies, killing that other guy without flinching."

"I'll let the sergeant know. But for now..." He threw open the warehouse door, letting the sunlight stream in. An ambulance was right on the other side, medics at attention. "You're going to visit those people."

I sighed. Might as well stop lying to myself. Hopefully I got some good pain meds out of this. I wanted to forget every moment of this day.

Twenty-nine stitches in the deeper layer of skin across my abdomen, forty on top, and eight in the face. But Ghira had been wrong about the scarring, at least according to the doc who'd put me back together. And she seemed to know what she was talking about when she was stitching me up, so I was just going to believe her.

I fidgeted in the seat next to Grayson. He'd insisted on staying with me until I was done, enduring two hours of debrief with the captain while I was getting sewn back together, and taking me home. While I appreciated it, a lot, I had something I needed to do. And not in front of him.

I watched out the squad car window as we got closer to my apartment. Everyone loved to talk about how much it costs to live in LA. They're right. I couldn't afford to live in a "good" section of town.

At least the place I was in now was more of a home than my last couple crash pads. Someone had taken an old house and split it into six apartments. It would have been drafty in any other state, but thankfully, this was California.

Grayson coasted to a stop outside of my house. He started to unbuckle his seatbelt.

I stopped him, putting my hand on his. "No, you don't need to come in. I'm fine."

He paused, but he stared at me.

"Seriously. It was just some stitches. The doc says I'm good to go back to desk duty tomorrow."

"You should stay home for a couple of days," Grayson said. "The sergeant saw what was going on. She's not going to make you come in tomorrow."

"I know what's best for me, Grayson." I pinched the bridge of my nose. "I'm sorry. That came out harsher than I meant it. I'll be fine. I'm going to go inside, call Kenzie, and then get some sleep."

Slowly he clipped his seatbelt back on. "Fine. But you better text me in the morning and be honest about how you feel coming back to work. It's just a job, Jay."

No. It was purpose. It was something to do other than sit in a lonely house, wishing I was playing with my daughter.

"I'll text you." I opened the door and clumsily got out of the car. Not being able to use my core made movement of any kind difficult. Thankfully, Grayson had sent one of the guys to get me clothes at Walmart, otherwise I would've looked like a murder victim stumbling into the house. He hadn't guessed well on the size, but I was grateful to be out of my bloody uniform.

I trudged toward the door of my apartment, trying not to drop the bag of fast food that Grayson had bought me after my trip to the ER, and digging for my phone in my sweatpants pocket with my other hand. I hit the unlock button on-screen, then had to adjust my belt on my shoulder, the service weapon weighing it down and pulling on my stitches. But there was no way that gun was going out of my sight for a couple days.

Not that Grayson's had helped at all during the fight, but at least my Taser was on my belt as well.

The door unlocked and I waved to Grayson, who had stayed to make sure I made it into the house. He nodded and took off, probably headed straight for the station to get the gossip on our newest prisoner.

Ha. If I ever saw her again, it would be too soon.

I clicked the deadbolt back into place, sat my food on a small table in the entry, and leaned down to pull at my boot strings. Dang. I couldn't bend over well enough to get them loose.

Someone pounded on the door right behind me. I jumped and halfway pulled my gun.

"Jayla! Jay! Open this door right now!" My neighbor, and co-worker, Phoebe. Fifteen years older than me and in the business far longer than I had been, she'd taken me under her wing when I'd moved in beside her. Today she'd been working dispatch, meaning her being here might not have been Grayson being a snitch.

Might not.

I punched the unlock button on my phone and let her in. There was no use trying to keep her out.

"Girl!" The door crashed open and Phoebe's hands went to her black-clad hips. "You look worse than I thought you would! You tell me exactly what happened. I want to hear it in your words."

Something inside of me broke a little. I bit my lip to keep from crying. "Can we go somewhere comfortable?" I headed for the small living room, glad the couch cover I'd ordered from Amazon had come in yesterday. Yeah, Phoebe and I were friends, but that didn't mean I expected her to sit on the old stained couch that had come with the place.

I collapsed into the dish chair I had sitting beside the window to leave Phoebe with the couch. I ignored her dark eyes trying to probe my soul and bent down, working on my laces again.

Still no luck, even sitting.

Pretending to just knock some dirt off my boot, I held back a groan and sat back up.

Phoebe took a look around the room, and did a pretty good job of keeping the distaste off her face. Yeah. I still hadn't picked up any of my personal stuff from my dad's place, and the landlord didn't seem too keen on decorating.

A couch, a chair, and a TV with my gaming systems. What else did a living room need?

"Girl. Enough stalling. You tell me what happened today. When I heard officer injured on the radio, somehow I knew it was you."

My smile probably wasn't very believable. "It was crazy. Some insane fae chick killed a fae guy, then drug Grayson and me into Faerie. I thought we were both going to die."

Phoebe's eyes bugged halfway out of her head, and she fell onto the couch. "You went to an entirely different world? And you aren't freaking out right now? Girl, you might be the first human who's been there! Like, ever!"

Did I admit to her that I was freaking out, just on the inside? That now that I wasn't fighting for my life, all of the terror that should have been going through me earlier had hit me, hours worth of fear smashed into the last few minutes when I'd had a chance to be alone?

"It was quite an experience." We hadn't known each other long enough. Not yet. Not for all of those feelings, all of those fears to get vomited all over her.

"But you're okay?" She asked, concern in every word. "You're not hurt, are you?"

Ah, this seemed like a trick question. With the way gossip spread around the station, I didn't see any way possible that she didn't know I'd gone to the ER.

"Got bumped around a bit, but I'll be fine."

Phoebe raised her eyebrow in that way I'd only seen in movies until I'd met her. She totally knew. Good thing I hadn't lied completely.

"Okay then. Let me whip you up some supper." She bounced on the couch, working her way to the edge. Yeah, a new couch should be on the priority list.

"Nah, Grayson grabbed me something." I hadn't looked in the bag yet, but it was from In-N-Out, my favorite place to grab a late night snack when Grayson and I were working overtime. I had no doubt that all of my top picks were in that bag. It was near bursting.

"Do you need anything else?" Phoebe asked. "Something to drink? Pain meds?"

"I'm good."

She gave me a look again.

"Seriously. Don't you have to work early? I'll be fine. But thanks a bunch for checking in." When she started for the door, I leaned down to work on my boots again. Still no luck. Before I could decide if to ask for her help or not, she had the door wide open.

There was an awkward silence, so I struggled to my feet to follow her and find out what could have made Phoebe stop talking.

Grayson stood on the other side of the open doorway, hand in the air like he was about to knock, mouth hanging open. "Phoebe?"

"Yeah, who's asking?" Phoebe went hands on her hips again. Whenever she got the slightest bit uncomfortable, she went all gangster. She had quite the interesting teen years to back that up.

"Uh, yeah, sorry," Grayson's words stumbled over each other. He'd had a quiet crush on Phoebe since I'd met him, always talking about how good her voice sounded over the radio. Apparently, he'd heard her through the door and recognized that voice. He tipped to the side so he could see me without getting into Phoebe's space. "Jay. We need to talk."

"That doesn't answer my question." Phoebe swung around to look at me. "Jayla, who is this man?"

"It's okay, it's my partner, Grayson. What's up?"

He eyed Phoebe like he didn't know if he should say anything in front of her or not. "Maybe you should sit down. Get off your feet."

My stomach sank. I didn't want to hear what he had to say. It couldn't be good. But I mustered what strength I had left and gave him a look that probably rivaled Phoebe's from earlier.

He sighed.

"I don't know how to tell you this. I'm just going to say it. The fae. She escaped."

CHAPTER FOUR

The words reverberated through my head at least four times before I could choke an answer past the lump in my throat. "Escaped? How? It's only been like half an hour."

"Forest and Joss pulled up at the station, opened the back door, and she was waiting. Hit them both instantly. Somehow she had her cuffs off."

I registered Phoebe's gasp through a haze.

"Are they okay?" Phoebe asked.

"Yeah, banged up a bit, but no hospital trip like this one." He stuck a thumb out in my direction, then kept going. "The fae knew not to stick around. Even someone who can fight like her can't take on an entire LA station. I think the captain had every off-duty cop in for the transfer since we didn't know what to expect. Once she was out of the squad car, there was no stopping her."

Grayson had been right. I should have sat down.

How did a person just deal with this? My throat tightened and I started for the living room, mostly to put my back to the other two.

I was a cop. An LA cop. No one could see my fear. No one could know how my mind raced a million miles a minute, going through every possible scenario, every option, every choice.

"Jay?" Grayson asked from the doorway. "We have no reason to believe you're in any danger. She doesn't have any reason to come after you, and even if she did, no way to find you. LA is a huge city-"

"Shoo, shoo," Phoebe waved her hands at him. He backed up, and she shut the door in his face. "You wait there," she yelled through the thin wood. "I'll come get you when she's ready."

She bustled after me, but I'd already fallen back into my chair.

"Do you want him in here? Because if you want him here, I'll go back and get him."

"Just give me a minute, please." I closed my eyes, but that just made my entire body hurt. I reached to get my boot laces, but couldn't stay bent over long enough. Tears of frustration welled up.

"Oh honey, let me get those for you." Phoebe leaned down and untied my boots, then slipped them off one at a time.

My feet had to reek. I didn't know if to give her a grateful smile or die of embarrassment. I settled on a "Thank you."

"You should have mentioned this earlier," she scolded. "I got you."

Now I did give her a grateful smile. I didn't have people I could count on in my life. Maybe that was changing. She was here, and Grayson... "Uh, maybe let Grayson in now."

"If you say so," Phoebe marched toward the door. I'd probably told her too many stories about how Grayson had been tough on me in the beginning. She didn't seem to like him, and she had just met him. He wasn't that off-putting.

Grayson awkwardly shuffled in, past Phoebe. This was the first time he'd been in my house. He wrinkled his nose, but I was fairly sure his house wasn't any better. Just from knowing him. "I've got people on your house tonight." Unnecessary. But sweet. "I can sleep on your couch, if you'd like." His face was red as he got the words out. He was still in uniform, and looked exhausted. He'd been through the wringer today too.

"Nah, I'll be okay." I waved him over to the couch. "You bought me way too much food though." I moved to go grab the bag, but Phoebe clicked her tongue at me and brought it over. "I think there's plenty for all of us."

Grayson's eyes lit up at the mention of food. It didn't really matter when the last time he'd eaten was. If it was offered, he was eating.

I pulled a burger out, followed by way too many fries for one person, then a grilled cheese. It probably was minus the tomato, like I always ordered it. Someone had thrown in cheese sticks and chicken from Arby's as well as unlabeled tacos.

"Grayson! This is way too much food!"

He swiped the burger, held it up and waited until I nodded in approval. "I didn't know what you'd be craving. So I just had people pick up some of your favorites." He held up the burger to Phoebe. "You want this? It'll be gone in a second if you don't speak up."

Phoebe checked out the fast-food-smorgasbord. "I'll take the grilled cheese."

That saying about was it a bad day, or a bad five minutes popped into my head as I watched my only two friends get to know each other over a fast-food buffet, sitting on my old couch.

This one could go either way. A homicidal fae had almost killed me multiple times, and now was out on the run.

Phoebe laughed at something Grayson said, and I realized I hadn't been listening to them at all.

But seeing them happy took the edge off the stress. We'd call it a bad day with a good ending, and hope for better things tomorrow.

My phone went off at five a.m., same as every morning. But this morning, instead of groaning and rolling over in bed, I groaned and set down my Ps4 controller. Normally I didn't let myself game on a weekday, because I got too caught up in whatever I was playing and didn't get any sleep, but I wasn't getting any sleep last night anyway and needed something to distract me from the fact that there might be a crazy fae woman hiding in any shadow around the house.

The electric bill next month was going to be through the roof if I started a pattern of keeping every light in the house on overnight.

I'd spent the first three hours of not sleeping last night researching the fae. I'd determined around one am that it was useless. Everything online was just speculation. Or, at least, I had no way of telling fact from myth.

I checked my stitches for the fifteenth time, poking at my skin. So far so good. The grittiness in my eyes was actually almost as irritating as the wound at the moment.

I pulled my phone over by the cord to shut off the alarm. There were several notifications on the screen.

The stupid thing had gone off all night. But I hadn't been able to deal with it. I scrolled through the messages. One from my captain, telling me I could have the day off. Nope. I wasn't sitting around here all day. Some funny memes from Grayson, his way of checking on me. A message from Phoebe. And four from my estranged husband, Travis.

"Ah, nooo," I groaned and rubbed my face with my free hand. I'd never called Kenzie last night. At least Travis wasn't being petty in his messages, just trying to make sure I was alright. But that made me feel like an even bigger pile of crap. I called her every night to tell her to sleep well and sing her a lullaby. She was probably freaking out right now. If she wasn't mad at me.

I struggled to my feet and the balance of pain between my stitches and my blurry eyes shifted sharply. I hissed at the tug in my stitches, glad no one was around to see it, and straightened up most of the way before grabbing my service belt with my handgun and shuffling to the bathroom.

"Ugh." One look in the mirror, and I was ready to go back to the couch and hide under a blanket. I looked terrible enough on my good side. When I turned my face and checked out the stitches along my jaw, I cringed. As good as going back to bed sounded, the smell was bad enough to stop me. Fear was a strong smell, and though it had faded, it had left behind a terrible odor that didn't mix well with the hospital smell and sweat.

And I couldn't even take a shower for another twenty-four hours because of the stitches.

It took me forever, but I finally got to where I found myself acceptable. The hospital had done pretty well cleaning me up, but there was still some dried blood on my abdomen that took some time to dab off. My uniform pants rode too high and rubbed my stitches, forcing me to change into jeans. I swallowed the pills the doctor from last night had given me on an empty stomach, which was supposed to be a no-no but I didn't want food right now and knew from experience that I shouldn't let the pain get ahead of the pills. Especially when I was going to be lugging my service belt around over my shoulder for the day.

By the time I was shambling out my front door, it was after 7:30. Unacceptable under normal circumstances, but decent for a morning like today.

The sun was already partly up, beating on the sidewalk. Good. I paused outside my door, hand on the knob, not closing it until I had a good look at my surroundings. Everything seemed okay. A squad car sat with two cops at the street. One of the officers I didn't really know from another shift raised her hand in a half wave.

I waved back even more half-heartedly. I started down the sidewalk on my daily routine of taking the train, but the officer waved me over.

"Hey. Want a ride?" she asked.

"Thanks." I walked over to the car and paused, deciding if the train or the back of the car was worse. Ah well, this car looked fairly new. Hopefully, no one had puked or peed in it yet. I slid awkwardly in, trying not to use my core.

"Where we headed?" the other cop in the front seat asked.

"The station."

The two of them exchanged looks, but neither argued. The woman shifted into drive, and I collapsed back against the seat. Deep breath in, deep breath out.

It was time to find a fae murderer.

"So..." the male officer said from the front seat. He was pretty new, a recent transfer. I couldn't remember his name either. "Did the woman really have pink eyes?"

"Edwards!" The woman driving said. "They told us no questions."

No questions. That made sense. Not until I was debriefed. But this one made sense. They should be on the lookout. "Yeah," I answered. "Pink eyes."

The two up front exchanged glances. After that they tried some idle chitchat, taking turns asking me how I was doing, if I was in much pain. I gave them short answers, grateful I didn't live far from work.

When we pulled up in front of the station, the entire parking lot was full. That wasn't normal. I slid out of the backseat of the patrol car, and banged on the top once. "Thanks. Appreciate not having to take the train today."

"No problem," Edwards answered.

I gave them a little wave and headed for the steps up into the building.

The station was always busy. But today, it was a different kind of energy. People rushed around the room, many faces grim.

Maybe I should have been checking the news this morning, instead of playing Horizon Zero Dawn. But I hadn't been in the right mental place to see any more bad news at the time. Too late now.

Cops I recognized but didn't know slowed their frantic pace and watched me walk by, like I was some sort of celebrity.

Nah. It was LA. Even celebrities didn't get this kind of stare down. "Still kickin'," I yelled, just to clear it up for the whole room.

A cheer went up and some of them clapped. My face started to burn and I hurried toward my desk, ignoring the attention. This was the normal reaction when one of us got back from leave after getting shot or pummeled to a pulp, but it felt a whole lot different on this side of things.

I laid my service belt on my desk, first thing. It would probably be awhile before my abdomen could take its weight.

"Don't sit down." Grayson startled me. I almost glared, but then noticed a whiff of coffee. A cup steamed in his hand. Everyone relied on him to make the coffee here. Somehow he got the machine to put out drinkable stuff, and I wasn't even that into coffee. "The captain wants to see us. She wants to hear your side of things."

I sighed, but I was grateful that he'd stopped me before I sat and I didn't have to try to get back out of the chair in front of everyone. "Let me get a bit of that in me first."

Grayson held up the coffee. "Wait, you think this is for you?"

I glared. We both knew it was. Though he had bags under his eyes and looked like he'd aged a couple years since last night. Maybe he needed it more.

He smirked and handed me the cup, then turned and left, knowing I'd be right behind him.

A sip burned my tongue. Coffee would have to wait a couple minutes.

Instinctively, I grabbed my gun belt. Interesting. Even here, in the middle of the station, apparently I didn't feel safe.

I didn't fight the feeling. I threw the belt over my shoulder, took another small sip of coffee, and followed Grayson.

Grayson waited until we were down a hallway, out of earshot of the din in the big room. "So. How you feeling? Your message didn't get much across this morning."

"Like you're ever open about how you feel."

He stopped walking and crossed his arms in front of his chest. "I complain about how I feel all the time. You complain about me complaining."

I poked him in the chest. "Yeah, sure, you complain about your knees, but don't think I haven't noticed how stiff that shoulder has been." He'd taken a bullet a year before I showed up to annoy him all the time. I didn't know how long those deep wounds took to truly heal, but I didn't need to. It was a good distraction at the moment.

Well. A good try, anyway. Grayson wasn't buying it. "Four words really don't count as a check-in. 'Alive. Coming to work.'"

"It's more than I got from you when you bruised your ribs going over that fence you had no business going over." I brushed past him. I didn't need him to go into the captain's office with me. "Two days, Grayson. You didn't answer me for two days."

He turned to follow me, for once ignoring the pictures of fallen officers hanging on both sides of the hallway. "You know as well as I do that I couldn't let that punk get away. If you'd been the one behind him instead of the one circling around, you'd have done the same thing."

"True." I turned and smirked at him. "But I would have made it over the fence." I left him with his mouth open and paused outside the captain's office.

Maybe I didn't want to go in alone. Surely she just wanted to hear my version of events in person. Our entire department's first brush with the fae. I hadn't done anything I could get myself in trouble by doing, had I? This would be my first one on one visit with the captain.

Grayson moved up beside me. Well. One on two.

I rapped on the door, making sure it had just the right amount of authority, but wasn't aggressive. Hopefully.

"It's open," Captain Harlow called, standing behind her desk. She turned to look at us, and I got a good look at her face. The laugh lines that usually stood out were faded, hazel eyes tired. Her normally impeccable posture was gone, leaving her shoulders slightly bowed. Had she gone home last night?

Papers were strewn everywhere across the massive metal beast of a desk. The captain herself looked rather disheveled, chestnut hair frizzing out of a normally immaculate bun. Both things were extremely unusual.

"Nofsky. Glad to see you looking better today." She nodded to me. "Anderson." A nod to Grayson. "Sit." She didn't wait until we were seated to keep going. "You've gotten me into quite the mess."

"But–"

Her deadpan stare shut me down quick. "I know. It's not your fault. You did the best you could under the circumstances you were in. I'm not blaming you. I'm just stating a fact." She sat down and put her elbows on her desk, lacing her fingers and studying them for a second. "As you can imagine, there are a lot of people who'd like to speak with you. Honestly, I was hardly able to keep them from beating down your door last night, even after going over everything we talked about at the hospital with them. It does help that I make sure none of my officers' home addresses can be easily found, for security reasons."

She paused, then glanced down at my waist, where a bulky dressing stood out under my shirt. "How's your wound? I wanted to stop by your house personally this morning, but I got the call that you were out of there before I could get off the phone with the president."

"Of the United States?" Grayson got out.

The captain nodded.

Of course. Of course this had blown up. This was the second place in the entire world where the fae had made themselves known. It was a big deal. A wave of thankfulness started at my toes. I wouldn't have handled being interrogated by people I didn't know very well last night. She'd taken the hit for me.

"They are, of course, aware that you're here now. Several agents have been waiting to speak with you." I followed her gaze over my shoulder. Two men and a woman stood just outside her office, observing us through the glass. "I hope you've recovered enough to speak with them." She leaned over the desk, and I met her partway. "I would really like to get them out of my hair."

"Yes, ma'am." As if I could say no. We both knew it, but at least she was letting me pretend I had a choice. I should have known there would be questions. Lots of questions.

"Grayson bore the brunt of their questioning last night. You should thank him. He's honestly the only reason they didn't force my hand and make you answer their questions yesterday, and if he hadn't told us that you'd been basically unconscious half the time, I'm not sure even his testimony could have stopped them from knocking down your door. I wouldn't have the authority to tell the federal government no if they really pushed."

"Why didn't you mention this?" I asked Grayson.

He shrugged. "Didn't want to by text, and didn't get a chance to this morning."

"You could have found a way to warn me!"

"You should have expected it," Grayson answered.

"I've never been in a full debrief situation. I didn't know what to expect! You could have-"

"Nofsky," the captain said.

I snapped my mouth closed. She was right, of course. And huge on partner trust, which meant I shouldn't be questioning Grayson's decisions in front of her. "Okay, then. Let's get this over with." I rolled my shoulders back, straightened my spine, and turned to face the federal agents waiting to talk with me.

The captain waved to them, giving them permission to enter. Two walked right in. The third moved to guard the door, keeping the flow of traffic moving against the far wall, out of earshot.

Oh, good. This was going to be on our turf, under our terms. Here, I had people who had my back.

The woman caught my eye first. Short. Dark hair. Possibly Native American, but I couldn't tell for sure. Probably in her fifties, though that was also hard to be certain about. Her height didn't take away from the air of control that surrounded her. Out of the two of them, she was definitely in charge.

The man with her was about my age, maybe a little closer to thirty. He looked like he thought he was Bond, but was probably her rookie.

Maybe he was as good as Bond. I didn't know him.

"Officer Nofsky," the woman said, sticking out her hand. "I'm Agent Bylilly. I've been assigned your case."

I shook her hand.

"Agent Brenner." The man stuck out his hand too.

They both nodded at Grayson, who seemed pretty chill. They must not have been too hard on him last night.

"How about you have a seat? I hear you were injured yesterday." Agent Bylilly gestured toward one of the chairs at the captain's desk. Maybe I should have protested to show that I was fine, but I didn't know how long we were going to be talking, and the stitches were starting to pull.

Agent Bylilly sat on the corner of the captain's desk, ramrod straight. Agent Brenner moved over to stand behind her, where he could keep one eye on the situation and the other eye on the door. Okay. Maybe he wasn't a rookie. It would make sense that they would only send experienced agents to deal with a situation like this.

Though no one had experience with the fae.

Wait. That was actually a big assumption. The federal government could very well have extensive experience with the other world and had just never told us.

"I've heard the story from Officer Anderson," Bylilly said. "And your version of the events that transpired through Captain Harlow.

Now I'd like to hear it straight from you. Please start with when you arrived at the warehouse."

So I did. She made notes as I told her about the walk into the warehouse. About the woman on the ground, acting like the victim. I grabbed the arms of the chair I sat in and squeezed, hiding the tremble as I told her about Ghira and her sword fighting 'lesson.'

"Stop," she said, tapping her pen against her notebook after I told her about Grayson's break for the portal. "Officer Anderson. You didn't mention that you left your partner in the other world."

Grayson looked a little sick. "I didn't have a choice. It was her, or the city. Trust me, I didn't want to."

"I told him to," I interrupted. "It was the best choice we had. The only choice."

Agent Bylilly continued to stare Grayson down. "I agree. That's not what I have issue with. Why didn't you tell us?"

Grayson ran his hand through his hair. "I didn't want you to know I'd left my partner to die."

Finally, Agent Bylilly took her eyes off Grayson, but only to make another note.

"Is there anything else you aren't telling us?" Agent Brenner asked, his tone decidedly less friendly than before.

"No, no. That's it. It happened just like I said. By the time I got back from calling for backup, she'd gotten herself out of that place and was about to take on Ghira herself. Again." He looked at me, eyes moist. "Sorry."

He didn't need to clarify that the sorry was for leaving me, and not about omitting some things from his report. This explained all the extra food and time he'd spent at my house last night. We took care of each other, but I wouldn't have called us friends. Until now.

"It is what it is," I said. "You did what you had to do."

He nodded, but looked away. Maybe he felt better, maybe he didn't. I couldn't tell.

"Officer Anderson, we'll need to have a talk after this," Captain Harlow said.

He nodded again. If there had been something I could do to help him out, I would have done it. But there wasn't at the moment, so I continued my story, finishing with me leaving the hospital looking like a voodoo doll, sewn back together.

Agent Bylilly studied me hard for a moment, like she could see anything I was hiding. Like I would hide anything. I'd seen what this crazy woman was capable of, I wanted her caught more than anyone. "Did you see anyone other than the dead fae, and the other one that was helping Ghira?" Bylilly asked.

"No," I answered. "No one."

"Think about your answer."

I settled back in the chair a bit, doing as she'd ordered. I ran every painful memory back through my head, straining to remember. "No, sorry. No one else."

Agent Bylilly relaxed. "Don't be sorry. That's good news. No other fae escaped into our world while the portal was open."

She could have told me that was why she was asking.

"Now, I have a few more questions for you..."

Her few more questions turned into an hour of being grilled. How any suspect held up under her interrogating, I had no idea. I wasn't even on the hook for anything, and she made me sweat. My head pounded, and no matter how many sips of water I forced down, my mouth was as dry as the Sahara.

"Agent Bylilly," the captain finally broke in. "I believe Officer Nofsky may be struggling a bit. She was injured in the line of duty yesterday."

"I'm truly sorry, Officer." And Bylilly actually did look sorry. "It's a matter of not only national security, but global." She stood and straightened her jacket. "But that doesn't mean the individual doesn't matter." She handed me a card. "If you think of anything, any tiny thing, you call me. I don't care if it's the color of a flower or a blade of grass, I need to know." She nodded at the captain, but continued to ignore Grayson as she'd done the entire interview. "Captain. Thank you for your time. I'll be in touch soon about when we can have some time for follow-up questions."

And just like that, they left.

I finally allowed myself to melt into my seat, fully exhausted. Not sleeping on top of mental and physical trauma from the day before had hit me hard about ten minutes ago, but there hadn't been a thing I could do about it. How long had we been in here anyway? Far too long.

"Am I free to go?" I asked the captain. I checked my watch. My shift hadn't even hit lunch. But I needed to get out of here.

"I told you not to come in today. They didn't get any info out of you that you didn't give me yesterday. This could have waited." She lifted an eyebrow and stared me down. "Yes. Go home. Get some rest."

I stood, awkwardly, but I made it to my feet.

"Oh, wait one moment." The captain stood also, and walked over to a large locker against the wall. She unlocked it and pulled out the sword I'd kind of used yesterday.

"The labs ran every possible test on this all night long. There isn't anything special about it, no unknown metals, no strange hides for the hilt, nothing. It could easily have been made here on Earth." She walked over and held it out to me. "In my opinion, it's yours. Thank you for being a cop I can be proud to have in my station."

I hesitated. Did I want a reminder of what had happened hanging in my house? The picture of Grayson shooting straight at Ghira and missing her popped, unwelcome, into my head. Yes. I did want it. I took the sword from her. "Thank you."

Grayson eyed us both, but didn't comment.

"Anderson," the captain said. "You and I will have our talk later. You're home for the day too, after getting Nofsky home."

"Yes, ma'am." Grayson's voice didn't sound right. A tone I'd never heard from him before. But I couldn't worry about it right now. I had to get out of here.

Officers whooped and hollered for us as we walked out of the station. At least today, we were all a family. I stepped into the sunlight and paused for a moment, face toward the sun.

"I'll go grab my car, just stay here," Grayson said, then trotted off. He never ran unless absolutely necessary. He really must have felt bad. Which made me feel bad. I'd told him to leave me. And I'd meant it. It was the only thing that had made sense in the moment.

It was less than a minute before Grayson pulled up beside me. I tossed the sword in the back seat and slipped into the front, ignoring the belt. Grayson pursed his lips. He hated the dinging sound. I gestured to my side. The seatbelt would lay directly over my wound. He sighed and threw the car in drive.

"Your place?" he asked.

The thought of going home and sitting alone... No. I couldn't handle that. "No. I need to see Kenzie."

He studied me for a second. "Are you sure that's wise? You and Travis..."

"We've been getting along better. And it's Saturday, so Kenzie will be there as a buffer." I leaned back against the seat of the car, closing my eyes. "I need to see her." My reason for living. Her, and this job, trying to help people. Purpose. Everyone needed purpose in their lives.

"If you say so." Grayson coasted out onto the street. "But I'll stay in the car."

CHAPTER FIVE

The drive was quiet. Neither of us was in the mood to talk. Grayson didn't care for Travis very much, some of which was my fault, and some was his own baggage with his divorce years ago.

When I'd moved out of our home, I'd been bitter toward Travis. Far more than he'd deserved. I'd told my side of the story strong and often, and Grayson still looked at Travis like the reason I'd left had been all him.

When really, he'd done his best. I'd needed more, but I'd never told him, trying to be perfect, trying to be everything I thought he needed me to be, the mother I needed to be, until I'd nearly lost myself.

I knew it wasn't great for Kenzie for us to be apart. But it had to be better for Trav.

As Grayson and I pulled up to the small two bedroom house I'd used to share with my family, the front door flew open. Out came my three-year-old, just out of the toddler stage. She grew every day I didn't see her. I swiped at a tear as her little pink sneakers pounded the pavement, in a full sprint toward us, her dark braids flying behind her.

"Mommy!" she shrieked. Her voice was the sweetest sound I'd ever heard, even through the window.

I wriggled my way out of the car. She launched herself at me before

I could stop her, and I couldn't stop the oomph that went out of me when she hit. But it was worth it. I swept her up into my arms, breathing in that comforting scent of watermelon shampoo. She always picked out the same kind when we went shopping. Or, now, when she went shopping with Travis.

"Oh, Kenzie, I've missed you so much!" I said, squeezing her tight. I sat her down, biting my lip to keep from crying out.

Kenzie took a step back and studied me, face going stormy. "You didn't sing last night."

Grayson rolled down the car window and leaned over the passenger seat. "Hey there, kiddo! How ya doing?"

Kenzie lit back up and jumped up and down to get a better look into the car. "Uncle Grayson!" She ran in a little circle, unable to contain her excitement.

Looking over her shoulder, I saw Travis step out onto the porch. My still-married-but-not-really-husband's handsome face was blank, but not hostile. He had a five-o'clock shadow, which was normal. He didn't like to shave on Saturdays. His body language was relaxed, which was good considering I didn't have any right to see Kenzie today. I'd never tried when it wasn't my weekend before.

As he walked over, his green eyes zeroed in on the fresh stitches along my jawline.

"Rough day at work?" he asked, his voice concerned, even with the two of us not sure where we stood at the moment.

I nodded. "Occupational hazard. That's why I missed your calls last night."

"And you couldn't call this morning?" he asked. There was no accusation in his voice, but that didn't stop me from taking it to heart.

"She was a little busy," Grayson snapped out the open window.

Kenzie looked disturbed. She always knew when things were tense, even when I thought we were hiding things well. Supposedly that was a trauma response, which just made me feel like a worse mother.

"What did I miss on our call, munchkin?" I asked, bringing the conversation back to her.

Kenzie launched into an excited account of her week, especially about some new books at the library. Her little voice bubbled with joy, momentarily easing the knots in my shoulders.

I leaned back against the car, exhausted. Coming here after the morning I'd had probably hadn't been the best idea. But it had been exactly what I needed.

Travis studied my face for a second. I looked down, hoping he hadn't noticed the dark circles under my eyes. But he didn't push for details. "Come on in," he said. "I just put on a pot of coffee."

My heart clenched, hard, dropping right down into my stomach. I hadn't been into the house since I'd left them. Left them, and almost... No. I couldn't handle that right now. "Not right now, thanks. I just wanted to stop by and say hi."

I couldn't even squat down to give Kenzie the hug she deserved. I just pulled her in as close as I could. Her little bottom lip stuck out. "You're leaving?"

I nodded.

"Why?"

That was a great question. I chanced a look up at Travis. He was getting mad. This was the only time he truly got angry with me. When I hurt Kenzie. I didn't want to hurt her. It had been selfish coming here when it was about what I needed, and not what she needed. Every time I thought I was doing better, that I might be ready to try and reconnect our family, I did something dumb. I didn't deserve them.

"Mommy had a really bad day yesterday," I said. "I need to go home and get some rest."

"This could be your home too," Kenzie protested.

I almost agreed with her. I'd improved a ton since I'd had terrible issues after she'd been born. But I wasn't where I needed to be yet. I avoided looking Travis in the eye, giving Kenzie another half hug, half pat on the back, and awkwardly got back into the car.

"I love you, baby," I said out the open window, and then flapped my hand at Grayson, hoping he would know what that meant.

He did. He pulled away from the curb.

It wasn't hard to keep it together. A large part of me had learned how to be numb in the two and a half years since Travis and I had separated.

Grayson didn't question me. Didn't talk at all. He just started on a tour of the city, checking on me now and then as I laid my face against the window, eyes closed against the sun.

Eventually he pulled up in front of my apartment. He turned off the car, and we sat in silence for a few minutes.

"You'll feel better after a nap." Grayson finally broke the silence. "I always do."

A nap. Naps had been how I'd dealt with things after Kenzie had been born. They'd never made me feel any better in the past, but I didn't need to let Grayson know that. "Yeah, sounds good." I slipped out of the car. The pain meds were starting to wear off.

Grayson got out of his side.

"What are you doing?" I asked.

He opened the back door and pulled out my sword. "I was thinking we could watch that movie you've been talking about. The one where that woman is trying to get on a game show or something?"

Comedy. His least favorite type of movie, but my favorite. I always said the world was dark enough, why would I want to watch movies that made me think it was worse than it is, but really, the dark movies just made me too depressed sometimes.

"You don't want to watch that movie." I started up the sidewalk toward the house. "Go home."

He slammed the back car door, it always stuck, and followed me, carrying the sword. "Nah. I don't feel like being alone right now."

I paused. Sure, maybe he was being nice. But he'd been through a lot yesterday too. We'd seen a man get killed in front of us, and been completely powerless to help. Maybe he did need someone. His daughter would probably be busy, and he didn't really have anyone else in his life.

"Okay, fine. But I get to choose where we get takeout from."

Grayson grimaced. "Fine. As long as I can get something that isn't too spicy."

I grinned at him, a weak grin, sure, but the fact that we needed each other lifted my mood a bit. "Getting old?"

"You wish." He walked past me onto the porch. "You're stuck with me for a good long time yet. I might even be on the force longer than you are."

I hit the unlock button on my phone and followed Grayson into the house. "Nah. I couldn't be *that* unlucky."

Grayson went straight for the TV while I headed to the kitchen to pop some popcorn. Grayson was truly trying to be a great friend. But right now, I just wanted to be with my husband and daughter. Kenzie had the best way of just making me forget anything else was going on in the world. But they didn't need to see me like this. Didn't need to know that I let the world, the job, affect me.

Dumping half the popcorn in my one bowl, I walked back out into the living room. Grayson already had the movie up and ready to go. He'd propped the sword up in the corner of the room. I avoided looking at it. I handed him the bowl, and sat down with what was left of the popcorn still in the bag.

It was a good thing I'd seen the movie before. As soon as I got into my bowl chair, I started to nod off. I checked on Grayson whenever I startled awake. For as much as he liked to complain about my movie choices, he was sure laughing a lot.

After finishing one movie, I called in for takeout, and let Grayson pick the next one. A full stomach and a boring old western was all it took to knock me completely out.

"Jay?" Grayson said quietly.

I snorted awake. "Huh?"

The credits were rolling on a different movie than the one I'd fallen asleep to.

Grayson stood and stretched. "I'm gonna head home. You gonna be alright?"

I waved him off, struggling to stand up. The movement sent a sharp pain down through my side, and I gritted my teeth, trying to not let it show on my face. Having him here for the day had been fine. All night? Not so much. "I'll be fine. Get some rest."

He nodded, rubbing his eyes before shuffling to the door.

"Don't fall asleep while you're driving!" I yelled after him. He held a hand up to acknowledge he'd heard me, but then closed the door. The latch clicked shut behind him, leaving me in silence. I took the trash from our takeout into the kitchen and threw it away, then rinsed our glasses before slowly working my way back to the living room and collapsing on the couch.

I sat motionless for a few minutes, listening to the hum of the refrigerator and the occasional car passing by outside. Maybe being left alone wasn't as great of an idea as I'd thought. Every time I closed my eyes, I could see Ghira, her pink eyes boring back into my soul.

A sharp rap at the door nearly sent me flying off of the couch. I got myself up, grabbed my gun, and shuffled over to the peephole. Phoebe stood on the other side of the door, her face pinched in concern.

I swung the door open. "What are you doing here?"

"Just wanted to check on you." She walked right past me without an invitation. She was still in her dispatcher's uniform and had probably come here straight from work.

"Did Grayson use me as an excuse to get your number?" I shut the door and locked it, following Phoebe back into the appropriately named living room. It was basically the only space I'd used in the last twenty-four hours. "You know, so he could check in?"

Phoebe bustled about, tidying up and pushing me gently onto the couch when I tried to help. "You need to rest," she insisted. "Have you taken your antibiotics?"

I squinted at a clock. Somehow it was after seven. I must have napped more than I'd thought.

Phoebe's eyebrow went up.

"No, I didn't realize what time it was," I answered. "Grayson? Number?" Maybe some good could come out of this.

The pill bottles were on the end table. She walked over and grabbed them, tossed them to me, gave me a look that said stop asking questions, and then went into the kitchen. "Where do you keep your glasses?" She slammed cupboard doors around for a second. "Never mind." She came back out of the kitchen, glass of water in hand.

Shoving the cup into my hand, she stepped back and crossed her arms, waiting to watch me take my pills.

"I'm not a kid," I grumbled. "Trust me, I want the pain meds."

Her face instantly went soft. "How bad is it?"

"A thousand times worse than a papercut, but not as bad as losing a limb," I answered. I didn't know that from experience, but logic said it was true.

The eyebrow went back up until the pills went down. "Did the doc say how long it's going to take to heal?"

"No. I'm supposed to make a follow-up appointment with my family doc."

"And when's that?" Phoebe asked.

I could feel my jaw twitch. We were work friends, not this close of friends. "I don't have a family doctor. I'll have to find one and then I'll figure it out." If I ran out of pain meds before the pain went away. Otherwise, the ER doc had seemed to do a lovely job, and the stitches were dissolvable.

"Is that the sword you brought back with you?" Phoebe asked, walking over for a better look.

"Yep," I answered. There were probably more questions behind the question, but I didn't have the brain power to figure that out right now.

Phoebe kept talking, but I could hardly hear her. For some reason I was exhausted, even after sleeping all day. The wound hurt, sure, but it shouldn't have done this to me. Phoebe paused, and I looked at her, a dumb look on my face, no doubt about it.

"I'm sorry," she said. "You look exhausted. Let's get you to bed." She shooed me toward the bedroom, following along. "And find me some blankets."

Blankets? "Why?" I asked, feeling like I was underwater.

"I'm sleeping on the couch tonight. Just in case you need something." She held up a finger and shook her head. "Uh uh, I don't want to hear a no. That's what's happening."

I didn't try to argue. There was no real arguing with Phoebe. She helped me get my shirt off and then left while I got around for bed.

"Goodnight," Phoebe called from the living room.

"Goodnight," I called back. "I'm just going to call my daughter real quick."

"Okay. Sleep well."

I got out my phone and hit the video chat button. Time for the highlight of my day, every day.

. . .

As the first rays of morning light filtered through the curtains, I groaned and rolled over, my eyes fluttering open. The next thing I noticed after the light was the endless throbbing of my wound. Grr. How long was it going to hurt like that? I sat up slowly, wincing as my side protested the movement.

I hit the bathroom and ran a brush through my hair just in case Phoebe was still out on the couch, then made my way toward the living room.

The couch was empty. Time for more pills. I'd need food before I took them. I shuffled into the kitchen. There was a plate with an omelet on it sitting on the table, a note next to it.

I limped over to the table, picking up the note. It was Phoebe's neat handwriting. "Had to run early. Eat something, and take care of yourself. -P." I smiled faintly, then loaded up a quick bite of the omelet.

Grabbing my phone, I stuffed more eggs into my mouth. I was famished, which didn't make sense. I normally skipped breakfast. Going through my messages, I went past a text from Grayson telling me how much he'd hated my movie choice last night, and another from Travis just checking in, then opened one from Captain Harlow. "Meeting with Agent Bylilly at 9 a.m. at the station. Don't be late." I glanced at the clock. It was already past 8:30. She'd sent the message at just after eight the night before, but I'd already been in bed. Growling under my breath, I hurried to get ready, each movement sending jolts of pain through my side. I stuffed my pill bottles in my pocket. Who knew how long today was going to take.

On my way out the door, I paused, looking at the sword still leaning in the corner. Sure, I had my gun. But that didn't really make me feel safe anymore. I'd take the sword, but just in case Bylilly had any questions about it. That way the captain didn't get in trouble for sending it home with me.

Sure. Made perfect sense.

Despite having absolutely no reason to think Ghira cared about me even a little, I couldn't help but think that if we ran into each other, it wouldn't end well. Surely we wouldn't run into each other, right? Not when she was trying to avoid the LAPD.

The same two officers were parked outside my apartment this morning. I moved as quickly as I could over to the car, not even asking before sliding in. Edwards gave the sword a weird look, but didn't ask.

"Station?" the female cop said.

"Yes, please. And fast. I'm late."

She grinned over her shoulder. "You got it. Just don't tell the captain."

While she sped toward the station, I tried to figure out what other questions Bylilly could possibly have for me. I couldn't come up with any. But, that's why she was a federal agent and I was just a beat cop.

We pulled up in front of the station in record time. I held my side as I climbed out, then reached for the sword. "Thanks again."

"You got it," Edwards said. "Anything for the cop who went to Faerie and back."

"The "and back" is the important part," the other cop said, grinning. I was going to have to learn her name.

I'd just started up the steps when a familiar figure caught my eye. Grayson. Good. I wasn't going to be alone today.

Reaching the top, I moved in to stand by him. He didn't say anything.

"Come on, you can't still be sore about the movie," I said. "It's a good movie!"

I looked up when he didn't answer to find Grayson's eyes intent on me, like a junkyard dog on an intruder. But something was wrong. Very wrong. Pink. Those weren't Grayson's eyes staring at me. They were pink. His lips moved, and I almost missed the beginning of what he said. "Your Grayson is not here at the moment. I think we should talk."

I stumbled back. The voice was Grayson's, but had another voice overlapping it. A voice I would never forget. Ghira. "You'd better leave his body," I snapped at Grayson. My voice came out strong, even as my heart tried to leave my chest. What was happening? How was this happening? "Now. We have nothing to talk about."

"Wrong." Grayson walked away, headed down the stairs toward an alley on the other side of the road.

I looked wildly around for help, but the street was empty. Was this some fae ability? What could I do? How was she controlling him? What could she make Grayson do? He'd risked his life for me the day before yesterday, throwing himself into danger to save me. My grip tightened on the sword.

Today I'd return the favor.

CHAPTER SIX

Following Grayson, possessed by Ghira, into an alley may not have been the most stupid thing I'd ever done in my entire life, but it was definitely up there, right under losing Kenzie and Travis.

Grayson stopped, turned, and waited for me. He stood completely still in a way that was so un-Grayson like that I would have known it wasn't truly him even if Ghira hadn't spoken. Or I would have thought he had a stroke. My fingers tightened around the hilt of the sword I'd been given as a memento of the last time I'd clashed with Ghira.

"I now know anything this one knows," Ghira said once I was in earshot. "Keep that in mind as we chat."

Chat. That's what she was calling this. A chat. A fae being was inside one of two people I called friend, and speaking out of his mouth, and she thought we were just having a chat.

"If we're going to chat, why don't you come out and face me?" I asked. Was all of her in there? Just her consciousness, and her body was somewhere else? Was she off buying a coffee and controlling Grayson at the same time? What else could she do? My body went cold as a thought hit me. Why wasn't she just controlling me? Why was she forcing someone else, and not just making me do what she wanted?

"I'll get right to the point," she said, ignoring my demand that she actually face me. "You closed a portal I spent an inordinate amount of time building. I'm unhappy. I want it back."

So much for the she had no reason to go after me thing that I'd been telling myself for the last twenty-four hours. "Because you want to unleash your crazy husband on the world."

Grayson smiled, but it was way too creepy for Grayson. My stomach turned, and it wasn't just the rotting garbage strewn around the alley causing it.

"Do my intentions matter? They shouldn't. Not when you have far more important things to worry about. And I think you got the wrong impression. My husband isn't crazy. He's just a little... sadistic."

What exactly could she make him do? Would he be able to stop if she told him to injure himself? My gut said no. "Don't hurt him." I wasn't giving anything away. If she could see his memories, she knew how much I cared about Grayson.

He paced, but it was a lithe, controlled movement that wasn't his own. "I won't, if I don't have to. Keep your sword sheathed. I have something I need you to do for me."

My stomach sank. This wasn't going to be good. "What do you need me for? You built your portal without me once. Why spend the time tracking me down, forcing me to help you?"

"Time," Grayson spat out. "Time is exactly the problem. I've been building that portal for fifty years. The items necessary to complete such an intricate gateway are nearly impossible to find."

Good. The thought of her husband joining her on Earth almost made me shiver. I didn't know anything about the man, but if he was anything like her, we didn't want him here. Why did he even want to come? I held it together so she couldn't see how much the thought scared me, but barely.

"Kienthall has waited for years. Cut off from Earth, starving. And now, with the new queen, Faerie has become a dangerous place for him."

Starving? My attention stuck on that one word. Okay, yeah. This was super scary.

Grayson stalked over and leaned into my personal space, not blinking. "Opening a new portal would take far too long. But to reopen the old..." He crowded in closer, making me stumble back. "All I need is you."

I scrambled away, getting out of reach. All she needed was me? I bit my lip, keeping my face still.

I stepped back farther, with more control than the frantic movement of a moment ago. Grayson didn't follow. "There's no use running, girl." The voice was Grayson's, but the mocking tone was not. "I know everything about your life now. Everything about those you love. If your blood doesn't open this portal, I will ensure that theirs seeps through the ground, an offering to the fae you kept from their destiny."

She was bluffing. She had to be. No way she could just know everything. She was a bully. If she'd wanted to kill me, I'd be dead.

"Where's your real body?"

Grayson grimaced. Apparently, that was a question she didn't want me to ask.

If I stayed, Grayson and I might end up hurting each other. I had to call her bluff. "I'm walking away. And you'd better leave Grayson."

Turning on my heel, I closed my eyes, waiting for a sword in my back. When it didn't come, I took a step away.

The sword didn't come, but the words that did cut deeper than a sword. "I think I may pay a visit to Kenzie. Surely she would love to meet a superior being, wouldn't she?"

My throat tightened, and I had to fight to keep myself from whirling around to face her. I couldn't let her know how deeply her words had cut.

"I told you. I know all things this one knows. Including the home the two of you recently visited. And I promise you, that if you don't help me achieve everything I want, your daughter will suffer."

Once I had my face under control, I turned back toward Grayson. His face twitched when he saw me, and for a second I saw my friend. He was fighting back. His eyes shifted, pink to brown, brown to pink.

"I know you. I know the places you visit, where you sleep. Everyone you call friend. Make it easier for us both and give yourself over now." The words were nearly growled. Grayson stumbled, fighting himself.

"No. Now leave my friend alone." I stalked closer, glaring. What could I actually do? Nothing came to mind. I couldn't hurt her, not without hurting Grayson. My chest tightened, the feeling of helplessness I knew all too well working its way up my neck, trying to take control.

"If you resist, they will die. One by one until you have no one left. Starting with the one you care about the most. Now which one is that?"

His voice was deadly serious. No bravado, no show-boating. Complete sincerity. I could give myself over, die, and doom the city, if not the world to a maniac with superpowers, or I could let the people I loved die.

I got up in Grayson's face. "Touch a hair on any of their heads, and you'll regret it. You'll never reopen your precious portal without me, and if you hurt any of them, you'll never see me again."

Grayson literally growled at me, a guttural sound that nearly sent me packing. But then his eyes went back to brown, and he collapsed to the ground.

I dropped down beside him, rolling him over. "Grayson? Grayson!"

He blinked at me, his eyes staying their normal beautiful brown.

"Are you okay?"

He blinked several times, and I sat back into a squat, looking down at him. This had happened because she was after me. He could have gotten killed, because she wanted me.

And now, the rest of my loved ones were in danger too. And there was nothing anyone could do about it. Not if Ghira could control people.

"I'm so sorry, Grayson. I don't want this coming back on you. I'll send help. Please, don't look for me."

He fought his own body, struggling to get up. But I wouldn't let something happen to him. Not because of me.

I walked away, not looking back. Because if I saw him helpless on the ground a second more, I wouldn't be able to leave him like that.

Running was out of the question. I was still in too much pain. But I could get away from here. Go somewhere else, give myself a chance to make a plan.

I couldn't just leave Grayson there on the ground. Maybe Ghira controlling him had damaged him somehow. He needed help. I walked away from Grayson, playing perfectly confident in case Ghira could still see through his eyes. I was anything but confident. But I marched toward the station to find him help.

There. Phoebe, uniform perfectly pressed even though she worked from behind a phone, was just walking inside.

"Phoebe!" I jogged over, an awkward gait, but still faster than a walk. "Grab someone and go check out that alley. I think I heard something weird going on. I'd check it out myself, but..." I gestured toward my abdomen, the stitches there a great reason for me to not get into a scuffle and giving me an easy out.

"Hendricks just walked inside! Give me one second!" She ran for the station door, somehow able to move faster in platforms than I could in boots.

As soon as she yanked open the door, I split. Well, split as fast as a recently injured person could.

If that monster could control people, everyone was safer with me gone. Could she control them indefinitely? Could she make them do anything she wanted? Would her ability work on more than one person at a time? Why wasn't she just forcing me back to the portal, why mess with Grayson at all? Tons of questions, and no way to get answers.

My forehead broke into a cold sweat. I ducked down an alley on the other side of the station and leaned against the wall for a second. Blaming the churning in my gut and the way my body protested that short jog on the trauma I'd sustained the day before yesterday was a whole lot better than admitting the truth.

I had no idea what to do. No idea where to go. And the thought of Ghira hurting someone I loved... I turned my face to the cool brick wall and let the roughness ground me.

I couldn't stay here. I had to go somewhere.

And I had to warn the people Ghira could use against me.

Panic knocked the air out of my lungs. I scrambled for my phone, fumbling with the unlock code before punching Travis's name in my recents list.

"Hey, Jayla. Everything okay?" His voice nearly made tears spring to my eyes. He made me feel safe, even though we weren't together anymore. It was probably weird to him, me calling at this time of day.

"Travis, listen to me." He went silent on the other side of the phone. He had to know something was wrong, just by my tone. "I need you to get Kenzie and get out of town. Go visit your parents, go on a mini-vacation, whatever. Just don't tell anyone where you are."

"What's going on?" His voice went hard. That meant he was in processing mode. Good. I wasn't one to overreact, and I'd never done anything even close to this. He'd know it was serious. "What's wrong, Jay? Where are you? Does this have something to do with the stitches in your face?"

I put a hand to my stitches on my abdomen, the pressure helping with the throbbing, just a little. "Don't think about me right now. Think about Kenzie, and get out of here."

"How far away does she need to go?"

That was a great question, actually. Could Ghira control him from anywhere? Could she make him hurt our daughter? Did she have to be within a certain radius to push her will on others?

I looked around at that thought, sure she'd jump out at me at any moment. "As far as possible. I gotta go." I clicked the end call button while he was still talking. A year ago, that would have made me feel good. Now, I just felt alone. Very alone.

"Jayla?" Grayson's voice snapped me back into the moment. "Jay!"

"Jayla!" Phoebe's voice joined his. "Jayla Nofsky, you get out here this instant!"

No, no. I couldn't let them find me. Were they even in control of themselves right now? Or was she using them to get to me?

I stumbled up the alley, away from the voices. Did Grayson remember what had happened to him? Or had he just woken up in that alley, unsure of how he'd gotten there?

I needed to start making notes. Looking for weaknesses. But for now, I just needed to get somewhere safe.

Pausing at the end of the alley, I leaned against the building again as I checked the road. No one. I had one more call to make. One more person to worry about.

My hand trembled as I dialed my dad. He definitely wasn't in my recent calls. Limping along, I listened to the dial tone until it dumped me in his voicemail. I couldn't stop the wave of relief that hit me. I wouldn't have to talk to him.

Convincing him to leave home would be nearly impossible anyway, but at least this way, I'd tried.

"You've reached the voicemail of Reverend Raymond Elric. Please leave a message, and he will return your call as soon as possible. If this is an emergency, please call the church," his assistant's voice told me.

"Dad. I ticked off an extremely dangerous criminal, and now you aren't safe. Get out of town for a few days, do some fishing or something. I'll call back when it's safe." I paused. "I... I... love you, Dad. Bye."

I moved out of the shadow of the alley and limped forward into the sun, my side hurting more than it had even in the initial injury. I didn't have a destination in mind, I just needed to get away from here.

A cop car cruised around a corner, and I ducked back into the shadows for a moment. Grayson probably had the whole force on high alert. Not only was I avoiding Ghira and anyone I cared about, but the whole LAPD until I could explain why I'd run.

The squad car turned, and I inched back out onto the street. I needed to find a base of operations. Somewhere to lick my wounds and figure out my next move. Somewhere no one would think to look for me, but where I'd be relatively safe.

And then it hit me. I had just the place.

The chop shop I paused in front of was the exact opposite of what the movies showed. Catering to the elite of the city, the store front looked more like a vintage car dealership than a criminal base, with old classics behind two-inch-thick tempered glass. Not that anyone would be dumb enough to try and pull off a smash and grab here.

All the better to fool anyone who came this way. Sure, Abeyta's Timeless Classics made plenty of money from legitimate business. But Mr. Abeyta didn't seem to think it was enough, and sometimes you just couldn't get parts for an old car in any legal way.

A friend had introduced me to Ricardo Abeyta back when I'd joined the force. The old man ran his shop with honor, and gave the LAPD enough leads that they left him alone.

Mostly.

The front door had a large sign that stated Visitors By Appointment Only. I ignored it and shoved my way inside, awkwardly dragging the sword I still somehow had a hold of. There wasn't any obvious announcement when I walked in, but I'd probably set off fifteen alarms around the place.

Cool air hit me, along with the smell of cedar. That was new. Mr. Abeyta didn't like to pay for air conditioning. Maybe he was getting soft in his old age.

The showroom hadn't changed in the year since I'd been here. Millions of dollars in inventory lined the walls, shined until a person could see them from outer space. Not a speck of dust. I'd eat off of this floor with less thought than eating off the plates at some of the diners Grayson insisted we go to.

I didn't know a lot about cars, but the baby blue one on the other side of the room was enough to catch my attention.

No one in sight. But there were footsteps in classy sounding shoes clicking closer and closer from one of the hallways. I leaned the sword against a wall and made sure to keep my hands in sight, wandering over to get a better look at the blue car.

Not that I probably looked like a customer, but I didn't know who would be coming to greet me.

A hulking boxer type sauntered out, perfectly casual. He wasn't tall, but he didn't need to be to make me know I'd be in trouble if he came after me. I would have thought a man like him would be uncomfortable in the suit he wore, but he seemed perfectly at ease.

He nodded to me. "Mr. Abeyta will see you."

Without waiting for an answer, he spun on the heel of his fancy shoe and clicked back up the hallway.

I, of course, grabbed the sword and followed, without even questioning how he knew what I wanted.

Rows of doors lined the hallway. The whole place gave off more of the feel of a hospital than a car dealership, with no names on the doors and everything the same bright white.

Muscles opened the last door on the left and gestured for me to go through.

This was the farthest I'd ever been into the place. Mr. Abeyta had met us up front the time I'd stopped here with Hank.

Stupid. Stupid! Why had I thought this was a good idea? Only because I needed someone Grayson didn't know, someone no one I cared about really knew. But asking a criminal for a safe haven? Was I insane?

The office did nothing to put me at ease. This space couldn't have been more different than the sterile hallways. Dark wood covered the walls, heavy drapes blocking the light from the window behind a massive wooden desk at the back of the room.

Behind it sat Mr. Abeyta himself. Elbows on the desk, fingers steepled in front of him. He wore a dark suit, custom fit to his frame. The man was old enough to be my grandpa, but he looked younger than Grayson. He didn't speak, leaving us in uncomfortable silence.

"Ah, Mr. Abeyta..." I stopped there. I should have come up with something when I was out in the showroom instead of gawking at the gorgeous cars. Somehow leading with a crazy fae was after me and I needed a place to crash until I figured it out didn't seem like a good opening.

"Jayla!" He stood and swooped around the desk. "So nice to see you. How's Hank?" He paused for a second to eye the sword, but then pulled me into a hug.

"He's fine, sir," I managed to get out while trying not to flinch away. "I just saw him last month. I'm surprised you remember me."

"Of course I remember you." He leaned back to study my stitched up face, less intimidating now that he was standing and smiling. The smile especially. He took another look at the sword I was holding, but still didn't mention it. "If you are family with Hank, you are family with me. Now come on over. Tell me why you're here." He moved back around the desk and sat primly on the edge of the chair behind it, just for a second, before giving in and putting his elbow on the desk and resting his chin on it. "Are you needing information on someone? Do you have something juicy for me? It's been too long since I heard a good bit of gossip."

How honest did I get? Really, other than him thinking I was crazy, there wasn't any reason to hold back, and I had the news of the century for him. "I do have a warning for you."

He snapped up straight, face cold.

"There's a fae woman loose in the city," I said. "She's trying to build a portal to let more fae into the world. And from what I gather, they aren't very friendly."

Thankfully his face softened a little, and went thoughtful. "That is interesting news. I'll have more questions in a moment. What are you hoping to trade for?"

"Somewhere to stay for a couple days. To just lay low and look into it, that's all I'm asking."

He stroked his chin, freaking me out a little while he considered my request. After a moment, he nodded. "I can offer you a room in the guesthouse. It's not too far from here and you'll have plenty of privacy. But," he leaned forward, his eyes on mine, "I'll need you to keep me updated on anything you find out about this fae woman. Information like that is valuable to me. I don't know how much I like the idea of getting involved in fae business, but it seems like we may have the choice taken from us. If you stay, I need you to promise me something."

"Anything," I said immediately. Desperation wasn't a good negotiator.

He raised an eyebrow. "You don't know me well enough to make that promise. But I'll tell you what it is anyway. If this fae woman comes knocking on my door, I need you to leave. Even the guesthouse. I can't risk my family for someone else's problems."

"Of course." I tried to hide the absolute relief that almost covered my face, but probably hadn't stopped it before he'd seen something, the shrewd old man. If he figured out I wasn't going to be some fountain of information, I had no doubt I'd be out on the street again, friends with Hank or not.

"Though, on second thought, it may be better to put you somewhere other than the guesthouse." His shark smile showed off several gold teeth. "There are others staying there that aren't as, shall we say, friendly toward police as I am. Now. Shall we have a little chat about this fae woman?"

How much did I tell him? I needed to have information to give him to make him believe he needed me. For once the fact that all that the news had playing for the last few weeks was videos of the fae in Indiana had actually been a good thing. Apparently it freaked out the criminal world as much as it did the law.

"I don't know a lot more than what I just told you, actually. But I'll keep you in the loop."

He cocked his head and eyed me for a second. "Strange that you need a place to stay if you don't know much. But that's your business, not mine." He let the quiet try to force me to say something for a long moment. I didn't let it. "I have a friend. One who knows far more about the fae than anyone else I can find." He pulled out a pad of paper, wrote something on it and then tore the paper free. "He may be able to help you with... whatever it is that you need." He stared me in the eyes, not blinking. "But this is not a favor. I expect to be compensated."

I had to fight against my dry mouth to get any words out. "Of course, sir. We made an agreement."

"Good, good." He smiled, cheerful again. "Carlos." The door swung open and Muscles politely gestured for me to walk through into the hallway. "Good luck, Ms. Nofsky."

He even remembered my last name? I couldn't remember the first name of ninety percent of people I met. Maybe coming to him had been a worse idea than I'd thought. What kind of favor would he ask of me? Would he let me free after only giving him info on Ghira?

Only time would tell.

As I followed Carlos out of the dealership, I looked down at the slip of paper. An address, hopefully of the place where I was supposed to stay, and two phone numbers. One with no name, which I assumed was Mr. Abeyta's, and a second one. Dr. Ian Thompson, fae expert.

Fae expert? That seemed like an exaggeration. The human world had only learned of the fae last month. But I wouldn't argue. I would take any lead at this point. I had nowhere else to go, no one else to ask for help.

My life, and the lives of my family, could very well rest in his hands.

At this point, my bumps and bruises from getting knocked around by Ghira were competing with my stitches on the pain scale. I needed to get to the safe house, lie down for a few minutes and make a plan, then call this fae expert.

How could he even help me? What did I want to do about Ghira? Locking her up would be ideal, but would she stay there? Did I kill her?

How could I even think about intentionally killing someone? That was murder. But look at what had happened the last time she'd been arrested. Yeah, maybe the LAPD would be better prepared this time, but how could they really prepare when we didn't know anything about the fae?

I made a note on my phone. Ask about weaknesses. Oh, and why guns didn't seem to work right around the fae. Abilities.

Yeah, I did actually have a lot to talk with the doc about.

I shuffled out into the street.

"You okay?" Carlos, Mr. Abeyta's goon walking behind me, asked.

I waved a hand.

Apparently, he took that as not okay. He popped his phone out, and made a call in Spanish. As I put the safehouse address into my phone, a sedan pulled up in front of the dealership.

Carlos stepped forward, opened a back door, and gestured for me to get in. "He'll give you a ride to the safehouse. But he doesn't speak any English, so leave him be."

I glanced at my phone. A mile, according to the map. Yeah, not walking a mile in the heat right now would be much better.

"Thank you." I repositioned the sword I'd been hauling around for no good reason, threw it into the car, and slipped past him to slide in. The driver didn't even wait for me to put my seatbelt on, just pulled away from the sidewalk as soon as Carlos had the door closed behind me.

I leaned back against the warm leather seat and closed my eyes. Food should probably be pretty high on my priority list right now, but I didn't feel hungry. At all.

If I knew for sure this guy didn't speak English, I'd just call the fae expert now. But that was actually a bad idea, because it would probably be a long conversation, and I'd need a pen and paper.

I shifted in my seat, trying to find a position that didn't hurt.

There wasn't one.

Thankfully this section of LA wasn't as busy this time of day, and the mile only took us ten minutes. The car cruised to a stop, and I slipped out. "Thank you," I told the driver. He may not speak much English, but he would get the idea.

He nodded, then started to pull away, barely giving me a chance to pull the sword out and slam the door.

The house he'd dropped me in front of could only be described as dilapidated. I didn't care at the moment. As long as there were no bugs, I could probably fall asleep on a bare floor and not wake up until tomorrow.

I limped to the front door. Did I knock? I didn't really want to surprise anyone, so I rapped on the door twice.

A woman yelled in Spanish, but I didn't catch what she said. There was a small commotion on the other side of the door before it swung open. A Hispanic woman in her fifties stood on the other side, wiping her hands on her apron. She lifted an eyebrow at either the sword I carried or my sewn up face, but didn't mention either thing.

"Come in, come in. Ricardo already told me you were coming." And then she turned and walked away.

I'd never heard anyone call Mr. Abeyta Ricardo before, not even

Hank, the friend who'd gotten me interested in becoming a cop. It was weird.

The house was almost as warm inside as it was outside when I stepped through the door. But for everything else, the difference was nearly magical. The interior of the house was clean and well-kept, decent furniture and polished wood floors. The aroma of something cooking filled the air, but I couldn't place what it was.

"Hello?" I asked. The woman was gone.

"Just a minute, I don't want to burn my custard." The voice came from the back of the house, down a hallway.

Did I follow her? Were there things here that, as a cop, I really shouldn't see? I didn't know. I just took stock of the living room where I stood, being careful not to look nosy. Nothing special about it, other than there wasn't anything personal. No pictures of family, no books or knickknacks.

The woman bustled back out. "I'm Valeria. You can call me Tia Val. I'll show you to your room, let you rest a few minutes." She looked me over even harder than she had at the door, gaze critical. "And then you must eat." And just like that, she took off again.

I followed her down the hallway, past a kitchen much too large for a house this size, and into another hallway, this one lined with doors. She threw open the door to the first room and gestured me inside.

As soon as I stepped into the room, Val slammed the door behind me. I jumped about a foot in the air, nerves shot, pain keeping me from thinking straight.

A glance around the room showed a small one-person bed, a tiny wooden desk hardly large enough for the chair that matched to fit underneath, and a lamp. As minimalist as a bedroom could get, but immaculate. I'd take it for sure.

I stumbled over to the bed, propped up the sword within reach, dropped my service belt beside it, and sat down, resisting the urge to just flop across the blankets. The last thing I needed right now was to pop some stitches.

I placed a hand over my bandages. They were hot to the touch. Weirdly hot. Surely the wound wasn't infected. With as many antibiotics as the ER doc had put me on, that didn't seem possible.

Thankfully I'd taken them to the station with me this morning, not knowing when I'd be home. It was about time for another dose, and my pain meds.

But first, I needed to see what was going on under those bandages. I peeled back the top layer, and heat radiated from the skin beneath. Maybe it wasn't as hot outside, or in here, as I'd thought. Maybe it was me letting off all the extra heat.

I peeled back the second layer of gauze, and light burst from the skin underneath, blazing around the entire room.

CHAPTER SEVEN

What the...

I touched my bare, glowing skin, and jerked my hand back. How was my skin that hot without burning away?

This was not good. Really, really not good. I sat on my hands to keep myself from poking at it again, not able to look away and hyperventilating a little. What did I do about something like this? Who did I call? I couldn't go to the hospital. What if I'd brought some weird disease back from that other world?

I scrubbed at my abdomen, like that would help something under the skin, yelping when I bumped a stitch.

No, no, no, this couldn't be happening. Not after everything else I'd been through this week. All the wild possibilities went through my head. Maybe the ER doc had left a light in there. Ha. And it just hadn't shown up until now? This had to be something to do with Faerie. There was no other explanation. I'd never seen anything even close to this, even in movies.

Okay. Okay. No hospital. They might lock me up, keep me there in case it was something dangerous, and leave Ghira easy access to me. No contact with friends, not ones that Grayson could have accidentally revealed to Ghira.

That left... The fae expert.

I literally had no other options. I fumbled with my phone with one hand, and shoved my shirt back down with the other.

Nah. I pulled my shirt back up. Yep, the light was still there.

I hit the send button next to the doctor's contact info that I'd saved in the car. The phone rang twice, then went to voicemail.

"You've reached Dr. Thompson. Leave a message." Cryptic, and in a young woman's voice. Maybe his daughter or assistant? Mr. Abeyta had specifically said the doc was a man.

"Ah...," I sat on the line, stupidly not knowing how much to say. "Hi, Doc. Mr. Abeyta gave me your name and number. I have something very important to discuss with you. If you could get back with me as soon as possible, I'd greatly appreciate it." I paused again. Did I leave my name? It didn't seem safe. And if I said anything else, he might think I was crazy and refuse to meet with me. Just my number, then. "Thank you." I hung up.

Now what? I couldn't just wait around. I could be a ticking time bomb right now for all I knew. I peeked under the hem of my shirt. Still a bright glow, but not enough to hurt my eyes at this point. Was it actually better, or was I getting used to it already?

I unlocked my phone to do a quick search for the doc, and noticed six missed calls from Trav. Yeah, I'd probably given him quite the scare earlier. He deserved better. I'd call him as soon as I looked up the doc.

Google gave me ten million results for Doctor Thompson. Obviously that wasn't going to work. I tried Doctor Thompson + fae, but that didn't help at all. Doctor Thompson and fairy tales, Doctor Thompson + myths gave me the same results. I should have asked Mr. Abeyta for more information. An address, where the man worked, what he was a doctor of. But I'd been too exhausted, too out of it to think like a cop.

Nothing for it then. Either call Mr. Abeyta and ask for more specifics, something that didn't sound like a good idea at all, or just wait. I didn't want Mr. Abeyta regretting giving me his number and blocking me. Waiting a bit it was.

I brought up Travis's contact info. My hand trembled for a moment as I stared down at the screen. I'd never changed the picture I had saved for him. Me, Kenzie, and him, at her first birthday party, frosting on my chin and smeared across her face, the biggest grin covering his. What I wouldn't give to have this back right now.

I tapped his name.

He answered on the first ring. "Jay? Are you okay? Where are you? What's going on? I'm coming to get you. We'll get you out of the city-"

"No, Travis." His voice filled me with desperate need. Need to see him, to see Kenzie. Need not to see them, to keep them safe. "I just called to tell you I'm still alive. That I'm getting things handled."

"What things? No one knows anything. Grayson won't say a word, but he sounded mad when I called. Did you run out on him too?"

I almost snapped back an answer, but a little voice stopped me.

"Mommy? When are you picking me up?"

I froze, hot tears prickling in my eyes. "As soon as I can, baby. You know I miss you and want to spend every minute with you, right?"

"Miss you bigger, Mommy." I almost couldn't take the sadness in her voice. Sadness that was there because of me.

"Are you both somewhere safe?" I asked.

"We're in the car," Travis answered. "We're-"

"No," I interrupted. "Don't tell me."

We sat there in awkward silence for a moment. "I'm taking Kenzie somewhere. You don't even know the place. But then I'm coming back for you. And if you make me search that entire city Jayla, I swear..." he stopped himself, probably for our daughter's sake.

"Please. Just stay gone," I answered. "I'm going to hang up now. And you might not hear from me for awhile." The silent moment we shared this time was sad. Fearful that this would be the last time we talked. "If you don't hear from me again... I love you. Both of you."

"We love you too." Travis's answer was instant, without a pause. He'd always said he loved me, even through everything a couple years ago when I'd lost custody of Kenzie.

"Love you, Mommy!" Her little voice made the tears I'd been trying to hold in begin to fall. They had to stay safe. Had to stay away from me. Ghira was terrifying enough on her own. What if this light was something contagious? They *had* to stay far away from me. I'd never forgive myself if something happened to one of them because of the mess I was in.

"I love you to the moon and back, Munchkin. I'll see you as soon as I can."

Somehow I found the strength to punch the end button. But then I collapsed on the bed and let the tears flow, the stress of the last twenty-four hours too much to handle.

My phone buzzed, making me roll over and pat the bed, trying to find it. What time was it? I squinted at my phone screen, trying to read the clock. Two p.m. I'd slept two hours.

I rubbed at my eyes. A text. From Doctor Thompson.

If there is something you'd like to discuss in private, please meet me at my office. The short sentence was followed by an address. He must have heard the hesitancy in my voice when I'd left him that voicemail.

The text had come in over an hour ago. Crap. Would he still be at his office?

I hit the dial button and tried to call. It went straight to voicemail.

Now what? Did I go, just hoping he would be there? Try calling again in a few minutes? What kind of hours did professors work?

I moved to get out of bed, bumping my stitches. I winced automatically, but after a second, realized it hadn't hurt. I pulled up my shirt slowly, not sure if to be more afraid that the light I'd seen earlier had been a fever dream, or that it was actually there.

Okay, yep, still there. I closed my eyes, taking a deep breath in through my nose. It was still there, and I still felt fine. Nothing to be afraid of.

Did it have something to do with why my stitches didn't hurt as bad anymore? Was it a living thing? A disease? I couldn't wait and just hope that this fae expert would call me back again. What if this thing was eating me from the inside out?

I stood and tucked my shirt firmly into my pants. I needed to get some different clothes. And a burner phone. The last thing I needed was for Grayson to show up here with the entire police department, all targets for Ghira to possess.

The sword was still tipped up against the desk. Did I take it, looking like some weirdo, or leave myself defenseless? There were plenty of weirdos in LA, I was probably fine carrying it around. People would think it was a fake. But at the same time, it wouldn't help me much against Ghira anyway.

Leave it. But I stuffed it under the bed before heading out of the room. No reason for it to sit out in the open.

"Hello?" I called as I walked toward the kitchen, not wanting to startle anyone I shouldn't. No answer. The house was empty, but there was food sitting on the table. Tia Val must have left it for me.

I checked the address the fae expert had texted me online while mowing down some pasta salad. Almost on the other side of town, near the museum. Of course. At this time of day, it would take me an hour to get there.

If I stopped for a burner now, there was a chance I'd miss the professor. If I didn't, there was a very good chance that the LAPD would have a warrant to track my phone and I'd have officers on my doorstep.

Worse, officers on Mr. Abeyta's doorstep. Hopefully I wouldn't have to come back here, because it would be too easy for them to find at this point. Which meant I could lose the sword. I froze for a second, undecided. Then went back to the room and fished it out from under the bed.

I made a quick call for a cab, then turned my phone off. A cab I could pay for with cash. Uber or Lyft would tell anyone with access exactly where I was going.

The wait for the cab was excruciating. Falling asleep, no matter how badly I'd needed it, had been a dumb move. If I missed the professor because I'd needed a nap...

Finally, the cab pulled up.

The driver waved me in impatiently. I hid the sword, like he hadn't probably seen it when he pulled up, as I slipped into the back seat and gave him the address. "And I need to stop at a gas station on the way."

He shrugged. No doubt he got a lot of stranger requests every single day. Being a cop in LA put all the crazy on display, but cabs were actually the front lines.

The stop at the gas station was as fast as I could make it. I bought some jerky even though I wasn't at all hungry. I should be by now, it had been hours since I'd eaten anything but pasta salad, but my body was numb.

Thankfully there was an ATM sitting right outside. I'd taken out the max cash allowed. After the phone, jerky, and some caffeine, I still had plenty for the cab with some left over.

We pulled up right at 3:13. With the pit stop to buy the phone, my estimate of an hour had been spot on. Being a cop was good for knowing traffic patterns and estimated time frames. Yay for those little superpowers, right?

I paid the driver. He raised an eyebrow at my low tip, but I didn't have anything extra at the moment. Who knew how long I'd be on the run, and going back to the safehouse would be a big risk. It was a last resort if I didn't have any other choice, but if I could help it, I wouldn't be going back.

The building he dropped me in front of looked like it used to be some college or government offices. There weren't any signs announcing what the building was used for. I straightened up and marched toward the front door, no doubt looking a little crazy with my service belt thrown over one shoulder and my sword over the other.

I caught myself reaching for my stitches and put the energy into flexing my hand instead. I didn't need anyone seeing that weird light. Some things couldn't be explained away, and this was one of them.

The main door was unlocked. I walked in and paused, a hallway stretching out in front of me with no reception desk. I let the door swing closed, and the sound boomed down the hallway, marble floors making the sound reverberate. I cringed, feeling like a librarian was going to come out and yell at me.

But there was no one in sight. It was late for this kind of place. Maybe they were closed.

Fancy brass lights were spaced along the wall, every six feet or so. The doors were covered in ornate carvings of plants. This had to be a private institute of some kind.

At least the doors had placards in here. Greek Mythology. Egyptian Archeology. History of the Mayan Civilization.

Ah, here we go. Celtic Legends. This had to be it. I paused in front of the door. Did I knock?

Nah.

I pushed the heavy door open and slipped into a small waiting room. Murals of old fairy tales I mostly didn't recognize covered the walls. One looked familiar, but I couldn't place it. Finally. A person. A young woman with bright red hair sat behind a desk at the end of the room.

I walked over, and she looked up from a book she was reading, blinking at the interruption.

"How may I help you?" she asked.

"I'm looking for Doctor Thompson. I left a message for him earlier, and he said to come on over."

"Oh, yes." Her face brightened into a huge smile. "He's expecting you. Right this way."

She slipped a dollar bill into her book as a bookmark and stood, walking over to another door behind the desk. She waved for me to follow her, not acknowledging the sword. Maybe it was normal around here. Educated types got away with weird stuff like medieval weapons.

Nothing about this situation felt out of place. But for some reason, I had the jitters. I ran my hand over my belt, just to reassure myself that my service weapon was still in place.

In place, and ready to go.

Ghira had no way of knowing I'd end up here. She couldn't, right? Not unless she found Mr. Abeyta, and I really couldn't come up with a way she could have done that. I hadn't even known where I'd go when I'd fled the station.

The receptionist led me through two more small rooms, these

completely unlike what we'd been in so far. Sloppy, with bookshelves overflowing with old tomes and artifacts.

We stepped through a doorway into yet another room. On the other side, a man in a white medical jacket stood with his back to us.

"Doctor Thompson. The woman who called earlier has arrived," the receptionist announced me.

"Thank you, Denise."

Why did that voice sound oddly familiar? I couldn't place it.

I shifted, uncomfortable. Something was off. I'd learned to listen to my intuition over the last year being a police officer. My hand went to my gun.

"I was hoping our paths would cross again, Jayla." How did I know that voice? Doctor Thompson turned around, and I got my first look at his face. Not Doctor Thompson. Wenslo, Ghira's henchman. "We have much to discuss."

CHAPTER EIGHT

Seriously?

Doctor Thompson and Wenslo were the same person?

I jerked back, my gun coming out of its holster on auto-pilot. The receptionist squeaked and jumped away from me.

This couldn't be. I didn't have anyone else to turn to. This was literally the only option I had to find help. My only chance of not dying, or worse, letting an insane fae into the world.

Well. Another insane fae.

"No need for that," Wenslo said.

"At this range, it would be impossible for me to miss," I said. "Even with all that weirdness from before. What do you want? Why are you here?"

The receptionist backed away more, but in for a penny, in for a pound. I swung around and motioned for her to move over by Wenslo. Did she know who he was? Was I giving him a hostage?

"Stop!" I yelled. "Don't get any closer to him!" I probably looked crazy at this point. But it didn't matter. The receptionist froze, about five feet from Wenslo.

"Truly, we don't need to have this type of stand-off. Allow Denise to leave, and you and I can discuss why you're here." Wenslo didn't seem bothered by my gun. At all. Or my attitude, either. I doubt the sword would make him pay any more attention than the gun. He just seemed like that kind of guy. I set the sword on a nearby table, making sure I had an extra hand to brace my gun, never taking my eyes off of him.

He looked significantly better than the last time I'd seen him, and wasn't showing any signs of the injuries he'd taken that night in the warehouse.

"I can't let her go. If I do, she'll call the cops," I said.

"Aren't you a police officer?" Wenslo asked, eyebrow up.

"Well, yes." He had me there. "But I don't want any others here for this conversation." None of them could know I'd brought something back from Faerie with me. I didn't want them knowing anything that they could accidentally pass on to Ghira.

"Denise," Wenslo said gently. "Would you please go into the other room and shut the door? Don't try to call anyone. The officer and I are on amicable terms."

Amicable terms? We were far from amicable terms. Sure, he'd let me escape Faerie, but he hadn't done anything to help while Ghira beat on me during my sword "training." Of course, he hadn't defended himself against her either. What had been with that?

Wenslo gestured toward another door in the back of the room. "There is no other exit from that room. It's used for storage. How about Denise heads in there, gets a nap, and forgets you were ever here?"

Holding a civilian hostage made my insides crawl. Not as much as when Ghira had described her husband, but enough to make me want to agree. I held out my hand to Denise. "Phone."

Denise looked from my hand to Wenslo. When he nodded, she dropped her cell in my hand. I motioned toward the room and followed her over, keeping an eye on Wenslo. Denise opened the door, and a quick peek showed a small room with random crap spread around in it.

No second exit.

Denise went in and shut the door behind her. I whirled to face Wenslo, tossing Denise's phone on a desk. I let the barrel of my gun point down, but only because I didn't want to let my arm get tired. I knew what this man was capable of.

"We haven't been properly introduced," Wenslo said.

"I don't have a habit of introducing myself to murderers. Makes it harder for them to find me if they start thinking of ways of getting back at me for locking them up."

"Murderer?" His eyebrow lifted again, and I got the distinct impression he was enjoying this.

"You killed that other fae." My teeth ground together. I didn't like feeling helpless. And seeing that guy die hadn't really processed yet, with all of the other things going on over the last twenty-four hours. "Right in front of me."

Wenslo walked toward a shelf on the other side of the room.

I jerked my gun back up to train it on him.

He just held up a pitcher of what looked like sweet tea, grabbed a tumbler sitting beside it, and poured himself a glass. "I didn't kill him." He took a sip, watching for a reaction.

He wasn't going to get it. What a drama queen.

"I clearly saw you choke the man to death."

He took another slow sip. "I'm going to give you one of the secrets of the fae. Just to prove to you that we can work together. But you mustn't tell anyone. Ever."

Like I'd agree to that.

When I didn't answer, he sighed in disappointment. "Fine. The fae can't die in the human world. His body remains here, but he is now chained to the realm of Faerie."

"What? Like a ghost?" That was a lot to take in, but nothing would really surprise me anymore. The guy was probably lying, but I had no way of proving it. And I needed him. I lowered my gun.

"Let's say I believe you. Why'd you do it?"

He moved over to a chair and settled in, draping himself over the back. "Ghira told me to. And until she reached Faerie, I had to do as Ghira wished."

"Why?" This guy gave off the vibe that he didn't do anything he didn't want to do.

"I'd told her I would. And so I had to."

That was a bad excuse. "You'd just do anything she told you to? Hurt anyone she wanted?"

His jaw twitched. I'd gotten him there, just a little. "I think that's enough one-sided questioning. What do you plan to do about Ghira?"

I bristled a little, but this was the entire reason I'd come to find him. "I don't know."

Wenslo laughed, and it almost made me squeeze a round off to get him to stop.

"What? What's funny?"

"A human, admitting they don't know something." He smirked. "I find that highly amusing." He sobered. "Ghira, on the other hand, is no laughing matter."

"Don't you work for her?"

"No!" He threw his glass, shattering it against the wall. The scent of mint filled the air as he struggled to calm himself.

I kept a safe distance, but these displays were a normal part of a cop's life and I'd seen similar things a thousand times. I just waited it out. And made a mental note of how I'd accidentally punched one of his buttons.

"I was coerced into helping her reach Faerie. Now that she has achieved that, I am free." He tugged the collar of his jacket straight, his face going back to neutral. "Now, it is you and I who share a mutual goal."

"Oh really?" I asked. "What's that?"

"To kill the witch, and not allow her knave of a husband to enter your realm."

Kill her? My heart dropped and bile rose up in my throat. Sure, that had come up as an option, but to actually name it as our goal? I'd never killed someone before. Never seriously harmed someone. Protect and serve. That's what we signed up to do. There were terrible exceptions, but most of us took that very seriously.

Protect and serve. There was probably no greater service I could do for the human race than to remove Ghira and the threat of her husband from the equation. But first I needed to know more about who we were dealing with.

"Tell me about the husband," I said, leaning back against the table behind me. It was amazing how one little slash across the abdomen could make me exhausted all of the time. Or maybe it wasn't that at all. Maybe it was the weird light. But I couldn't ask Wenslo about that until I knew he wasn't going to just run off and tell Ghira about it.

"Kienthall?" Wenslo asked, like that word meant anything to me. He must have seen my thoughts on my face. "That's his name. Her husband." He looked serious now. "He's... more of what your human horror stories like to create than Ghira. She's only driven. He's..." Wenslo paused again. "Shall we say, he enjoys the pain of others, and leave it at that?"

"No," I said. His eyebrows shot up, like he was surprised I didn't just go along with what he'd said. "I need to know everything I can about him. If I know about him, I can work on a plan for if he does make it to Earth. Does he have an ability like she does?"

Now he smiled, more of a smirk, really. "You met Ghira's ability, did you?"

When I didn't answer, he continued.

"Yes. Kienthall does have his own ability. And he'll use it to have his fun, if he makes it here." Wenslo leaned forward to meet my eyes. "Trust me. You don't want to see what he thinks is fun."

I shivered. I didn't trust Wenslo on many things, but I got the feeling that this? This I could trust him on. "How am I supposed to trust you when you tried to kill me?"

"Tried to kill you?" he asked, tapping his chin. "Oh, you must mean at the warehouse. I wasn't trying to kill you." He smiled that weird smile again. "Trust me."

Ugh. Trust me. No one who could actually be trusted would be saying it over and over, and I'd never heard someone use that phrase so much. And I'd probably never trusted anyone less. I knew what Ghira's motives were. "So. How do we stop her before she can bring him through a portal?"

Wenslo smiled. A creepy, serial-killer level smile.

"We visit the museum."

Visit the museum. Visit the museum, he said. Like that was going to solve my problem of a visitor from another world with superpowers, who happened to be trying to kill me.

"And that will help how?" I asked, after he didn't continue.

"There's an item there that will be most helpful when it comes to fighting Ghira." He walked over and knocked on the storage room door. "Miss Denise? You're free to leave as soon as you hear us head out. It'll only be a moment."

She didn't answer. Hopefully she wasn't too traumatized. Maybe she was taking that nap Wenslo had mentioned earlier.

"You just expect me to waste my time following you around?" I asked. "You haven't even told me what we're going to see."

"I thought that in the interest of saving time, you'd prefer we walk and talk." He headed for a chair. "But, if instead you'd prefer we stay here…"

He had me there. Was I on some type of timeline with this light under my skin? I couldn't ask him about it now, with Denise on the other side of a thin door. If I even wanted to ask him about it. What if he thought it was something terrible and killed me? Forced me through a portal somewhere to take it back to Faerie? I was torn. But that could wait. It wasn't threatening my family right now. "No, no. Let's go. The sooner we get this over with, the better."

He gestured for me to go ahead of him out the door. I hesitated a second, but then started that way, grabbing the sword off the desk. I stopped. I couldn't very well carry a sword into the museum. In fact, I'd have to leave my handgun here as well. Maybe that's what Wenslo wanted, why he'd chosen the museum. There would be decent security there.

Nah. He didn't seem nervous of my gun at all, and if the whole scene with Grayson trying to shoot Ghira was an indicator, he had no reason to be.

I shivered, the thought of being defenseless clawing at me. Surely I could hit him if I was this close. He'd been hit before, at the warehouse, even if he seemed fine right now, I knew what I'd seen.

Wenslo walked up beside me. "Ah, my old sword."

I hadn't thought of that. He might want it back. I was strangely possessive of it now, after earning it by getting myself thrashed in a different world. But it was his.

As if he felt what I was thinking, Wenslo raised his hands. "It's all yours now. But it does have a spell on it that you may find handy." He raised an eyebrow, as if asking permission.

A spell? Not only did the fae have abilities, but they could also affect inanimate objects? Not sure what else to do, I nodded at Wenslo, who patiently waited for my answer.

At my nod, Wenslo commanded, "Wane."

And the sword shrank. I nearly dropped the tiny object that was left, jumping enough in place to make Wenslo smirk.

"Whaa..."

"Gain." The sword, thankfully still in its sheath, grew back to normal size, weighty in my hand.

Could I do that? Without asking permission, I said the spell word out loud. "Wane."

Nothing happened.

I glared at Wenslo.

"It's not enough to say the word. If so, it could come up by accident. You must put force behind the word, and prove to the sword that you know what you're doing."

Prove to the sword? Whatever. Here went nothing.

"Wane," I commanded.

And the sword obeyed, shrinking to the length of my thumbnail.

"Ahh, very good," Wenslo grinned at me, like I was his best student and I'd won the science fair.

I stared down at the sword resting in my palm. "I'm going to lose it at this size."

"Hmmmm." Wenslo took the sword from me. "Gain." It was the right size, instantly in his hand. He walked over to a workbench and set it down, staring at it. He walked over to a drawer in one of the cabinets and rummaged around for a moment, before coming back with a fancy carabiner of some kind. "This should do nicely."

He held the clip to the sheath of the sword, mumbling something that sounded like it could be in another language, but I couldn't tell because he spoke the words so quietly. The clip melded with the sheath, looking like it had always been there. "Wane."

He held out the shrunken sword. "Hopefully that will help."

I eyed it for a second. The clip was small enough it wouldn't fit on my belt.

Wait. The perfect spot, if it was still open. I hadn't worn earrings since I'd joined the force, but the hole should still be there. I found my old cartilage piercing with my finger, and awkwardly clipped the sword into place.

It fit perfectly, strangely cold against my ear.

Wenslo smiled in approval.

"Got somewhere safe for this?" I held up my utility belt, not quite believing I was going to leave my gun behind. But I didn't really have a choice.

"This room will lock behind us, and only I can open it from the hallway." He moved toward the door as he spoke. "It will be safe here. But if we don't leave soon, the museum will be closed."

I didn't trust this fae, but I was stuck in the position of having no other options. Again. I sat the gun belt down on the table, my hand spasming a little as I left it there. I had to physically tell it to not snatch the weapon back off the table.

The sword was nice, but the only thing that gave me any comfort right now was my gun. Not that it would do me much good against the fae, but it sure would against any humans that happened to be controlled by a certain pink-eyed monster. Was she tracking me now? Worse, tracking Kenzie?

"All ready then?" Wenslo asked, breaking me out of my spiral.

"Ready."

He gestured toward the door, but I gestured right back. He sighed, but didn't argue and went first, not seeming to be concerned that I was at his back.

"Bye, Denise! Sorry for holding you at gun-point!" I yelled.

"Not a problem!" her muffled voice made it through the door she hid behind, proving she could hear us.

I pulled the door shut behind me once I reached the hallway, then tugged at the handle. Locked, just like Wenslo had promised. I looked up to find him watching me. He cocked his head, like he was asking if I was ready. I nodded, and Wenslo and I were off to whichever museum we were visiting.

I followed him in silence for a few blocks. I had more questions but was starting to be afraid I'd run him off if I asked too many. He was the closest thing to help I had right now, and I'd just have to make do with what I had. Which sounded good, but so far nothing had stuck out as somewhere that I could get a tool that could save me from a homicidal fae woman.

"Where are we going?" I asked Wenslo.

Wenslo gestured ahead of us.

Of course. The Natural History Museum. He had to take me to one of the most public places in the city. And that was saying a lot. Hopefully security guards didn't get updates from the LAPD. I had to believe that Grayson had a warrant for my phone records and credit cards by now. No way he was letting me disappear without knowing why.

Let alone the feds and the captain. Grayson probably had the full backing of every government agency out there, if he was even allowed to be involved in the search.

Thinking about Grayson made me think about the weird light in my sword wound. My heart rate sped up a little. Should I ask Wenslo now? Nah. Maybe it was gone. I hadn't checked in awhile. And it didn't hurt. At least not any more than just the wound should.

I grabbed my stomach instinctively, and wished for a restroom or somewhere I could duck in and check on the thing. But then Wenslo would be out of sight. That seemed like a bad idea. Decisions, decisions.

We passed beautiful gardens, and well-manicured grass. Things I was definitely not used to seeing in LA. The water bill at this place must be crazy.

Kids streamed out from between stone columns. I checked my watch. Four o'clock. They were probably finishing up a late field trip.

We walked up to the ticket counter. Wenslo still hadn't given me a good reason for why we were here. To his credit, there had been people around the entire short walk to the museum entrance. We hadn't had a chance to speak without someone overhearing.

The ticket line, next to an impressive arch over the entrance to the museum, was empty. The only person in one of the little booths eyed us when we got close. "The museum closes in an hour. You may want to come back tomorrow."

"We'll be fine." Wenslo slapped cash down on the counter, and the first hint of impatience I'd seen from him flashed across his face as we waited for the guy to print out the tickets, put them in a brochure, and get them halfway to the little slot under the window.

"Right now our traveling exhibit-"

The brochure holding the tickets dropped from his hand and whooshed under the window, Wenslo snatching it from the air. "We can show ourselves around, thank you."

My eyes narrowed, and I let Wenslo pull me lightly away from the confused man behind the glass before stopping in my tracks. "Did you do that? That wasn't the wind. Not in a confined space like that."

"Yes. It was me. Now let's go." He lightly tugged on my elbow, smiling at a little boy watching us from a line of kids.

He definitely had powers of some kind, though they seemed to be different than Ghira's. He'd lifted that other fae in the warehouse. In all the horror of the things Ghira had done, I'd made myself ignore that, since he was an ally at the moment. I followed, numb.

The smile on his face looked so normal that it creeped me out. Were all fae like this? Murderers, possible psychopaths? Narcissists, at the very least.

Wenslo tugged me through the main entrance, and into a massive hall. It had been years since I was here. Probably on a field trip myself, as a teen. I should have brought Kenzie. She was old enough to be awestruck at a place like this.

Ornate walls, gorgeous flooring. Light spilled down on two dinosaur skeletons locked in battle. Those I remembered. And Kenzie would get a kick out of them.

"Your people are very odd, putting dead creatures on display." Wenslo just kept on walking as he spoke, strolling along at a pace more like the rest of the people visiting the museum than the speed-walking we'd done to get here. "It's time for you to start taking notes." He nodded to a security guard.

Taking notes? I stored that for later, while doing as he said and taking a thorough look around the room. "My people are odd for liking history, but you're okay with yours killing anyone they disagree with?"

He lifted an eyebrow, looking genuinely confused. "All things die. What does it matter if it's today or in a hundred years?"

I probably looked like a fish out of water, my mouth flapping open. That was his justification for murder? The people would be dead at some point anyway? He didn't even feel bad, at all? I needed to get whatever we were after, and get away from this man. As if I hadn't thought he was dangerous before.

He slipped into a smaller room off to the side of the entrance. I followed, but with a bit more distance than I'd allowed before. No one was in this room, except for us. Maybe this time of day was perfect for whatever it was he wanted to do. The school buses all leaving, people tired from being here all day.

"We're in luck." He strode over to a glass display case. "It's a rotating exhibit, but the bracelet is still here." He bent down for a closer look, and I joined him.

I couldn't see anything special about the bracelet he was talking about. In fact, it looked nasty. Spikes rimmed the inside, like they would bite into the wearer's arm. Even though it was- I checked the case- over a thousand years old, the metal looked fairly new. Other items supposedly from the same era sat on the red cloth around it, but Wenslo paid them no attention.

"What's this antique supposed to do for us?" I asked. "Especially from in there."

"This bracelet is imbued with magic from another world," Wenslo answered. "It-"

"Wait. Another world, as in Faerie, right?" I wasn't proud of how my voice came out. But the answer to that question... Did I want to know?

The side of Wenslo's mouth quirked up in an amused half-smile. "Another world. The magic of the bracelet will stop Ghira from using her power."

What a weird experience. I wasn't even questioning the" bracelet was magic part," just the whole "there's yet another world" part. Were the people there like humans? Like the fae? Or were they people at all?

"We can discuss that later." Wenslo did a quick check around us. "At this moment, be ready."

My stomach dropped. "Be ready for what?"

His little smile turned into a full-on grin. "I think you know." And then he smashed the glass.

CHAPTER NINE

An alarm started blaring instantly, nearly making me slap my hands over my ears.

Was this man, fae, whatever, crazy? No warning, no planning, just a smash and grab with this much security?

Wenslo reached in between shards of glass and grabbed the bracelet, tossing it to me. I reacted, catching it without thinking.

The odd metal was cool in my hand. Maybe it was just because I knew the thing had magical properties, but it felt... wrong. Like a strange buzz of current, just... wrong.

I didn't have time for those kinds of thoughts right now. I stuffed the thing in my pocket and assessed the room for the best exit. Hopefully security would think a kid set the sensor off or something. Was that possible?

"Did you take notes?" Wenslo looked like he found this whole situation amusing. Of course he did. A powerful fae, about to be arrested by some poor unsuspecting security guard. It probably meant nothing to him. I had to get the both of us out of here before this turned into a bigger mess than the one we were currently in.

Or, had to get at least myself out. It might solve some problems if Wenslo got caught.

No, that wouldn't work. Wenslo had shown he could definitely take care of himself. And in taking care of himself, could do something to make this bad situation into a terrible one. Like, kill someone. I had no doubt Wenslo wouldn't think twice about spilling blood to protect himself. I'd already seen him kill another fae, and I didn't even know why.

"Take notes? You didn't even tell me what test I was taking! If I'd known you were going to do something this stupid-"

"Ensure the bracelet gets out with you," he said, taking a step away from me, like he just expected to be obeyed. He probably did. But his comment was interesting. He was going to make sure I got out.

"Only if you swear no one gets hurt," I answered.

A security guard skidded into the room, gun already drawn.

Shoot. They probably had cameras. Of course they knew this wasn't some kid playing a prank.

Wenslo lifted an eyebrow, still not looking too excited.

"Swear!" I said.

"Hands above your head!" the security guard yelled from the other side of the room. He was about Grayson's age, but in better shape. Trim in his uniform, though short, even shorter than me. Still, I had no doubt he could take me if we got into a physical altercation.

I instantly obeyed his command, sticking my hands in the air, though it was a strange feeling to be on this side of the order.

"You don't know what you're asking," Wenslo said.

"Swear," I growled.

"But if I swear-"

"Swear!" I snarled.

"I swear," he grumbled, sounding extremely unhappy.

"Help!" I yelled. "We were here on a first date, and he just broke the glass! Out of nowhere!" The date part was a bit of a sell, but the glass part was true. If he'd have told me what we were doing, I wouldn't be here right now.

The security guard stalked closer, within easy hearing distance at this point. "Drop to the floor," he ordered Wenslo, gun trained firmly on him.

"Oh, thank you," I said, inching away from Wenslo, glass crunching under my boots. "This guy just smashed the glass with no warning!" Maybe I should dial it down a bit. Overselling would hurt more than help. I got brave and took a bigger step toward the exit.

"Not so fast," the guard said, his gun still on Wenslo, but his eyes on me. "You aren't going anywhere either. We're waiting until I've got some backup, and then we'll be going to the holding cell where we can frisk you and figure this whole thing out."

Holding cell? Man, this place was more prepared than I thought.

Wenslo moved slightly, putting himself between me and the guard. "Now, now. There's no reason to get excited." His voice was soothing, making my skin crawl. What if all fae could control people? I hadn't seen any sign of it from him before, but I also didn't necessarily know what to look for.

The guard's eyes bugged halfway out of his head. "No reason to get excited? You just stole an artifact! Just blatantly, in the middle of the day!"

"It's hardly the middle of the day. And stealing during museum hours is much more convenient. No loud alarms on the entrances, actually less guards, lots of distractions. Strange, isn't it?" Wenslo took a step toward the guard.

His gun popped up higher, finger tight on the trigger.

Oh, great. Wenslo might be fae and therefore nearly impossible for a bullet to hit, but I sure wasn't. This guy was about to start letting bullets fly, just because he was nervous. I'd seen his type before.

Wenslo gave me a look. I didn't know what that meant, but I took it as run.

So I did. The guard couldn't get both of us.

I darted down a hallway. Thankfully things were more twisty and darker in these back rooms than the main entrance.

The guard yelled behind me, but I couldn't make out what he shouted. Hopefully all the other guards were headed to that room too. They could all gang up on Wenslo.

For some reason, even fully against logic, I almost believed him when he said he wouldn't hurt anyone.

Almost.

A different guard skidded around a corner in front of me. I had just enough time to slide behind a giant whale head.

The guard didn't slow, charging toward the room where I'd left Wenslo.

Did I feel guilty about that? No, actually. Nice.

I moved cautiously out from behind the display. People were screaming on the other side of the wall. Apparently they were still evacuating.

Perfect.

My best move at this point would be to get myself hyped up and act like a scared tourist. Unless the original guard came after me, they were unlikely to be able to recognize me from a grainy security video. Most of them probably hadn't seen it, anyway. They would have been out patrolling, and wouldn't have had time to study the video before coming to help their friend.

Hopefully.

I took off at a run, rounded a corner, and crashed right into a security guard. We tumbled to the ground.

He cursed and shoved me off of him, then scrambled to his feet, towering over me.

I cringed back away from him, not even needing to pretend to be afraid. If they turned me over to the LAPD, they would make me change into a jumpsuit. The officer assigned to me would find out that part of me glowed. Worse, Ghira would have all kinds of people to choose from to carry out her will, and I'd be trapped, right there in a cage, waiting like an animal to be slaughtered.

The guard leaned down toward me, and I had to curb my instinct to grab him and jerk him down, to use my knee to break his nose and run off.

As if I would get lucky enough to make it away.

This was it. The moment of truth. Because there was no getting out of this on my own. I kept the side of my face with the stitches turned away from him. Somehow they made me feel like I looked guilty. Guilty of being a troublemaker or something.

The guard leaned down and offered me a hand. He jerked me to my feet, then took off at a run, never truly looking at me.

I limped forward, my side shooting pain all up and down my body. The ache had been easy enough to ignore while all of the crazy stuff had been happening, but getting jostled may have reopened the stitches.

The wound felt warm to the touch, even through my shirt. Because of the injury, or because of the weird light? That was the question.

I filed in behind a family of three, everyone crowding toward the exits.

Crap. A guard stood at the door, making everyone empty their pockets and bags. They didn't think anyone was in danger, which was good. That could stop anyone from getting hurt in the panic. But they didn't think anyone was in danger, which was bad because it made it more difficult for me to slip out.

What could I do with the bracelet? Thankfully the line was long. I stuck my hand into my pocket, reassuring myself that the bracelet was still there. Why couldn't this have been some piece of jewelry that looked like something a person would actually want to wear. There was no way I could pass this thing off as a fashion accessory. Wearing it wasn't an option.

Did the guards know what had been taken yet? They had to, didn't they? They would have an inventory list for what was supposed to be in the case. Had they captured Wenslo?

"Let us out!" someone in the middle of the line yelled.

"You can't keep us here, in danger!" someone else screamed from my left. "What set off the alarms?"

Of course they wouldn't know. Rumors were most likely flying through this crowd. I looked around. The mom of the family of three in front of me clutched her tenish-year-old's hand tightly, gaze darting around the room.

I moved up closer to her. "I heard there was a shooting in one of the upper rooms. What did you hear?"

I almost felt guilty when the little girl's eyes got big. But I couldn't afford those feelings. Not when I was protecting my own daughter.

"I heard someone got knifed in the ocean exhibit," the dad whispered back, looking a little more together than his wife, though not by much.

Wow, news traveled fast. Not accurate, but fast.

"It's terrifying that they're making us stay in here," I whispered.

"Yeah, but I understand why," the wife said. "They need to check everyone, make sure they aren't taking something out of the museum they shouldn't."

A gun went off somewhere behind us, making me jump and several other people scream.

Okay, that was not good. Probably for the guards. I wasn't worried about Wenslo. Okay, yes, I had to be, because I didn't know how to use this stupid bracelet, and I had no one else to turn to for help.

But he'd told me to run. And he seemed like the type that not only could take care of himself, but would.

The crowd pushed forward harder. Two security guards tried to hold back the wave.

I checked on the family quickly. The mom had the girl by the hand, and the dad was behind them, shielding them from the stampede that was forming at the back of the line.

"Please everyone, keep it together!" one of the security guards at the front yelled. "We're letting everyone out, but please form up outside for inspection!"

Another shot rang out, and this time the screaming didn't stop. En masse, the whole crowd rushed forward, knocking one of the security guards over.

A man to my left clipped me in the shoulder as he passed, spinning me to the right. I almost went down, but slammed into a woman in a hijab. She steadied me before continuing the mad dash for the exit.

Swept along, it was only a moment before I reached the guards. One was fighting against the crowd, trying to get to... The other guard. Still on the ground.

No, no, no. I couldn't stop. I needed to get out of here.

Two people trampled the guard in their panic, not even seeing her there. She was going to get killed. I could feel it in my gut.

I slammed into the person next to me, knocking them away and causing a brief moment of flow around the guard.

It wasn't long enough for me to get to her.

I fought against the heavy stream of people, getting close enough now to see a trickle of blood coming out of the guard's lips. I couldn't tell if it was from her mouth, or something far worse. She wasn't curling up for protection, just sprawled across the floor. That was a bad sign for sure. The only time she moved was when someone kicked her, and I couldn't tell if that was reflexive or just the force of the blow.

The other guard noticed me fighting my way in her direction. "Help her," he yelled. The panic in his eyes said they were probably more than work friends. He fought against the crowd, swinging at anyone close enough. They avoided him, but were still in the way.

Crap, crap.

A huge guy started to muscle past me. He would do nicely. I latched onto his arm. He dragged me forward but slowed, trying to shake me off. "Let go, lady!"

The screaming had subsided enough that I could hear him. "Help me help her!" I pointed toward the unconscious guard. He swiveled to look, and his eyes widened. He nodded.

"Hey!" he roared. His voice echoed around the huge hall. It didn't slow anyone down, but they did move away from us.

It would have to do. I shoved my way forward, the guy keeping me from getting mowed down from behind.

I reached the woman, and rolled her onto her back. Still breathing, but completely out of it. I'd rather not move her, but at this point, it seemed more likely for her to get killed in here than it did she would have a spinal injury.

"Can you carry her?" I asked my new friend.

He nodded and leaned down. I helped roll her onto his shoulder in a fireman's carry.

By now, the crowd had started to thin. But I wasn't leaving this poor woman on the marble floor. We fought our way toward the exit.

I held the glass door open for the man and followed him over to a section of grass. He rolled the guard onto the ground. I leaned down.

"Her breathing is steady." Her face had already started to bruise. Under her clothes she was probably pretty beat up. But there was nothing I could do about that.

"I couldn't even see her, with all those people stepping over her," the guy said, anxious sweat around the collar of his t-shirt.

"Thank you," I said, and straightened.

Sirens sounded in the distance. It always seemed to take forever for help to arrive when you were on this side of the emergency. I'd been here many times, waiting with someone for an ambulance. But it had always been for work, and I'd been able to distance myself a bit.

"Keep an eye on her," I said.

"What about you?" he asked, his eyes wide.

I looked up just in time to see a form jump from a third-story window. Security guards clustered around on the third floor, looking down through the shattered glass.

"I have someone I need to talk to." I ground my teeth, trying not to say more. That person was about to get an earful. He'd nearly gotten this woman killed. Who knew what else had happened in the mess Wenslo had created.

The chaos outside the museum worked in my favor as I worked my way around people, all trying to make sense of what had just happened.

I scooted around another crying kid and his dad, making for the back of the museum. It was out of the way if I wanted to go back to Wenslo's office, but I didn't care at the moment. I just needed to get out of sight.

Sirens wailed and tires screeched as the first cops arrived. They'd have to secure the scene before EMS was allowed in. Hopefully they dragged that guard to an ambulance quickly. As far as I had seen, she was the only one to truly worry about.

"Ma'am?" a voice behind me asked. "Everyone is supposed to stay here until they can be inspected."

I shuffled forward a little faster, pretending not to hear him. I wasn't in sprinting shape at the moment, the adrenaline draining from my body gave my side plenty of space to shout about the exertion of the last hour.

"Ma'am!" his voice was stronger this time, more urgent. He started after me. I wouldn't have long before he flat out grabbed me.

"She doesn't speak English," another man said to the first. I forced myself to keep walking and not look over my shoulder. "I checked her inside. She's clean."

The calls for me to stop didn't continue. I shuffled forward a few more feet before looking back. The male security guard from inside the museum sat on the grass, the woman's head in his lap. He didn't look up, but I nodded in thanks anyway.

The shuffle became more real the farther I went. That nap from earlier hadn't gone as far as I'd have liked it to. Exhaustion pulled at my vision, sending floaters across my eyes. I wasn't going to be able to take much more today. My safe house was probably blown, I had no cash. Mr. Abeyta could surely help me out more, but I didn't have any more info to give him.

Not, at least, until I talked to Wenslo.

I might be sleeping on the streets tonight. Ah well. There were worse things.

Ducking around a corner, I took one last look behind me. No one was following. Somehow with no plan and no prep, we may have actually gotten away with stealing from one of the biggest museums in the country.

Of course, having a magical being who could jump out of third-story windows didn't hurt.

Speaking of said magical being, there he was. Just casually walking out of the bushes ahead. I nearly punched him in the face, just because. "What were you thinking?"

"That we needed the bracelet." He brushed shards of glass from his jacket, completely unperturbed. "And now we have it."

"And your face is going to be plastered across every newspaper and channel in the entire country!" My voice rose, right along with my anger. "How are we supposed to get anything done with every cop and criminal in the city watching for us? You know that every crook in LA would take the bracelet from us too, if they could. They're all going to assume it's super valuable!"

"It is very valuable." Wenslo held his hand out. "Give it to me."

I crossed my arms in front of my chest. "Why did you give it to me in the museum in the first place, if you wanted to hang onto it? I'm the one who would have ended up in prison."

He sighed and started walking. It frustrated me to no end that I had to follow, but I did. He still needed to tell me how to use this stupid bracelet, and I still needed to grab my gun from his office.

"I wouldn't have been able to convince you to break the glass, true?" he asked without looking back.

I thought about my answer. True. I couldn't come up with one scenario that didn't include Kenzie dangling over a pit of lava that could have gotten me to break that glass.

"You also would have a more difficult time escaping the guards without a distraction, yes?" He didn't wait for my answer. "One of your jail cells wouldn't hold me, whereas I would have a difficult time getting the bracelet back if one of your law enforcement officers took it before locking me up."

"You just wanted me to be the mule."

"Precisely." He turned back to me and held out his hand. "And now, if you would give me the bracelet, we could be finished with this partnership."

"I still need my gun." I walked past him, leaving him standing there with his hand out. "Tell me how this bracelet works."

He sighed again, so long-suffering, and I heard his footsteps following behind me. More police cars flashed by, but he didn't seem concerned. What could he do, other than hold a person up in the air with his mind?

The fact that I didn't know almost made me leave my gun where it was and take off. Almost. He didn't answer my question. Didn't say anything.

We made it back to his office building. The place was quiet, even more quiet than my first visit. After hours, apparently.

We went back to his office, me trying to convince myself that I wasn't an idiot for following him here. But I needed him to tell me how to use the bracelet to stop Ghira.

His office was empty. His receptionist must have let herself out after we'd left. I grabbed my service belt as soon as we stepped through the door, the presence of my weapon making me feel better even though it didn't make sense.

Wenslo made his way over to a small coffee machine and started measuring beans. "This is one of the few things I find truly wonderful about your world."

Um, what? That's what he wanted to talk about, coffee? The machine was a monstrosity. It had probably cost him more than my rent did a month, and I lived in LA.

"How can I use the bracelet against Ghira?" I asked, straight to the point. If I didn't sleep soon, I was going to pass out.

He turned his dark eyes on me while the machine ground his coffee beans. "You'll be leaving that bracelet with me." He lifted a hand, face as serious as back at the warehouse.

I froze for a second, body going cold. But nothing seemed to happen. I pulled at the sword earring. "If you won't tell me, things are about to get much less pleasant."

He blinked in my direction, dumbfounded, by the look on his face. He stuck his hand up again.

Still nothing.

"Yeah, I don't know what that's supposed to be doing, but I don't like it." I unclipped the earring and held it up. "Gain." I threw every ounce of intention I could into that word, afraid the sword wouldn't obey me if I was planning on using it on its master. But it did, instantly.

The machine beeped loudly, sending steam into the air, but Wenslo didn't take his eyes off of me. "How?" he asked.

"How what? How to tell me? Just start with what I need to do to get this bracelet to stop her."

"No," he took a step forward, staring me down.

I lifted the sword tip, just a little.

"How are you not forced to stand in place?"

Oh. That. He thought his power should be working on me. The fact that it wasn't was almost as scary as if it was. Why had it before, but wouldn't now? I'd wondered why Ghira didn't just take control of me, but this explained it. Maybe she couldn't. But why? The only thing that had changed from when Wenslo had lifted me off the floor in the warehouse before to now was... the light.

Now I definitely couldn't ask him about it.

"If you won't tell me how to use this bracelet, I'm going to take it with me and find someone who will." I inched backward, moving toward the door. It wasn't really a bluff, because if he wouldn't tell me I would be forced to find someone else who could.

For Kenzie.

I paused in the doorway to give him one last chance. Hopefully he didn't use that chance to come after me. Because right now, I had no fight left in me. There was nothing I could do to stop him.

CHAPTER TEN

Stuck in a straight up stare-down, I reached slowly for my gun. Gun in one hand, sword in the other. Surely one of them would get the job done, if Wenslo did come after me.

He held his hands up, but didn't seem too worried. More intense. "Are you part fae?" he asked, studying me.

"That's a little personal," I snarked back.

He just lifted an eyebrow, waiting without saying anything.

Fine. I wanted to know what was going on as much as he did. "Not as far as I know."

He cocked his head, eyes narrowing. "Do you have a magical artifact?"

That one I knew the answer to. "Nope. All my stuff is cheap or LAPD issue. None of it is magical." As far as I knew. Was a secret magical artifact something that happened? "Oh, but I do have your sword."

He waved a hand dismissively. "If it was the sword, I would never have allowed it to leave my possession." He squinted, looking me over.

"Nope," I said. "No magical artifact then."

He crossed his arms and tapped his finger to his chin, like he was pretending to be human. It was such a stereotypical human move that it caught me off guard. So far he'd been very good at mimicking a real man. "Then why aren't you susceptible to my powers?" he said out loud, but didn't seem to be looking for an answer from me. "Or Ghira's for that matter. I've been wondering why she didn't just force you to her, but didn't think you would have any answers."

Of course she should be able to control me. If she could make Grayson do as she wished, there had to be some reason she couldn't just make me walk right over and find her. There was only one thing I could think of that could be stopping fae magic from working on me. And for some reason, I really didn't want to tell him about it.

Still, not bringing up the light in my side seemed stupid. Here was a person who probably had answers. Maybe the only person I had access to.

But he scared me. Far more than I'd ever admit to anyone. His total nonchalance while killing another fae made it impossible for me to trust him. That fear made me need to keep the light a secret, just in case it was the answer to why he couldn't freeze me in place or lift me into the air.

"Do you have a bathroom?" I asked.

He blinked at me, like I'd completely surprised him again. That made sense. My question didn't really follow our conversation. But I wanted to check on the light, and as soon as I'd mentioned a bathroom I'd realized how much I needed to go anyway.

"Just down the hall." He gestured to the left.

I hitched my service belt up on my shoulder and turned and walked out of his office, taking a left out the door.

He followed me.

"No privacy, huh?" I asked.

"Not while you have the bracelet," he answered. "Though I'll allow you to go into the room alone. There aren't any windows."

"Thanks a bunch," I muttered before walking into the bathroom and slamming the door in his face. I locked it behind me and leaned back against the door for a second. The bathroom was small, with no décor. But it smelled nice, which was unusual for LA.

While I needed to check on my stitches, a large part of me didn't want to look. Didn't want to know. Fine. I'd use the toilet first. It would probably be better if I washed my hands before poking at a wound anyway.

I scrubbed my hands for a full thirty seconds when I was done, then splashed water on my face for good measure.

A knock on the door provided a welcome distraction. "Is everything okay in there?" Wenslo asked.

"Fine," I yelled back. But that did prompt me to actually check my wound. I really didn't need a grumpy fae breaking down the bathroom door. Or even making a scene. The cops would have blown up pictures of our faces from the cameras by now. In fact, they may even have them out to the public.

No. They'd find out who I was pretty quick, and then they'd go to my apartment. And then off to see Travis. It was a good thing he wasn't home right now. He already thought I'd started to lose my mind back when I'd left them. Hopefully my dad had actually listened to me and wasn't at home. He definitely didn't need any more ammo against me.

I took a deep breath and pulled up the edge of my shirt. A faint glow covered my hand, more white now than the yellow of before. The light was changing, whatever that meant. I pulled my shirt up the rest of the way and got a good look.

Light leaked out from between the stitches, bright enough to see even in the well-lit bathroom.

"What are you?" I whispered.

The light pulsed a little. It seemed bigger than before, but I hadn't measured it. I needed to get a Sharpie and put a line where the light ended, so I could tell if it grew. My stomach growled. I needed a Sharpie and some food.

"Do you need assistance?" Wenslo asked.

I practically growled, shoved my shirt down and flung open the door. "Don't fae have any manners?"

He raised an eyebrow. "Thus she asks rudely."

"Fine, whatever." I shouldered past him and started down the fancy hallway toward the exit. I needed to get something to eat, and then I needed to find somewhere safe to sleep. Maybe not in that order, if I got lucky.

"Where are you going?" Wenslo called after me.

"None of your business," I yelled back. Part of why I was really peeved was probably because I was tired and my side hurt like the dickens, but a massive part of the irritation was real. He could have warned me that we were going to rob the museum we were "visiting."

"As long as you have the bracelet, it's my business." He caught up with me without effort.

I didn't slow down.

He grabbed me by the shoulder and spun me to face him.

"Everything about you is now my business. Until you tell me how you are able to resist fae abilities, we are going to spend a lot of time together."

I shoved his hand away. "Ah, no. We are not." I marched up to the big glass door leading outside and flung it open.

"You need a place to stay!" he called after me, catching up again. "I have a place."

I stopped then, to stare him in the face. "When Hell freezes over. That's when I'd stay somewhere with you." And then I started walking again. I didn't have any special destination. My only goal at the moment was to get away from the fae stalking me.

"I don't understand this idiom." Wenslo matched me step for step. "That's impossible."

I caught myself before stopping in my tracks again. "You believe in Hell?"

"I'm not sure how that's relevant, but yes."

That was a tidbit I'd consider later. But for now, I marched out onto the street. Well, it was more of a slink, really. I checked for cops both ways, and didn't see anyone that looked like they fit the bill.

Now what? I'd been all bravado with Wenslo a second ago.

"If I may, I actually have an apartment-"

"No," I interrupted him. I'd sleep on the streets before staying with him. Maybe one of the homeless people I dropped food off for during patrol would let me stay with them. It'd still be outside, but at least they'd know where to go to stay safe.

Actually, there was a shelter not too far from here. If I could make it there before they closed the doors for the night, at least I'd feel a bit more safe. Surely no one would be looking for a museum thief in a homeless shelter.

I started walking in the direction I hoped the shelter was in. Wenslo trailed behind me.

"You really should give me the bracelet for safe keeping," he said. "I hate to force you to give it to me, when we're just beginning our working relationship. But if I have to, I-"

I whirled around to face him for a second. "You try to take this thing from me and that will be the end of any type of relationship you might think we would have."

What would I do if he did try to take it? It was useless to me, unless I could figure out how to use it. But something told me handing it over to him was a bad idea.

"I'll need your help getting it on Ghira. I'm not going to take it from you unless you force my hand." He sounded sincere. Hopefully.

I turned and started walking again. His words didn't even deserve a response. It wasn't like I was going to change his mind. We walked along the road in silence. How did I get away from him? There was no way I would sleep with him around.

If I went to the shelter, did I put everyone there at risk? Could Ghira use the people there against me? Would Wenslo? I had no reason to believe he wouldn't, even if he couldn't use them the same way Ghira could. How did I protect everyone? I should be trying to figure out a plan with Wenslo right now, but my body trembled in exhaustion, my eyesight blurry, and head throbbing. I needed sleep.

Lost in my thoughts, I nearly missed a car pulling up beside us. The window rolled down, revealing a familiar face. Travis. I stared at him, too tired to process him here, out of our normal context.

"Jay! I've been driving all over this area looking for you!" His gorgeous green eyes were full of concern. He put the car in park and flung open the door, jumping out to grab me by the shoulders and look me over, checking for injuries or something, before pulling me into a hug.

"Who is this man?" Wenslo interjected from somewhere behind me, his voice cool.

"I'm her husband," Travis growled back over my shoulder, which was very unlike him. "Who are you?"

I wasn't going to look a gift horse in the mouth. I pulled away from Travis and jumped in his back seat, the closest door to me. He took the hint and got in the driver's seat, hitting the lock button.

Wenslo tugged on the door handle.

"I'll find you tomorrow," I said. "After I've slept."

"Jayla, we really should discuss this," Wenslo said, his voice muffled by the glass. He knocked on the window with his knuckle.

"I need time to think." I met his eyes, trying to reassure him that I was being honest. "I'll be back soon." And it was the truth. As much as I hated it, he was my best shot at protecting my family from Ghira.

Travis threw the car in drive. Wenslo didn't look happy, but he must have been okay with what I said, because the car moved forward without him holding it back telepathically. Or maybe his ability couldn't work on anything I was touching, not just on me? Or he could have made my clothes hold still before. Ugh, lots of things I didn't have answers to.

Travis looked at me in the rear view mirror, his eyes no longer worried. Now he looked furious.

Out of the frying pan, and into the fire.

My ex, or estranged husband, or whatever we were, looked over at me. "Who was that guy?" He didn't even sound jealous or anything. Not that he should, but it made my heart twinge. He did deserve to know though, since he'd just helped me get away from him.

"A fae. He's trying to help me with a problem." Where was the line with being honest? Even admitting that Wenslo was fae felt strange, let alone the fact that knowing could possibly get Travis in trouble. Trouble with the fae, trouble with the government, who knew. I didn't want to be too honest. If he knew about Ghira, he'd stick around to help out of duty. And that would make him a target.

"Fae?" he asked, eyes wider than I'd ever seen them. At least with the fae on the news constantly, he didn't think I'd lost my mind. "You told me to hide Kenzie. I did that. Then I saw you on the news. That you're a person of interest in the museum robbery. And now you tell me that the guy you were there with is fae. What's going on, Jay?"

His green eyes were sincere. I almost just spilled everything to him, right then and there. We used to share everything. But that was before...

"I've got it handled," I sat back against the seat, body language telling him to let it go.

Even though I was staring out the window, I could feel his whole body go tense. "Where am I taking you?" Travis asked, his voice tight.

"Somewhere to spend the night." I looked over long enough to see a muscle jump in his cheek. Yeah, it only did that when he was super mad. "If you'll let me borrow some cash."

Always playing it safe, Travis pulled over into an empty parking spot and pulled out his phone. He punched in something, which I assumed was hotels near me, but didn't speak.

"Trav, I'm sorry," I whispered. Thoughts of his eyes turning pink, and him dragging me to Ghira, maybe helping her kill me danced through my head. "Please, say something."

He tossed his phone on the dash. "You expect me to say something when you won't? What has you so spooked? Why did you tell me to stash Kenzie away? Why are you helping a fae rob a museum? I know you have to have good intentions, you always do, but I'm struggling to understand at the moment."

He didn't put the car in drive, just sat in the driver's seat, eyes boring into me through the rearview mirror.

I didn't have any answers for him. I barely had answers for myself. And at this point, it was a good thing I was sitting down, because my body trembled, on the brink of collapse.

After a second, his face softened. He had to see the pain and exhaustion on mine, even here, with only the dim streetlight above us to see by.

"I found a spot nearby. They say there are rooms available." He pulled out onto the road. "It's just a couple blocks."

We sat in silence for those couple blocks. He apparently didn't have anything to say, and I didn't have the mental capacity to try and make small talk. How had we gotten to this point, where I didn't know how to make small talk with my husband?

Rhetorical question. I knew how. It had been my fault, in some ways. In some ways not, but that part always escaped me somehow.

The hotel parking lot he pulled into didn't inspire a lot of confidence in what the rooms would look like. He squinted at the flickering vacancy sign. "They said they take cash." Raucous laughter drifted in from a nearby alley.

Loud music hit us right before the squeal of tires. I was too tired to even duck just in case. Thankfully it was fine, because it was just a couple of street racers burning rubber on the road. I'd have pulled them over if I was on duty right now.

A pang hit me. Was Grayson okay? Did Ghira's power cause any permanent damage? Oh to go back to the good old days that weren't old, when I could sit across the table from my partner and know my purpose and path. Not my reality now, where every moment was spent in worry and second-guessing.

Travis reached for the key in the ignition. "You aren't staying here."

I reached through the gap between the seats and grabbed his elbow, gently holding his arm in place. His skin was soft and warm to the touch. "I need you to get a room for me. I can't show my face, just in case the clerk saw the news."

He gave me a look, like he couldn't believe I was considering this place. "Won't they be searching around here for you?"

"Probably. But they aren't going to go knocking door-to-door. Once I get inside, I'll be fine."

He continued staring out the window at the dump of a motel, obviously not very happy.

"It's fine. I'll be fine." I tried forcing confidence into my voice, but it wasn't very convincing. "I just need some sleep, and then I'll be good to go. Tomorrow I'll get this whole situation sorted, and then things will be back to normal. Promise."

His look of disappointment hit me in the gut. He knew my lying voice. I'd used it on him enough times when I'd promised I'd stop drinking. That I'd be home at a decent time. The thousands of times I'd told him everything was fine, when it obviously wasn't.

And that had been before the weird hours at the police academy.

But he didn't say anything. He undid his seatbelt and reached for the door.

"Thank you," I told him, putting every ounce of truth that I could manage into the words. "For real. You might be saving my life tonight."

He nodded, but didn't say anything, getting out of the car and walking toward the office.

I closed my eyes, partially so I didn't have to read his disappointment in the set of his shoulders, partly because I could hardly force them to open.

He was only gone for about two minutes. He rapped on my window, nearly sending me into the driver's seat.

I glared at him before catching myself. It wasn't his fault I was about to collapse and couldn't stay alert to my surroundings.

In fact, he helped me out of the car when I could hardly use my abs, my stitches screaming. Even the ones in my face throbbed, and I'd barely felt them all day.

"You don't have to walk me up," I said.

He ignored me and opened the trunk, grabbing a bag. Then he walked away without checking to see if I'd follow, leading the way to the stairs and up to the second floor.

Already to the room before I made my way up, he pretended to continue ignoring me, but I saw him check and make sure I was doing okay.

The room wasn't terrible. It wasn't nice, by anyone's standards, but it would do. Travis dropped the bag he'd carried up the stairs onto the TV stand. "There are clothes in there for you. A toothbrush, deodorant."

He walked away to check the bathroom. I shut the door behind me and locked it. Even with Travis leaving soon, I wasn't going to take any chances. I went over and dropped my service belt onto the bed before checking out the clothes he'd packed for me.

A couple sizes too big. Old stuff from before I'd left him. I'd been fighting depression for over a year after Kenzie had been born, and I'd thought them better off without me. Now that I wasn't post-partum, I knew it had been wrong, but I didn't know how to go back after everything that happened between us.

Too big would be fine. But I did have to blink back tears. Travis did share fault in why we weren't together anymore, but that didn't make this any easier. Didn't take away the sting of memories that came up every time I saw him.

Travis checked his phone. I could hear the buzz after he pulled it out of his pocket, but he hit ignore and stuffed it back in. "The room seems fairly secure." He walked over and sat on the bed, reaching down to untie his shoes.

"What are you doing?" I asked.

He didn't look up, didn't pause. "I'm staying here. I'll sleep on the floor."

"You're a germ freak, you can't sleep on the floor."

He did look up then, and raised an eyebrow. "I don't think you're in the position to tell me what I can and can't do." He kicked his shoes off and went and rummaged through the drawers, probably looking for an extra blanket.

My emotions warred inside. To have someone I trusted completely with my safety take watch so I could get some sleep... Amazing. No words. But to put that same person in danger...

"You don't get a say in this." Travis didn't even need to look at me to know what was going through my head. "Unless you want to tell me what's going on." He pulled his phone out of his pocket again, glanced at the screen and hit mute.

"You should turn that off," I said. "Just in case they try to track it. It's suspicious that you went missing at the same time I robbed a museum."

"It's probably law enforcement that keeps calling," Travis said. "But I can't turn it off. Because of Kenzie."

I grunted. I couldn't argue with that. Whoever had her, had to be able to get a hold of him. I fought the urge to beg him to tell me where she was. I couldn't know. Barely able to move, I shuffled to the bed. Once I sat down, I probably wasn't getting back up. But I didn't even care right now. Very carefully, I tipped over to lean back against the headboard. Shoot. I'd forgotten my pills.

"Would you grab the prescription bottles out of my belt, please."

Travis tossed the pillow and blanket he'd dug out of the drawer onto the floor and grabbed my belt, pulling out the first bottle. He looked it over. "Did you get hurt somewhere other than your face?"

"Yes." A lie would only make things worse.

He tossed me the two bottles and went into the bathroom. The water ran and he reappeared with a plastic cup full of water.

I downed the pills, finishing off the water. I really should be drinking more, but that wasn't high on my list of worries at the moment.

I tried to reach for my boots, but couldn't bend. Pride would have made me sleep in them, but Travis saw the whole thing. He rolled his eyes at me and reached down, carefully untying and tugging my boots off.

"You're too tired to talk tonight," Travis said.

I grunted in agreement, eyes closed. I was half out already.

"But in the morning, we are going to discuss what's going on, and what your plan is to fix it."

It was my turn to ignore him. I pretended to have fallen asleep. Tomorrow, I'd have to make a plan to get away from him. But for tonight, I could sleep safe, knowing someone had my back. Tomorrow? That was a different story.

CHAPTER ELEVEN

Light streamed in through the threadbare curtains covering the hotel room window. I blinked several times, attempting to get the sleep out of my eyes. It took me a moment to place where I was.

Then the craziness of the last couple days slapped me right across the face. I sat up, shuffling back to lean against the headboard.

A blanket sat neatly on the end of the bed, a pillow on top of it. I patted around for my burner phone, just to check the time. When I finally found it, the battery was dead.

I squinted at the window. That was a lot of light. I must have slept in a lot longer than I should have. "Travis?" I croaked out, my throat incredibly dry.

No answer, but the shower was running.

I pawed around for my service belt, just in case it wasn't him in the shower. Sure, I couldn't think of anyone else it would be, but stranger things had happened in the last twenty-four hours.

There. My body relaxed a little at the coolness of the grip of my weapon. My hand bumped something else, metal and cool, but strange.

The bracelet. I'd clipped it on to my belt last night and forgotten. Finally awake enough to not think someone who wanted to murder me had gotten distracted and decided to take a shower instead, I pulled the belt over and took a closer look at the thing. Last night I'd been so exhausted I'd basically collapsed. Looking at the bracelet had been the last thing on my mind.

But now I had a moment to breathe. The bracelet looked just as terrible today as it had yesterday in the museum. I'd only gotten a quick look at it then, before Wenslo had busted the glass, and the thing looked even more wicked now as I studied it. The spikes were long, and the space between them far too small for an arm to fit without the spikes digging into flesh. Notches and grooves covered the metal, and didn't look like they were just for decoration, but I couldn't come up with a reason for them.

Maybe I didn't want to know what they were there for.

I ran a finger over the metal, and a shiver went up my spine. Something felt... wrong about this thing. Dangerous. How could a bracelet feel dangerous? Maybe I was just making things up because of how Wenslo had acted when we'd taken it, but I didn't think so. I had a ton more questions now than I'd had before.

A quick glance around the room showed that Travis must have run over to a gas station and bought breakfast burritos and coffee. While he was busy, I took a quick peek at my stitches. Yep, the wound was still there. The light had faded, nearly gone. It pulsed, completely blocked by my skin for a millisecond at a time.

That had to be good, right?

Yes. It had to be good.

I winced as I sat up, my abs protesting the movement. After shuffling over to the TV stand, I grabbed one of the burritos and took a bite. Cold, but I'd take it. I hadn't eaten a decent meal in what felt like forever.

The bathroom door opened, and Travis emerged, dressed in a black t-shirt and jeans, towel-drying his hair. He glanced over at me and gave me a small smile. "Morning."

"Morning," I replied, my heart melting a little. I missed his real smile. And the one I'd just gotten might not be his full force grin, but it reminded me of how much we had loved each other. I didn't try to say anything else, my mouth full of breakfast burrito a great excuse to not have to come up with something to say. I took a sip of the coffee. Lots of syrup, just the way I liked it. He remembered, and took the time to make it as good as possible under the circumstances. Cold like the burrito, but I didn't want to offend Travis, so I took another swig.

He walked over and sat on the bed. I handed him a burrito, and we ate in silence, the only sounds coming from the occasional rustle of the bag as I reached for another burrito or took a sip of coffee.

Travis crumpled up half of his burrito and threw it in the trash. He ran a hand through his hair, not looking at me. "So, about last night..."

I tensed, bracing myself for the lecture I knew was coming.

"I'm not going to ask you to tell me what's going on," he said. "But I am going to offer my help."

Um, what? This was a total reversal. "What do you mean?"

"I mean you're an adult, obviously. And we aren't together anymore. I don't have the right to tell you what to do, or force you to tell me anything you don't want to." Now he did look at me, his eyes so earnest it threw me back to high school when he'd first asked me out.

"But," he continued, "I care about you. And I know that something is going on, something scary. And I want to help you with that. Whether that means just finding a safe place for you to stay, or helping you figure out a plan to get out of whatever situation you're in."

I stared at him, my heart pounding. Travis had always been kind, but this... This was beyond kind. I'd married an amazing man. Long before I was ready to be married. "Why are you doing this?" I asked, my voice barely above a whisper.

He shrugged, a small smile tugging at the corner of his lips. "I guess I just can't stand to see you hurting. Especially alone. No one should go through a disaster alone."

Tears prickled at the corners of my eyes. Travis was right, of course. I had a hard time asking for help, which he knew. So he was offering without me asking. And offering instead of trying to force me to accept his help took all of the wind out of my sails.

"And I have to assume that this is a major disaster, if you were willing to rob a museum," Travis said.

Okay, he wasn't flat-out asking, but that was close. Not that I blamed him.

"What time is it?" I changed the subject.

"Three o'clock."

"Three?" I'd wasted most of the day. And he'd probably had to pay for a second night at the hotel. Crap. Was Wenslo still looking for me? Ghira was.

Shoot, Ghira. Always Ghira. Travis being so sweet was going to be difficult to shoot down, but I couldn't risk it. Couldn't risk him.

Having someone to watch my back with Wenslo would make me feel a lot better about being around the fae. Not that Travis would be much help, no human that I knew would be. What if Wenslo had gotten a hold of Ghira? What if he'd been secretly helping her, instead of me? Or, he'd given up on me and decided to turn me over to get back in her good graces? I didn't trust that fae, in the slightest.

No, I couldn't get Travis involved. But I could at least let him give me a ride.

"Are you free to take me back to where you picked me up last night?" I asked.

Travis studied me for a moment, frustrated and confused, assuming I could still read him. "The same place as last night?"

I nodded.

"You're meeting the guy from last night?"

I nodded again.

"The one you helped rob a museum?"

I raised an eyebrow. "How do you know he didn't help me?"

He sighed, no doubt regretting his promise to help me without questioning too much.

"Fine. But there's one thing you have to do for me first."

My face twitched, but I kept it under control. And here I was just thinking that this may actually work.

He held up a hand, no doubt knowing where my mind had gone, and went over to the TV stand. The poorly fitting drawer squealed as he wiggled it open. He pulled some clothes out and walked back, holding them out to me. "Take a shower. You smell."

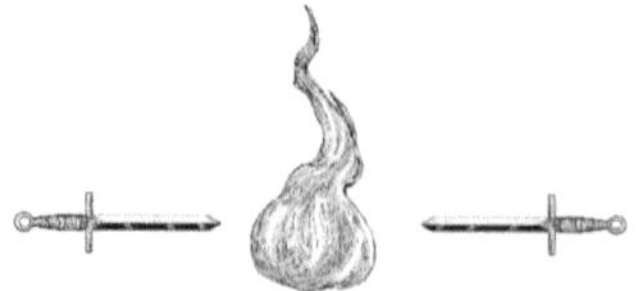

The shirt Travis had picked up for me at the gas station fit perfectly, but I tugged at it uncomfortably anyway. An *I Love LA* shirt might actually be a good way to blend in if we were in the tourist sections of town, but probably not going into an academic building. I was about to stick out like a sore thumb.

Travis pulled into a parking lot not far from where he'd picked me up last night. This was it. Where I had to tell him goodbye. "Travis, I-"

"I've got the hotel room for another night," he interrupted me, holding out a hotel room keycard. "And I hit the ATM at the gas station this morning." He held up a stack of cash.

Interrupting was rude. And out of character. But we were far out of our comfort zone, and he probably knew exactly what I'd been about to say. I didn't reach for the money. Couldn't reach for it.

But then, how could I not? What happened if Wenslo didn't have any ideas? If I had to be on the run from Ghira for another week? A month?

My stomach dropped. No. I couldn't go that long worrying. Couldn't go that long without seeing Kenzie. I might need supplies. And I'd definitely need food. I took the money from him and stuffed it into the pocket of a second pair of sweats he'd brought me.

Tonight, I was washing my other clothes in the sink. They were day after hospital comfy clothes, but at least I didn't look ridiculous in them, like I did in this.

"I'll pay you back," I said. "As soon as this is over. And with interest."

He nodded, completely serious. "I know you will." He nodded toward the spot where he'd nearly had a confrontation with Wenslo last night. "Do you trust this guy?"

Should I lie? No. He'd see right through it. I'd never been able to effectively lie to him, even when it had been about a surprise birthday party or a Christmas present. "No."

He nodded again. "Good. I'd have been more worried if you'd said yes."

The sun beat down on me as I stepped out of the car. With how late I'd slept in, it would have been easy to forget it was afternoon already if this wasn't California.

Travis leaned over the center console. "I'll wait."

"That's probably not a great idea. I don't know how long I'll be. I don't even have a real plan at the moment."

"No plan?" His face got all stubborn. "Are you sure-" He interrupted himself for a second, clenching his jaw. "I'll wait."

I slammed the door shut, then snapped my service belt around my waist, pulling my baggy shirt over it. The tug on my stitches was worth having my hands free. It was obvious I was wearing something, but hopefully it looked like a brace and not a bomb. I checked my ear for the sword. It hung in place, warm to the touch.

Without looking back, I marched toward Wenslo's building. No use trying to hide where I was going. It would be a waste of time, which I didn't feel like I had to spare.

Where was Kenzie right now? Was she scared? Confused? He had better not have left her with my dad. Sure, my dad would take care of her, but Ghira could figure that out too easily.

No, Travis was smart. And a little paranoid. If I'd been worried when I told him to hide our baby, then he would have hidden her well. Another reason I shouldn't be around him. If something happened to him, I'd have a hard time finding my little girl, even if I did find a way to stop Ghira.

And if something happened to both of us, she'd lose both of her parents.

The place was much busier today. I passed what looked like interns on the sidewalk, then a few men in suits. It almost made me wonder what type of place this really was, but I hadn't thought to look into it more before passing out last night, and had slept in way too long this morning to take the time.

I shoved past a couple people before realizing that this close to the museum, I really shouldn't be drawing attention to myself. Cleaned up and in different clothes, I looked entirely different than the woman who had robbed the museum the day before, but it wasn't enough to risk drawing attention to myself.

After that thought, I kept my head tucked down, not looking anyone in the face. I made it through the front doors and to Wenslo's office. Behind me, a man in a tweed jacket stared. I'd seen him facing me when I walked by, and could feel his eyes boring into my back. Was he just some creeper, staring at the stitches on my face, or had he recognized me?

I swung the office door open and flung myself inside, shutting the door behind me. Smooth. Real smooth. And not at all suspicious.

When I looked away from the door, I caught Denise staring at me from behind the receptionist's desk. She blinked, looking concerned, but not as freaked out as I would have been if the woman who'd locked me in a closet at gunpoint the night before had just flown through my office door like something scary was chasing her.

Straightening my service belt under my shirt, I smiled at her. "Hi. I need to talk to Wenslo."

She looked genuinely confused.

"Oh." I looked around the room until I found a nameplate. "Doctor Thompson."

"He's busy at the moment." Somehow her tone was super professional, like she dealt with crazy people every day. "If you'll take a seat, I'll let him know you're here."

If that guy in the hall had recognized me, I might not have much time until cops started to arrive. I'd forgotten about the stitches at first. They made my face rather recognizable. "I'm sorry, but this can't wait." I shoved past her and marched toward the back room, her trailing me and objecting.

And then for the second time in as many days, I opened the door and nearly freaked out, seeing who was on the other side.

Yes, Wenslo. That wasn't a surprise. But the person with him? Surprise didn't cover it.

Pink eyes. Check. Sword on her back. Yep, that too. Creepy smile? Perfectly in place.

Ghira.

CHAPTER TWELVE

"You!" I shouted. I didn't even know if I was shouting at Ghira or Wenslo, but it didn't really matter. They both deserved it. I reined in the instinct to make a run for it, my heart pounding in my ears. Showing weakness to this woman would be a very bad idea.

As if she hadn't already shown how much stronger she was than me, after knocking me around in that weird forest in Faerie. She probably only saw me as weak.

I fought down a weird sense of betrayal. I didn't even know Wenslo. Didn't trust him in the slightest. And yet, for some reason I did feel a pang. I guess robbing a museum together didn't make us friends.

"Have you gained the ability to lie?" Ghira asked Wenslo, ignoring my interruption.

"No," Wenslo answered. "Until this moment, I truly had no idea where she was."

Gained the ability to lie? What did that mean? I resisted the urge to feel for the bracelet hanging from my service belt. If I tried to grab it now, I'd just be showing our hand.

Now Ghira turned her attention to me. I couldn't stop the small shiver that escaped as her pink eyes looked me up and down. Hopefully she didn't notice my moment of extra weakness. While what she wore could pass for human, it had an other-worldly style to it. Leather pants, and a silk shirt of some kind. And then there was me, in my sweats and *I Love LA* t-shirt.

Wow, Jay, you have more important things to worry about right now than how you look compared to your arch-nemesis.

My side warmed in agreement. I bit my lip so I didn't jump. I'd thought that stupid light was going away. Or, more accurately, hoped. Thankfully it wasn't bright enough to see from under my shirt, but I could feel the heat. Why was it heating up right now?

"Why don't you obey me?" Ghira asked, her tone curious. This was the most civil she'd ever spoken to me. Were we actually going to have a real conversation?

"Why would I obey you?" I croaked out an answer, my mouth dry. Did the light heat up more when it was protecting me? Did Denise out in the hallway know how much danger she was in right now? How many other people were in the building? Could Ghira make them all come after me at the same time? Was Travis close enough that she could compel him to do her will? Just how far away did someone have to be to be out of range of her ability?

I shifted my weight, distracting myself to keep from spiraling.

"Because I told you to." Ghira stepped closer, studying me. Now I knew how those bacteria under a microscope felt.

"And that means I just obey you?" I wanted it to come out authoritative. It didn't.

"Usually it does," she answered.

The thought of Grayson's pink eyes almost had me backing away. But she'd admitted she couldn't control me, for whatever reason. Right now I needed to worry more about her bringing out a sword than mind-control.

"I need you to come with me." Ghira took a step in my direction, the intensity from Faerie back. "Since you are the one who closed the portal, I need your blood to reopen it." She raised a hand before I could protest. "Not all of your blood. Just a bit. Though it must be fresh. If you come with me, you will be fine."

Being fine sounded pretty good right now. If I could believe her.

For some reason I got the feeling she was telling me the truth. I'd always been able to read people well, even before I'd become a cop.

But if I went with her, helped her reopen the portal, then her husband would come through. The one that supposedly enjoyed feasting on humans. And if he had an ability like Ghira, they very well could be unstoppable. Even if she did let me live, I'd be unleashing something on the world that the world definitely wasn't ready for. Yeah, helping her reopen the portal? Not happening. I'd die before doing that. I didn't need to say my answer out loud. She read it all on my face.

"Do you know what I went through to make that portal?" Ghira hissed, moving around a desk in my direction. She'd transformed instantly from calm and curious to intensely angry, that quickly. "The years of struggle, the sacrifices? If making portals isn't your natural ability, then it's more difficult than you can imagine. Can you imagine how difficult it is to make a portal?"

She was in my face now, but I refused to back down. Running from a predator got a person killed. She waited, like she truly wanted to hear my answer.

"I imagine it would be extremely difficult," I finally answered.

"You're honest." Ghira answered. "For a human." She took a couple steps back and cocked her head. "Wenslo. Grab her."

I looked to him, trying to keep the panic off of my face. I couldn't take her by herself, let alone the two of them. He'd been injured the same day I was, but I hadn't seen one single sign that the injuries were bothering him.

Not that it made much of a difference. A weak spot would be helpful if it was just the two of us getting into it, but meant nothing when Ghira was here as well.

He sidled around Ghira, giving me a look I had no idea how to interpret. Was he under her control? Or just obeying her?

Wait. His eyes were their normal dark brown. They hadn't turned pink like Grayson's had when he'd been under her control. Wenslo was, at the moment, making decisions for himself. Would he secretly try to help me? How loyal was he to Ghira?

From what I'd seen, loyalty among the fae was severely lacking.

I raised my hands in the air, pretending to give in.

Unlike when we were in Faerie, Ghira seemed to get no pleasure from what was going on here. She just waited, intent, while Wenslo moved forward.

When he was between Ghira and me, blocking me from her view, I unclipped my sword earring, backed three steps until I was clear, and took off through the door into the hallway.

Behind me, I heard Ghira yell at Wenslo. "Bring her to me."

Wenslo bolted after me out into the smaller hallway that led to the reception area. I flew past the doors lining the space, heading straight for the one that would take me out into the larger hallway, where I could maybe, maybe, make it outside.

When I burst into the waiting room, poor Denise almost fell out of her chair.

"What is always going on with you?" she asked, her voice indignant.

"Run," I said, not taking the time to actually explain. I rushed for the opposite side of the room, and the doorway there, Wenslo close on my heels. Was he chasing me because he wanted to escape also? Or chasing me for Ghira?

I wasn't about to wait around and find out.

Skidding into the main hallway, I took half a second to look both ways. If there were people in the way, I'd try for a different exit. I didn't need to give Ghira any more ammo to throw at me than she already had.

Without an ounce of exertion showing, Wenslo followed me. "Out the back," he said, and I didn't argue. Travis was out the front. Sweet, wonderful Travis. Who I would probably get killed if I got him into this situation, even though ninety percent of me wanted to go running out there, just to have someone at my back I could trust.

I couldn't see his eyes go pink. Couldn't handle him trying to hurt me, when I knew for a fact he would never if he had the choice.

"Wait!" Denise yelled from behind us. It was her voice, but not her tone.

Crap.

I ran harder.

Wenslo stayed behind me, though I had no doubt that he could pass me like I was standing still if he was so inclined.

"Stop!" Denise yelled again. "Stop, or I'll damage myself!"

Okay. Yeah. That made me stop. I slid to a standstill on the marble floor and turned around slowly, keeping my earring sized sword gripped tightly in my hand.

Denise walked forward, smirking. She held a large pair of office scissors in her hand. The shears were definitely long enough to do some damage if she skewered herself with them.

"That's a really unprofessional face," I told her. "You're going to get yourself fired."

She frowned, confusion taking over the smugness. "Fired?"

"Why did you stop?" Wenslo mouthed to me.

I ignored him.

Ghira came out of the door to the reception room down the hallway, in no hurry at all.

Wenslo kept his back to Ghira. Hiding his eyes?

"As if you could escape from me with such little effort," Ghira said, tone as smooth as butter. She walked forward, stopping by Denise. "If you don't do exactly as I say, this woman will meet an unfortunate end." She cocked her head, gaze shifting to Wenslo. "I'm disappointed in you. Catching this human should have been easy work."

"She's faster than she looks." Wenslo continued to keep his back to her.

"Can I assume you'll be coming with me?" Ghira asked.

What choice did I have? I didn't know Denise. But could I just take off and let Ghira make her kill herself?

Denise lifted the scissors in her hand, eyes looking dead beneath the pink. Right as I was thinking that, Wenslo spun around, stabbing Denise through the stomach with his sword.

Denise slid off the blade, collapsing silently to the ground.

"What are you doing?" I yelled, dropping down and rolling Denise over. She was alive, but her eyes were still pink. She didn't even seem to notice me. I wadded up part of her shirt and applied pressure. She didn't fight it.

"Oh, Wenslo," Ghira clicked her tongue, like she was disappointed.

"How did you acquire immunity? This one didn't share something with you, did she?"

"As our contract was fulfilled the moment you set foot in Faerie," Wenslo said, finally looking up at Ghira. "I see no reason to answer that, and you cannot force me to."

Outside, far in the distance, the sound of sirens caught my attention. A small amount of hope fizzled through me, and was gone. First aid training hadn't covered a lot, but Denise wasn't moving. The bleeding was sluggish at this point, but she was pale, and her body starting to get cold.

"I think it's time we part ways, Ghira," Wenslo said. "The human law enforcement will be here soon. You can't control them all at once. And I would think you aren't ready for that kind of attention?"

Ghira snarled a little. "You don't know that they're coming here."

"Actually," Wenslo nodded at Denise on the floor. "I do. She had a picture of you with standing orders to call them if you were to show yourself. So you should go." He pointed the tip of his blood-coated sword at her. "Unless, of course, you wish to take me on." He nodded at me on the floor. "Oh, and her. She is armed. I realize she isn't much of a threat alone, but I'm fairly confident you would struggle to take on both of us."

A head popped out of one of the offices, took in what was going on, and disappeared. We couldn't get into this here. How many innocent people were in this building? Let alone the police officers and medics that were on their way.

The sirens grew louder. What a whirlwind, my relationship with the police department this week. One of them, to being wanted by them for a robbery, and now, at the moment, they may literally be saving my life.

Ghira literally growled, and I leaned back away from her, still holding pressure on Denise's wound. I could try to drag Denise away, but didn't want to move her.

"I'll find you again," Ghira snapped at me. "When you're alone. Or I'll find someone you care about. You can't avoid giving me what I want." She turned and stalked away. Right as she slammed into one of the double doors to go outside, the other opened.

I caught a glimpse of two police cars outside, before it registered who had come through the other door.

Travis.

I held my breath as he turned a little to give Ghira room to pass him in the doorway, praying that she didn't recognize him from Grayson's memories.

She didn't seem to. But maybe that was because she didn't think a human was important enough to look in the face.

"Let's go," Wenslo said, reaching down to tug on my arm.

"Hey!" Travis yelled from the end of the hallway. He started running toward us.

I looked down at Denise. Could I just leave her here? Travis was a Boy Scout. He wouldn't be able to run past her, not even for me. And everyone here would be safer with me out of the picture.

Leaning down, I squeezed Denise's hand, my own covered in slippery blood. "Hold on."

I looked up. It was a long hallway, but Travis was fast. He'd be on us soon, and I'd never get away.

Our eyes locked, for just a moment.

And then I ran.

With no destination in mind, I ran. Ran hard. My side ached after only a short distance. Travis was going to catch up with me if he didn't stop to help Denise.

Wenslo hit a door in front of us pretty hard, and it flew open, letting in bright sunlight.

I took a short second to look over my shoulder. Travis leaned over Denise, one hand holding pressure on her wound, the other holding a phone to his ear. He didn't notice me checking on him.

Good. The less contact we had right now, the better. Ghira hadn't seemed to know who he was, but if she noticed him... She could probably get me to do anything she wanted.

"Come on," Wenslo said, impatient.

I obeyed, nearly falling through the door to get outside. But I only got a couple steps before I caught up and shoved Wenslo, making him stumble.

He turned an indignant look on me.

"Why did you stab Denise?" I yelled. I clutched my earring tight, ready to order it to full-size at the slightest sign of him coming in my direction.

He held up his hands. "Would you have left if Ghira had control of her? If she was about to be forced to harm herself?"

I deflated a little.

"Of course you wouldn't. I've known enough humans to be able to tell what type you are. I saw what you did for that guard at the museum. Denise wasn't going to make it out of that altercation without something happening. If I caused the damage, I could control how much and where. The wound will bleed excessively, but if your medics get here in any reasonable amount of time, Denise will be fine."

Turning and walking away, Wenslo glanced back at me, probably to see if I'd still follow. I didn't for a moment, thinking. But I couldn't come up with a better option. I could feel how white my face must be, my body cold even under the hot sun. He waited until I caught up, then wrapped my arm on my good side through his, half helping, half dragging me forward.

"She could still be around here somewhere," Wenslo said, scanning the street. "She didn't want to take on a large amount of humans at once, but that doesn't mean she isn't still looking for a chance to get us alone."

Who the "she" was, I had no doubt. "I thought you could take her?"

He shrugged. "I'd like to think so. But in truth…" he didn't finish his sentence.

Wonderful. That didn't give me much comfort.

"Now what?" I asked.

"Now we come up with a plan for how to get that," he pointed toward my belt where the bracelet was still clipped, "onto her wrist. Then I say the magic words, and voila."

"And voila." That wasn't an especially strong confidence booster.

Wenslo ushered me away, checking over his shoulder. "We can discuss this at my place. She doesn't know where I live. It's our best chance of staying out of her clutches until we're ready."

Great. Back to the his apartment thing. He had just helped save me, but that didn't make me trust him in the slightest. No, he had his own agenda. Our interests had been aligned, but how long would that last?

After a second to think, I followed him. No better options were coming to me at the moment. Follow him, get more info, and then pivot if I needed to.

The first two blocks we rushed as much as my stitches would allow, me checking behind us frequently. But eventually, Wenslo slowed the pace a little. I tried not to let him see how hard the fast pace had been on me. How long had the ER doc said it should take for the stupid wound to heal? Like six weeks. Way too long. And all of this movement probably wasn't helping.

This was a good chance for me to get more out of Wenslo. If I could find a good way to ask, without making him suspicious. "Why couldn't Ghira control you?" I blurted out. Yeah, real subtle. But I wasn't a real subtle person, so it would have to do.

His grin rivaled the Cheshire Cat's. "The bracelet you carry wasn't the only thing we picked up in the museum yesterday. I wasn't entirely sure it would work, but it seems to be doing a satisfactory job."

Oh good. Not only had I helped steal one priceless artifact, but apparently we'd taken two. "What was it? Will it work for anyone against Ghira?"

His grin dropped. "That is none of your concern."

Okay. Touchy subject.

"How far is this apartment of yours?"

"Not far." He slowed his pace to match mine, which had slowed even more. I was fading.

I should have just stayed home from work yesterday. I should have spent the day playing *Call of Duty* and eating taffy, maybe drink some coffee in the mix. I could definitely go for a nice hot cup right now, if only to feel like something was normal.

"What are you thinking about?" Wenslo asked.

"Uh." Did I tell him? He was going to think I was ridiculous. "Coffee?"

"Ah," he nodded. "I often find myself thinking of coffee as well."

Did they have coffee in Faerie? If not, no wonder all the fae were trying to get here. "Why were you working with Ghira, before?" I blurted out. My curiosity was probably one of the reasons I'd become a cop. Now was the perfect time to ask questions, while we were just walking and while he needed me, for something. "Your eyes weren't pink in the warehouse," I added when he didn't answer. "You were helping her voluntarily."

A muscle jumped in his jaw. "I wouldn't exactly call it voluntarily."

"She has something on you?"

He forced a smile fake enough that even I, who didn't know him, had no trouble knowing it wasn't real. "She did. I agreed to something that I didn't fully understand, and was trapped. Too many years around humans made me lax and not wary enough of making a deal with a fae."

I considered that for a moment. "What did you get out of the deal?"

"That's a discussion for another time." He swung to the right, tapping in a code on the door of a nice apartment building. "We're here."

Shoving down my apprehension, I followed him in. He was my best chance at an ally who could help me take down Ghira. Possibly only chance, depending on how the captain and Bylilly felt about me robbing a freaking museum.

He unlocked an apartment on the first floor. Expensive in this area of town, and especially expensive to have a place near the exit.

He motioned for me to go in first, and I did.

The room was dimly lit, dark shades on every window. Definitely not giving off good vibes. Wenslo closed the door behind us. "Where are the…" I turned around to ask Wenslo about the light switch. He stared at me, face odd. "Lights?"

"What?" I asked. I looked down to see what he was staring at.

Shoot. The light under my shirt was back, and glowing brighter than ever.

Wenslo took a step toward me, eyes fixed on my abdomen. "What is that?"

That didn't bode well for him being able to help me figure out what had happened to me in Faerie. "Funny thing. I was going to ask you the exact same question." No use trying to hide it from him now.

I rolled my shirt up a little, letting the light shine even brighter. I peeled off the bandage covering my wound. Light burst out from between the stitches, even though the top layer of my flesh was scabbed over.

Wenslo walked over and knelt down, poking at my skin with his finger. The light pulsed, and he jerked back.

"Hey!" I said. "That's still really sore!" But it wasn't really about the pain. I didn't want him touching me. Did he have another ability, or did fae only have one? Could he do something other than throw people around with his mind? Could he do something to me if we made contact?

"When did this start?" he asked, not taking his eyes off the light.

"Yesterday," I answered.

Wenslo stood, and then he finally looked me in the eyes, his face unreadable. He didn't say anything.

"What?" I asked. "Am I dying? Did I pick up some weird disease in Faerie?"

He ran a hand through his hair, looking more agitated than when we'd been in the middle of robbing a museum together, by far. "No, no, nothing like that."

I slumped a little, relief making me weak.

"It may be worse. It wasn't a disease you picked up in Faerie, but a parasite."

I reached back, looking for something to support my weight and finding a counter to lean on. "What does that mean?" I got out.

"They're small creatures, made of light." He bent back down for another look. "I believe your people call them will-o-wisps."

"Will-o-wisps?" He was kidding, right? Did fae make jokes? So far they'd just seemed weirdly serious. "Aren't those some legend in like Ireland or Scotland or somewhere?"

"Will-o-wisps to the Scots, Ellylldan in Wales, luz mala to those in Uruguay and Argentina. Even the ancient Romans had a name for them. Ignis fatuus. The creatures are well known to your ancestors." He studied me like some puzzle he was trying to figure out.

I tried to shove down the panic. It worked pretty well, actually. An evil light living inside my body didn't seem that terrible after a hateful fae woman had been trying to capture me for over twenty-four hours. What could a light do to me, anyway? Yeah, the light wasn't nearly as bad as Ghira. Especially not with what had just happened. Would Denise be okay? Was she still alive?

"What do I do about it?" I held up my hand, stopping him from answering. "Wait. How do I prioritize? Will-o-wisp, or Ghira?"

Wenslo still looked a little freaked out, which, in turn, was making it difficult for me to keep the panic from bubbling up from my gut. These swings were going to kill me. I'd been keeping it together about this light, until someone who never seemed worried about anything started freaking out.

"I'm going to say Ghira?" Wenslo's answer sounded like a question. "I have no idea what to do with the will-o-wisp. I'll have to do some studying. It's unlikely to kill you."

"Oh, very reassuring," I muttered. But it hadn't killed me so far. We were back to not letting it freak me out. At least for the moment. I was just going to naively pretend that things were going to keep trucking in the right direction.

Sure. Like they'd done the last twenty-four hours. Were we at forty-eight now? I didn't even know. And I didn't have the brain power to try and figure it out.

"Okay then," I said when he didn't continue. "What's your big plan for getting this bracelet on Ghira?"

"Ghira is very strong." The words came out of his mouth way too happy. "But, she can only control one person at a time. If we have enough people, we will be able to distract her. Once her attention is elsewhere, you will place the bracelet on her arm. I'm allowing you to do it because you aren't susceptible to her power. Even with my trinket, I fear she may be able to control me if she prepares herself."

Wenslo snapped his fingers, excited. He reached forward like he was going to shove my shirt up again, and I slapped away his hand. He held them both up, proving he wouldn't try it again.

"I believe I know why you can't be controlled by Ghira." He pointed at my abdomen. "It's the will-o-wisp. It has to be. They have some powers of their own, though nothing like the ability of a high fae."

Great. He had to bring up the strange being living inside my body again. I'd been all set to focus on Ghira.

"Until it emerges, I think you're immune to Ghira." He walked away, toward the fridge.

"Until it emerges?" I squeaked out. What did that mean? What would happen when it did? It wouldn't make me explode, like *Alien* or something, would it? I reached down and placed my hand over my stitches. They were warm again. Really warm.

Unbothered by my tone of voice, Wenslo opened the refrigerator door and pulled out a glass bottle of milk.

I lifted an eyebrow.

"Yes. They are their own entities. It won't need you for long." He popped the top off his bottle of milk and took a swig, then leaned back against the counter, face pensive. "We'd better get this bracelet on Ghira soon, in case you lose your immunity."

"How do we find her?" I asked. "And how do we get her somewhere innocent people won't get hurt?" My stomach roiled at the thought of Denise, bleeding out on the ground.

"I can contact Ghira," Wenslo said. "And while I'm doing that, you can get our backup."

My heart dropped. "Who's that?"

He raised an eyebrow. "Your friends at the LAPD, of course. We won't be able to make a more detailed plan until we find out how much help we'll have, and where Ghira wishes to meet."

No. I couldn't see Grayson like that again. Couldn't have him hurt me, or worse, hurt himself. Or even worse than that, force me to hurt him. I crossed my arms in front of my chest, ready to argue.

"Do you have anyone else you trust to get the job done?" Wenslo asked.

I let out the pent-up anger. No. I didn't trust anyone else but Travis. And there was no way I was involving him in this. Maybe if it was just him. Maybe. But Ghira could send him after Kenzie, and he was the only person who knew where she was. Keeping Travis away not only protected him, but Kenzie too.

"Okay. I'll go down to the station," I said. Maybe the captain could make sure Grayson was somewhere else. Somewhere far away. I waited until Wenslo met my eyes. "After we get this bracelet on Ghira, I never want to see you again. Not after Denise."

Wenslo's face didn't even twitch, my words not seeming to bother him a bit. "We'll see about that."

CHAPTER THIRTEEN

Standing in front of the station felt... weird. Normal had changed drastically in the last couple days. So drastically, I wasn't sure it could ever become normal again. Joining the police department had saved me. I'd been in a bad place after Kenzie was born. No matter what I did, no matter what I tried, I couldn't get better.

I'd nearly lost everything. If Hank hadn't found me that night...

Being a cop gave me purpose. Provided me a way to put others ahead of myself, to focus on something other than my problems. I needed it. Desperately.

But standing here today, my feelings were mixed. Relief that it wasn't going to be just Wenslo and me taking on Ghira. Fear, that I wouldn't ever be viewed the same, that I wouldn't be able to explain the disappearance, let alone the museum.

And the worst part, looking Grayson in the face.

Wenslo and I had taken thirty minutes to toss ideas back and forth. He'd given me a better picture on what kind of man Ghira's husband was, without going into detail. I didn't need detail to know we didn't want him here.

Whatever else happened, we couldn't let him through.

I started up the steps, much more slowly than my usual jog. My pain pills were still at the hotel as far as I knew. And the ones I'd taken before getting into the car with Travis this afternoon weren't doing much at the moment.

Cops I knew gave me odd looks as I made my way to the front door. Only a couple days ago, they'd been cheering for me. None of them acted hostile, just like they didn't know what to do with me. The captain had probably told them I was coming in, and there was to be no contact. I'd called her to make sure she was here, and that Grayson wasn't.

The captain was waiting for me right inside the door. She ushered me into her office, all eyes on us as we walked past the other officers. She closed her door behind us. That didn't help with the eyes, but it did with the eavesdropping.

"Are you okay?"

Her question threw me. Of course I wasn't okay.

"Physically," she added. "You don't have any new injuries, do you?"

"No, nothing new." The old wounds were plenty. Especially now that I knew one had a living being inside it.

She nodded curtly. "We're going to treat you like you're in witness protection. But it has to be off the books, because the brass isn't happy we're causing trouble with the fae this soon after they showed themselves."

Wonderful. I'd made the higher ups upset. And I could see where they were coming from, if I wasn't in the middle of this, I'd be upset too. All of us would have benefitted from getting to know the fae better before going to war with one of them.

"And I'm sure you've guessed that Agent Bylilly is expecting to be notified as soon as you're located. Someone in this office is probably on the phone with her now."

Yeah. I'd already guessed that. There were too many cops here for me to know them all personally, and an in with an FBI agent would be hard for some to pass up.

The captain went behind her desk to sit, putting her elbows on top and leaning in toward me. "So. Do you want to explain the last twenty-four hours? Because I was beginning to think you were dead. Until you showed up on security video, robbing the freaking Natural History

Museum. That's going to be a difficult one for me to explain away, no matter what you have to tell me."

A pang of guilt hit me, but I shoved it down. I hadn't had a choice. Not really. How much did I tell the captain? Everything, probably. She needed to be prepared if I was going to ask her to send my co-workers into a situation where they may end up trying to kill each other, against their will.

"The fae that we captured. She can control people," I said. "She's after me now, and everyone I'm around is a liability."

The captain's face tightened, but she kept it together admirably well. I didn't even know if I'd believe it if some lowly cop came and told me a fae might make her friends try to kill her. Maybe Grayson had already tried to tell her, but she hadn't said anything on the phone.

"And why did you come back?" she asked.

I leaned forward, putting everything I could into my face, staring her in the eyes. "I can't take down this woman alone. Bullets can't seem to hit her. She's a pro with a sword. She has an ability that she can use to make innocent people throw themselves at me with no fear of getting hurt. I'm struggling here, Cap, and I've got a plan, but it's going to require some muscle."

Got a plan was a little generous. I could assume Ghira would want to meet at the portal, but until Wenslo got back with me for sure, I didn't know. It didn't really matter. We couldn't take Ghira on, not just the two of us. No matter where we met, we were going to need backup.

"How many cops?" the captain asked. Her voice was hard. I'd known her long enough to recognize the tone. She hated what she would be asking her people to do, but knew it needed to be done.

"If it was just for me, I'd never put them in danger," I clarified. But she already knew that. We all were the same in that way. "She's trying to bring her husband here. And from the sound of it, that would be bad. Really bad."

The captain leaned back, closing her eyes and pinching the bridge of her nose. She had to be exhausted too. A pang of guilt hit me harder than the first. Hopefully she hadn't been trying too hard to find me when I hadn't wanted to be found. "How many officers?" she asked.

"Ten?"

The captain opened one eye.

"The more there are, the more distracted she'll be," I answered her unasked question.

"And the more to pile on whoever she's controlling." She nodded. "A good plan. But what are you going to do with her once you have her? How are we supposed to contain her if she can control people?"

I grimaced. Here was the hard part. Wenslo and I had agreed that it would be better if I didn't tell the captain the whole plan. I had to lie, or convince her not to ask. "I can't tell you, Cap."

She raised an eyebrow, face tightening. She wasn't out yet, but I was losing her.

"If she gets in your head, she'll know. And she'll be able to stop us."

My gut clenched as she studied me, begging internally for her to trust me on this. And to not ask what happened if Ghira tried to control me.

"I feel completely unprepared for this," the captain said. I started to object automatically, not really wanting to believe that there was anything she wasn't ready for, but she put her hand up and I snapped my mouth closed out of respect. "I'm not saying your plan is bad. How can I when I don't know the plan? But this is above my pay grade. We're going to have to bring Agent Bylilly in on this. You're asking an awful lot."

And I had to ask one more thing, which would be even harder. "And the agents need to leave behind their weapons. Guns aren't reliable around the fae, and it could prevent casualties if Ghira takes an agent over."

"No weapons?" The captain's jaw tightened. "You're pushing it, aren't you, Officer Nofsky? The whole trust you thing?"

Of course. I should have seen this coming. Of course she wasn't going to let some low-level officer make a call like this. But I needed them. Wenslo and I could fail if it was just the two of us. And this was too important to allow the chance for failure.

I rubbed my side, the heat coming off my stitches somehow reassuring. "Let me talk to Bylilly about it. But firearms are just going to get people killed."

The captain pushed a button, and leaned back in her chair, staring me down, like I was the enemy now.

I waited for Bylilly, trying to convince myself that this was the right thing to do. It had to be. Wenslo and I couldn't take down Ghira alone. Bylilly probably had access to anything I could think to ask for, if I could convince her it was needed.

But the look in Denise's eyes... Did she remember what happened? Did she know that she'd almost died because of me? Or had she woken up, injured, with no idea how she'd gotten out in the hallway?

If she'd woken up at all. I could ask Travis. Would he forgive me for running? For leaving behind a badly injured civilian? It didn't matter. I didn't want to involve him even for as little a thing as asking if Denise was okay until Ghira was caught.

Or dead. The *or dead* was starting to look better and better. We were not equipped to hold her. In all the superhero movies they had secure prisons with contingencies for every type of super ability. But the movie always started after those places were up and running. How many failures did it take, how many lives, before they figured out how to stop Ghira's ability? Would it still work if her victim couldn't hear her voice? Being in the line of sight seemed to make no difference. It didn't matter at the moment. All that was up to people much higher on the chain of command than I was.

Agent Bylilly must have already been on her way, or in the building. She was marching through the captain's office door within five minutes of me agreeing to talk with her.

My guess was the captain had called her as soon as I'd called the captain. Probably what I would have done if the roles were reversed.

The captain stood and put out a hand. "Agent Bylilly. Thanks for coming."

Agent Bylilly shook her hand. "Of course." She looked at me. "I'm glad you're back. What's the situation?"

Wow. At least I wasn't getting yelled at by the feds. Very weird. But I'd take it.

"She can't say much," the captain answered for me. "The fae we're dealing with can infiltrate minds. And when she does, she can see anything you know." She looked at me for confirmation that what she was telling the agent was correct.

I nodded.

"What do you need from me?" Bylilly asked.

"Permission," I said. "Permission to take some officers in with me. I need the backup."

Bylilly studied me for a moment. Then turned to the captain. "Your thoughts on this?"

"At the moment? I'm not sure how we know that Officer Nofsky isn't being controlled by the fae as we speak, infiltrating the station. She's asked that we don't use firearms."

Oh shoot. I hadn't even thought of them figuring out that I couldn't be controlled. But there was no way I was going to tell them about the will-o-wisp, and my immunity. What if they found me a threat and locked me up because I had some type of parasite? Or worse, found a way to kill it, making me vulnerable to Ghira's control. No, the will-o-wisp was going to have to wait until Ghira was taken care of.

"The eyes," I blurted out. "You can tell by a person's eyes. They turn pink."

Bylilly studied me for way too long. How could she trust me? How could she know I wasn't lying? There wasn't a way she could know. But she was just going to have to risk it. The alternative was far worse.

"Did you talk to Grayson?" I asked the captain.

She lifted an eyebrow. "About what, specifically?"

She didn't know. Did I throw him under the bus? Did he remember what had happened when he was under? I didn't have a choice. "He knows what being controlled is like."

The captain pushed a button on her phone. "Bring me Officer Anderson."

That dirty... She'd had him here the whole time, after I'd specifically asked her to keep him away. If he didn't hate me for running off, there was no way he would let me go to the warehouse without him. Probably even if he did hate me.

I closed my eyes for a moment. I couldn't blame the captain. She was trying to figure out what was going on, what to do, as much as I was. I was just the one who'd had the misfortune of getting tangled up in the situation first, and much deeper.

The door opened and footsteps came in my direction, pausing behind my chair. I took a breath and opened my eyes.

Grayson didn't look at me. His eyes were solidly focused on the captain, and thankfully, solidly brown. "I'm here, Captain. What do you need?"

I dropped my gaze. I couldn't meet Grayson's eyes, even if he did deign to look at me. I hadn't been treating him like much of a partner. It wasn't truly my fault that he was in this danger, but at the same time, I had been the one that had gotten us here. If I'd had more time at the scene to make a good choice, I probably would have waited and gotten the higher ups involved before destroying the portal. But in the moment, I hadn't seen any other good option.

Even now, the thought that Ghira may have gotten her husband through before the LAPD contacted the feds, and then the feds got around to deciding the portal was actually there and a threat sent a shiver through my body.

"Please tell Agent Bylilly exactly what you told me yesterday," the captain said.

"I was following Jayla out of the building..." His eyes went unfocused, staring at nothing. "When suddenly, I couldn't control my body. I kept following her, but I tried to stop. I couldn't."

My heart broke a little more. He remembered. He remembered the whole thing.

"Whatever was controlling me forced me to talk to Ja- Officer Nofsky. And then-" his voice got rough. "She tried to make me hurt her."

Tears stung my eyes. This I hadn't known. He'd fought back.

"And why didn't you tell me this before?" Captain Harlow snapped. She took a deep breath in through her nose, not seeming to expect a real answer. "Just continue."

"The woman in my head laughed at me." Grayson stared over my head. "She would have gained control back, but Jayla was already gone."

The room went quiet for a moment, everyone weighing his story, and hopefully, the options they had before them.

"This plan of yours," Bylilly said in my direction. "What are our odds?"

Even though I'd been through the plan a thousand times in my head, I went through it again. My weapons didn't do much against Ghira. My gun was basically useless. Letting the cops with me go in heavily armed would be a huge mistake. By the time we figured out someone was possessed, they would have already taken out half of the rest of us if they were armed with anything that could possibly take down Ghira.

Wenslo would keep her talking, and I would slip in and snap the bracelet on her arm.

No, there was no other good option. Cops as a distraction, Wenslo to keep her from killing me, and me, with the bracelet. I couldn't think of anything better, not right off the cuff. Not one that would end this quickly. Other than bombing the warehouse, and I didn't even know if that could hurt her or not. I would have the best chance of getting close enough to get the bracelet on.

"I don't see any other way," I answered.

"Guns blazing?" the captain asked.

"No," Grayson and I said at the same time. We glanced at each other, and I got just a second to see how much he was hurting. He had to hate me. It was my fault he was in this situation.

"Guns don't work correctly around the fae," Bylilly said for us. "No one has much experience with the fae, so it's hard to even guess what her weakness is. I've seen some die as easily as a human, but if she is anything like the fae I know in Indiana, there won't be a way to kill her. Firearms are a risk, but one we are going to have to take."

No way to kill her? This was much worse than I thought. "Please," I said. "I don't want anyone to get hurt. A Taser was the only thing that stopped her last time, and it didn't last long."

"People are going to get hurt," Bylilly said. "Come to terms with that. We'll do what needs done anyway. There's no way my people are going into that warehouse without a way to protect themselves. If she has that portal back open, who knows what could have come through it by now. The monsters we've seen in Fort Wayne..." she trailed off.

I couldn't imagine what she'd seen. I only knew about what they'd allowed to make the news, which included a dragon and some troll things.

"We're going in armed," Bylilly finished.

I nodded, unable to force myself to answer verbally.

"You grabbed something at the museum, didn't you?" Bylilly asked out of nowhere, studying me as she waited for an answer. "That's what your plan is?"

I didn't give her one. The less she knew, the better.

After a moment, she gave up waiting for an answer and nodded. "Okay then. I'll get a team together. We leave in ten."

Unmarked cars blocked the road in front of the precinct. Bylilly and the captain stood at the front of a small group of heavily armed and armored agents.

This was it. We would hit her fast, and hard. And that had to be enough.

"Listen up," Agent Bylilly said. These people were all hers, not LAPD, except for Grayson and me. "You all have the info that Officer Nofsky was able to give us. It isn't much, but it's what we've got. We know this woman is extremely dangerous. Don't turn on your fellow agents just because of the possibility of them being controlled. But if their eyes go pink, do what you have to. Hitting her with a round isn't going to be easy, even for those who are experts here. But we don't have any better weapons to use against her, so on sight, just fire at will. With that many rounds going through the air, something has to land."

My gut clenched. Taking guns seemed like a big gamble. But what were we supposed to carry, swords? The people around the circle shuffled uneasily. These were the best of the best, but even they probably hadn't had much interaction with the fae. It was a huge relief to have people here that I didn't know rather than friends from the station, but every one of them still had a family and every one of them was here because of me.

"Okay then. Stay safe," Bylilly said. "And come back." She smacked the top of her black SUV, then moved to climb into the back seat.

I waited until everyone else loaded up, and went to an empty car. I needed just a little peace before we went back into one of the worst experiences in my life. But Grayson followed me.

The car ride was awkward. I couldn't look Grayson in the face, and he still didn't seem to want to look at me either. I'd practically begged the captain to make him stay behind, but she hadn't listened, and here we were.

Where we were going, there was a good chance one of us wouldn't be coming back. We needed to get this worked out, but I didn't even know where to start. The captain and Agent Bylilly were sitting up front, the captain driving. Five unmarked SUVs followed us. Bylilly hadn't been exaggerating when she'd said ten minutes.

The dread in the pit of my stomach grew as I watched the blocks pass by. We would be to the warehouse soon. Once there, I wouldn't have the chance to talk to Grayson alone again.

"So..." I said. "How was your day?" Well, that was pathetic.

Grayson looked at me and lifted an eyebrow. "Better than yours, I'm sure. But still not good. Sitting around waiting to see if my partner was dead or alive."

Okay, we were getting somewhere. He was admitting he was mad at me. "I didn't want you hurt." It came off sounding like an excuse, and in a way, it was. But he was still alive. That had to count for something.

Grayson went back to looking out the window. Things were worse than I'd thought.

"I'm sorry, Grayson. I don't know how to tell you how sorry." I didn't add that I wished he wasn't here today. That I was afraid that he would look at me like Denise had. That he would hurt someone because of me.

Finally he turned to me, and actually made full eye contact. "You think you need to say sorry?" he was agitated, voice rising. I tried to shush him a bit, afraid the captain would hear him through the divider, but he just ground his teeth, frustrated. "It isn't you who needs to say you're sorry." He dropped his head, avoiding my eyes again. "I would have killed you, Jay. I could feel it. She wanted you alive, but hated you enough I wanted you dead. For her. Of course you couldn't trust me enough to call me. I get it. I wouldn't have called me either."

The record level of anger I'd felt toward Ghira until this point just got blown out of the water. How could she just do this to people? Casually ruin their lives? I reached out and grabbed his wrist.

"That is not on you. They weren't your intentions. They weren't your thoughts. They were hers. If you ever need to talk about it, I understand. But as far as I'm concerned, it wasn't you who did anything. We're square, and if you never want to think about it again, that's fine by me."

Grayson teared up. Something I'd only ever seen one other time, when we'd gone into a house on a domestic, and there had been a kid, dead on the floor.

I leaned over and gave him a quick hug. He wouldn't stand for any more than something short, and pulled away. "You haven't said anything about your stitches. Are they doing okay? You sure you should be doing this?"

The last thing I wanted to talk about right now was my stitches. But it was very sweet of him to ask. "I'm sure." Sure I didn't want to have anything to do with Ghira, but also sure I was the only one that had any real chance of stopping her right now.

"Okay," Grayson said, but he didn't look too sure.

The SUV crunched to a stop. I looked out the window.

Crap. The warehouse. Already.

The captain and Agent Bylilly opened their doors. I gave Grayson a moment to compose himself.

"You good?" I asked.

"Yeah," he answered, running his sleeve across his cheek.

Someone knocked on the window, nearly sending me out of my seat.

The captain opened my door. "You ready?" she asked.

"Ready," I said, though it wasn't the truth. At all. How did someone get ready for something like this?

She nodded and turned to go, checking her bullet-proof vest. I followed suit and checked my own, though it was probably useless. If I didn't have Wenslo waiting on me, I wouldn't be going in. Not with all of these armed agents. I should feel completely safe, surrounded by some of the best in the business. But I felt every emotion that was the opposite of safe.

I forced myself out of the SUV, and walked to the end of it, pausing for a deep breath before taking that last step and facing the warehouse. I clenched and unclenched my hands, trying not to turn and run the other direction. So far, in every meeting, Ghira had won. Maybe not exactly in the way she had wanted, but she'd definitely come out on top.

If she won today, it spelled disaster.

Wenslo stepped out of the shadow of the building. I took a deep breath and then took the lead, walking toward the warehouse.

No going back. For Kenzie.

"What's he doing here," Grayson hissed to me, hand on his gun.

"He's here to help." I hoped. I should have told them about him earlier, but I'd thought he'd stay hidden until we jumped Ghira. I should have known not to assume.

Grayson looked at me like I was an idiot.

"I know, I know," I said. "But we need all the help we can get right now."

He stayed strung as tight as a guitar string. "If you say so."

I grabbed his arm, making him look at me. "I say so."

We stared into each other's eyes for a moment, and I could see the moment he gave in. He nodded at me, not saying anything, but I knew. He was going to trust me on this.

"Nofsky?" The captain said, moving up beside me. "Who's this?" She nodded toward Wenslo.

"He's here to help," I repeated. "He doesn't like Ghira either."

"Why weren't we briefed on this?" Bylilly asked, stepping up beside the captain. Now I had them both ticked.

"I didn't know he was going to show up like this. But trust me, he's on our side." Again, I hoped.

"You're asking that a lot," the captain said, but then she walked away. They were in an even worse position than I was, trying to handle this with no real intel, hoping they could trust me.

They could. But there was no way of proving that.

All of us gathered around at the entrance to the warehouse. I nodded to Wenslo, and he nodded back. No one knew who he was, or how he'd been obeying Ghira the last time we'd been here, except for Grayson, who kept a close eye on the fae.

"You're early," I hissed at him when we got far enough ahead that no one else would overhear.

"I wanted to make sure everyone knew I was on your side, so I didn't get shot," he answered.

Okay. Valid. A little of the tension went out of my shoulders. "Is she in there?" I asked.

"Yes," he answered.

The tension in my body sky rocketed right back up. And I hadn't thought I could get any more wound up about this.

Wenslo sidled in closer to me. "Are you ready for this?"

"No." The answer was quick, honest. I was ready for it to be over. I wasn't ready to risk the lives of all these men and women. But one didn't happen without the other.

"Do you need a minute?" Grayson asked.

"I'm fine. Let's get this over with," I said.

"Okay then." The captain must have been eavesdropping. "You're sure she's in there?" she asked Wenslo. He gave a curt nod.

"Then cue the distraction," Agent Bylilly said. She nodded to the agent in front and he moved over to the door, paused a second, then flung it wide open.

I couldn't stop a slight pause. But I hid it well. And then pushed forward, the first one into the warehouse.

CHAPTER FOURTEEN

Walking back into the warehouse brought a strange sense of déjà vu, even though this time was very different than the last. I had a full squad backing me. Men and women who had probably seen all kinds of things in their careers. I had Wenslo on my side, instead of trying to kill me. That was nice. And we were much better prepared, knowing what Ghira was capable of.

Yet, somehow, this time felt even worse.

A laugh started up somewhere ahead of us in the dark warehouse. A laugh I knew all too well. She already knew we were here. It made sense that if she could control people, she could sense where everyone was.

The agents' lights swept the room, but with the echo, it was impossible to tell where the sound came from.

"All that work to try and force you back, and here you are, of your own volition," Ghira said from somewhere to my left. Or, at least it sounded like it came from my left.

A gunshot rang out. I jumped, looking wildly for the shooter. One of the agents ahead of me turned, and her eyes glowed pink in the dark.

Without pause or sound, the two agents closest to her jumped her, dragging her to the ground, fighting. Another agent knelt down, and in the light of his flashlight I could make out a body on the floor. The one who'd taken the bullet. The agent kneeling shook his head toward Bylilly.

The downed agent was dead.

I gripped my gun tighter. It wouldn't do me any good against Ghira. But it would against the others.

The agent who had shot the other slumped against her people, blinking. Her eyes were back to blue. I knew the moment she got with it enough to see the agent on the ground. Her eyes went wide and her hand went to her mouth, stopping a scream.

We had to keep moving. I waved everyone forward, but no one paid attention to me. They all eyed each other, stopped in place.

Finally, Bylilly stepped out in front. "Forward," she commanded. Everyone obeyed, even the trembling agent who had shot one of her friends.

The weird laughter started back up, and the group stalked forward, out for blood. They left the fallen agent on the ground.

One of the men to my left jumped the agent in front of him. They both went down, fighting for their lives. I couldn't make out much of the scuffle in the near dark, but it was violent. Then suddenly the aggressor threw his hands up. The other man on the ground gripped him in a chokehold.

Bam. A shot rang out. An agent on the other side of the formation crumpled to the ground.

She was jumping from agent to agent, keeping everyone freaked out. Darting from person to person quickly enough that it was impossible to know at any moment who she had control over. This was our distraction. We had to use it while we could, or it would be too late. All of these agents would be dead, and then she'd be after me, and only me.

I slid out of the group, moving behind a wall of boxes. Wenslo moved beside me, staying within arm's distance. A small jolt of relief went through me. I tugged the magic bracelet off of my belt, gripping it tightly enough that one of the spikes bit into my skin. The flesh went tingly, like I'd sat on my hand too long.

I moved agonizingly slowly through the warehouse. If we drew Ghira's attention, we'd have agents on us instead of fighting each other. More gunshots rang out, and I bit my lip to hold back the scream that wanted to break free. People were dying.

Grayson, stay safe.

We weaved through the warehouse, checking every nook and cranny, until finally I saw movement. I tapped Wenslo's arm and pointed. He studied the area for a second, then nodded.

The darkness around me somehow felt both overwhelming, and comforting. It covered me, but also hid any contingency plans Ghira might have in place. She'd proven herself to be a planner.

I worked my way around, coming at Ghira from behind. Wenslo waited in the shadows, a bigger distraction for Ghira than the team coming at her. I took a second, closing my eyes and taking a breath. I couldn't wait too long. The team was killing each other. I holstered my gun, needing two hands to work the bracelet closed.

A nod told Wenslo I was ready. He stepped out from behind a row of crates and directly into Ghira's vision.

"Wenslo!" I couldn't see her face, but her tone was gleeful. "You didn't completely betray me."

"How was I to know a swarm of humans would descend on you at this time? Do you know how they found you?" he asked. His non answer didn't give him away quite as quickly as the truth, but surely Ghira would notice he hadn't denied it.

I inched closer, crouched low to avoid her peripheral vision.

"Did you bring her?" Ghira asked.

"She's here," Wenslo answered.

"I can't sense her. Do you know why?"

I didn't give him the chance to answer. I didn't need her, or anyone else in the room who might overhear, knowing that I had a Faerie parasite growing in my body. I jumped forward, attempting to snap the bracelet around her arm before she had a chance to notice me.

I failed.

Cat-like, Ghira dodged, knocking me off target.

Wenslo didn't give her a chance to recover. He was on her in an instant, taking her to the ground. They exchanged blows, rolling across the floor.

Waiting for an opening, I prayed that while she was distracted, no one was dying. A rush of feet was coming toward us. Hopefully not of someone possessed.

There. An opportunity. I jumped in, grabbing Ghira's arm. She spit and tried to bite me. I rolled sideways, using my weight to pin her arm under me.

Super agile, Ghira kicked me in the back of the head, nearly knocking me off. But I wasn't going that easily. I put my knee on her shoulder joint, pressing all of my weight into it. She shrieked and tried to kick me again, but this time, I knew what she was going to do and braced myself, taking the blow without flinching.

I forced the bracelet around her bare arm, and rammed it closed, blood pouring over my hand from the spikes being forced into her arm.

Ghira screamed, in pain or anger, it was impossible to tell, and thrashed twice as hard as before, nearly throwing Wenslo off of her.

He recovered, and yelled something in another language. It didn't sound human.

The bracelet sparked, and Ghira instantly stopped fighting.

I stayed in place. No way I was letting this maniac go free until I knew for sure the bracelet had worked. Or, if I was about to die from friendly fire, which was a very real possibility.

"Don't move," Wenslo ordered.

We both took another second to breathe, and evaluate. People from the team made their way toward us, moving into place around Ghira, weapons solidly pointed at her. I checked every one of their eyes.

No pink.

Grayson came to stand next to me, gun trained on Ghira.

"Ghira?" Wenslo asked.

"Yes," she answered, her voice muffled from being pressed into the ground.

"Let her up," Wenslo said.

"Are you sure?" I asked, like she couldn't just toss me across the room if he wasn't in control.

"I'm sure," Wenslo answered.

Reluctantly, I shifted my weight back. She rolled over and took a deep breath.

"Stand," Wenslo said.

Ghira obeyed, eyes almost glassy. What was wrong with her? Was she reacting this badly to having no magic? Why wasn't she fighting physically, even if she couldn't use her powers?

"What's going on?" Bylilly called out, walking up behind her agents.

Wenslo turned to her and smiled, a slimy smile that I hadn't seen him use before. "She's no threat anymore." Was this it? Was the nightmare truly over?

"I've heard she's formidable, even without her powers," Bylilly countered.

"If someone can't shoot her, she could probably kill at least half of us with her sword before getting taken out," I said.

"What do we do with her?" The captain asked. I hadn't even seen her come into the room, I'd been too focused on Ghira. I looked over real quick. She had a split lip and was going to have a nice shiner but otherwise looked okay.

"She's mine now," Wenslo said. "I'll be taking her."

"I don't think she'd be very happy about that," I said. "We'll take her, now that she can't use her ability. We'll lock her up."

"I don't think so." Wenslo stepped back, dusting himself off. "Her ability is too rare. Too valuable. I can't allow you to take her."

What he wasn't saying dawned on me. "You told her to stop fighting, and she did."

Wenslo smiled, like a teacher proud as their student figured out an algebra problem. "Yes."

"You told her to stand, and she did," I said, sounding dumb. But I needed to be careful. Very careful.

"Yes," Wenslo answered. "The bracelet does a bit more than block the flow of magic."

I raised my gun at him. "Traitor. You got me to help you take control of her. What are you going to make her do?"

"Right a wrong," Wenslo said. "Not that it's any of your business."

Wenslo stepped in close, looking Ghira over. "Right, Ghira? You want to help me, don't you?"

She didn't say anything.

"Answer me!" Wenslo yelled.

She still didn't answer. Wenslo's face went pale, and I swung my gun toward Ghira. The team reacted to my movement and followed suit.

We all stood there in tense silence, staring Ghira down.

"Are you under my control?" Wenslo finally asked.

An ugly smile instantly covered her face. "No."

A shot went off behind me, so close my ears rang. My stomach dropped to the floor faster than the rest of my body and I flinched, expecting pain. But there wasn't any. That was almost worse. Who else had just gone down? Ghira grabbed me under the armpit and dragged me toward the other room. I flailed, getting my earring out, but not asking it to grow yet. More rounds went off, filling the warehouse with the smell of gunpowder.

I struggled against Ghira, but she was far stronger than me. Frantically looking back for help, I noticed blood pooling on the floor next to a body. It took a moment for it to register who it was.

Grayson.

After all I'd done to get away from this place, here I was. Here we were. I hadn't been able to protect the people I loved. I nearly retched, my stomach heaving. That had been my only true goal, and I'd failed.

Ghira shoved me from behind and I stumbled forward, numb. I walked through the empty doorframe.

The spot where the portal had hung before I'd destroyed it was still empty. Relief hit me in the gut, followed by regret.

If things went wrong, it wouldn't stay that way for long. Were the others still alive? I flinched. A gunshot from the other room said probably at least two of them were. I didn't know where Wenslo had gone. Or if Grayson was still alive.

Grayson. All that I'd done to protect him, over in an instant.

"Over there," Ghira pushed me forward again, closer and closer to where the portal had stood. "I only need a little of your blood, but I'm tempted to take every drop after all the trouble you caused me."

I cringed away from her, but she would have none of it. She

grabbed me by my hair and pulled me forward. What did I do now? If I fought back, she'd probably just kill me. But if I didn't fight back, I'd be allowing evil into the world. A new kind of evil that we weren't ready to deal with. As if there wasn't enough here already.

Patting around for a brief moment made my stomach drop. In the confusion, I'd lost my sword. Our previous fight had proven how useless my gun would be against Ghira. I'd never felt more helpless than this moment.

"It's time," Ghira shoved me down until I was kneeling in the empty portal space. She raised her sword.

"Wait!" I threw my hands up. I had just been stalling, but in the quiet, I noticed that the sounds from the other room had stopped. Was everyone dead?

No. The shuffle of booted feet moved toward us in unison. At least three sets of boots. I didn't know who to hope for, I was just glad for the help. As long as none of them had pink eyes.

Agent Bylilly, the captain, and an agent burst around the doorway, guns raised. Ghira grabbed my shoulder and pulled me in front of her, touching a knife to my throat.

At this point, I fully expected I would not make it out of this situation alive. All I wanted to do was protect the people here, and the people I loved out in the world. Kenzie would miss me for awhile, but she was young enough that she would be fine. Especially with Travis there to take care of her. I grappled with the thought of my daughter growing up without me, but I saw no better way.

"Shoot her!" I yelled. "I don't care if you have a clean shot or not, shoot her!"

The captain got her gun up first, and let off a round. She cared about me, about all of her officers, but she knew what was at stake. Or at least had a good idea.

The shot flew wide, which I had expected. But if there were enough bullets flying, one of them had to make contact. The captain did not get the chance to shoot again. The agent I didn't know stiffened and his eyes went pink.

I had to keep her distracted. I had to give them the chance to attack. "Look out!" I yelled, in case the captain and Agent Bylilly had tunnel vision on Ghira.

My three allies, or, at least my two allies and Ghira's minion, scuffled together, fighting over the agent's rifle.

Ghira started speaking in some other language, and the air started to feel strange, cold, loaded, like I was about to get struck by lightning. Another round of shots went off, but I didn't have the ability to look right now and see who was coming out on top. I could kill Wenslo right now. Maybe if he hadn't been so intent on controlling Ghira, he might have noticed something was wrong. And even if that wasn't the case, I could shoot him anyway, for devastating the fragile amount of trust I had in him.

I felt the pain before I even heard the shot. Heat spread across my rib cage, followed by the feeling of wetness. A bullet must have grazed me.

Ghira cackled and shoved me to the ground. "I didn't have to do it myself at all." Blood from the wound dripped on the floor and sizzled the way no human blood should sizzle. I waited in horror, but after a few seconds, nothing had happened.

Ghira shook me, causing the bleeding to start up again.

I gritted my teeth and slapped at her arm.

A deep laugh started from the shadows of the warehouse. Wenslo stepped out. "Ghira, Ghira. This just shows how little you know." He moved close, looking down at her. "The one who destroyed the portal must be willing to help you recreate it. You aren't getting that portal back open. Now you can pay for what you did to me."

I'd kill him. It would have been really nice to know that I had to be willing to reopen the portal. He'd manipulated me again.

Behind me, the fighting had stopped. Bylilly and the captain had the other agent handcuffed. How many were still alive in the other room? Was Grayson?

If Ghira couldn't open the portal without me willingly helping her, my fight was over. She could kill me. I couldn't stop her. But she wouldn't be able to get the portal back open without my help, and that wasn't happening.

Suddenly, the captain attacked Bylilly.

Ghira wasn't done. She lunged at Wenslo, her sword in front of her before she got to him.

They clashed, swords ringing in the large, mostly empty room.

I almost laughed. We'd won. By accident, but we had. I struggled to my feet. I had to check on Grayson. Wenslo deserved whatever came to him. He had his secrets, and hadn't included me in them. Had manipulated me to be here. If he'd told Ghira earlier that I couldn't be forced to open the portal, maybe Grayson wouldn't be bleeding in the next room.

"Wait!" Ghira yelled. She wasn't even winded.

I ignored her.

Bylilly had the captain on the ground. I stepped around them. It looked like she had it well in hand.

Ghira knocked Wenslo to the side. He hit the ground. Hard. And he didn't get back up. Ghira was on me in a flash. "Reopen the portal! Now!"

Peace went through me. Whatever happened, it would be okay. "There is nothing you can do that will make me help you reopen this portal."

She leaned forward, like we were friends, all in my space. "I think you'll change your mind."

She touched my arm and the world swirled around me, nearly knocking me to the ground. Except, it was no longer me. I blinked several times, trying to get my bearings, but it didn't help much.

I looked down and there was my daughter, coloring a picture. I took a step closer, and bent down. Except it wasn't me making the choices, and the body felt far too heavy.

When the picture Kenzie was diligently coloring finally came into focus, I got my first good look. She'd drawn a woman in strange dark clothing, holding a little girl's hand. The woman had dark hair. And pink eyes.

How had Ghira found my daughter? How could she control someone so far away? I didn't even know where Kenzie was. Did this mean... Did Ghira have Travis? He would die before he would tell her where to find Kenzie, if he had full control of himself. But, unfortunately, control was something no one seemed to have around Ghira.

Did Ghira even need someone to tell her how to find a specific person? No one I knew understood the fae yet. Maybe no one was hurt and she was just trying to get me to do what she wanted in a different way, since she couldn't control me. Maybe Kenzie and Travis were both fine.

"Is Travis okay?" I asked. My voice came out hoarser than I'd expected. I'd known I still felt something for him. But after he'd taken care of me yesterday, I had a better idea just how strong those feelings were.

"I think you have more pressing things to concern yourself with," Ghira answered. The woman whose eyes I was looking through reached down to the picnic basket sitting next to Kenzie, and pulled out a knife. She held it down beside her leg, blade ready. "Are you really worried about your man right now, when your daughter is about to die?"

She was right. There wasn't anything I could do for Travis right now, except to protect our daughter.

"What do I need to do?" I asked. Opening a portal to Faerie hadn't been one of the things covered at the Academy.

Ghira's smirk was smug. Oh for the chance to slap it off her face... But not while Kenzie was in danger. "It's very simple. Just put your intent into the universe. It will do the rest." Ghira tipped her head, considering me. "And just in case your daughter's life isn't enough for you," she waved a hand and the captain walked through the door tugging Grayson across the floor. A trail of blood smeared along behind them, staining the cement.

"No!" I ran to Grayson, sliding down beside him, the floor slick with blood. I pulled his jacket open and found the wound in his chest, applying pressure. I'd known he was likely down, but thinking it had probably happened and seeing him here, bleeding out, were completely different things. My soul was pulled in all directions right now, the only people I truly loved in the world all within moments of disaster.

"Now, now," Ghira said. "I don't have all day. Leave him."

Hot tears formed in my eyes. I looked down, but Grayson was already unconscious. If he didn't get help fast, he was dead. Intent into the universe. I gritted my teeth, trying to force him to heal.

Nothing happened.

"If I stop holding pressure, he'll die!" I screamed in her direction, not taking my eyes off of him.

"And here I thought that was the idea all along." She pointed at me with the tip of her sword. "Open the portal. Or you'll lose your partner and your daughter."

Grayson stood very little chance of living until an ambulance got here. This much blood... The air was filled with the scent, making me sick to my stomach. I stood, looking at my blood-covered hands for a moment. A glance at the captain proved that she would not be any help. Her eyes glowed pink, a strange color in the dimness of the warehouse.

At least Grayson was unconscious. Unless he found out about my betrayal after death in whatever happened when we left Earth, he would never know that I'd left him to die alone, lying on the cold concrete.

Were any of the others alive? If I walked through the portal with Ghira, would someone be able to save Grayson? Because there was nothing I could do to help him.

I glared at Ghira. "This had better be over soon. Or I'm going to kill you."

Ghira smiled. "Very soon." She gestured toward where the portal should be with the tip of her sword.

The bleeding from my gunshot graze had mostly stopped, drying my shirt to my hip. Apparently that wasn't enough. Ghira pulled a knife from her pocket and tossed it to me. It clanked and slid across the floor. I clenched my jaw for a second, but no other ideas popped into my head. This was it. The moment. The choice. Let two, maybe three, of the most important people in my world die, or let loose a maniac.

The knife bit into my forearm. It was sharp, and I didn't even feel the wound for a moment. I let blood drip on the floor where the portal had once stood and as Ghira commanded, closed my eyes, willing the portal to open. When I opened my eyes again, a surge of hope went through me. It didn't look like it was going to work. Nothing had happened yet. But then a few sparks lit the air. The sparks flew around multiplying until they formed a circle. My side heated up, and the portal flared to life.

I watched in a mix of hope and despair as the swirling light of the portal grew stronger.

Ghira grinned, in obvious satisfaction. She thought it was functional. She thought she had won.

Maybe she had.

The enormity of the decision I'd just made hit me. Hard. To save Kenzie, I may have caused the deaths of countless others. It was a terrible bargain, one I wasn't sure I could live with.

Ghira's grin widened, and she pointed her sword toward the portal. "It won't be long now."

My heart pounded in my chest, torn between the life of my daughter and the fate of the world. I had to find a way to make this right, to prevent Ghira from causing further destruction. If I took down the portal again...

I'd be right back in the situation I'd been in a few minutes ago. And I'd already made that decision. We hadn't been able to find a way to take out Ghira, and now she would have backup. Of an entity possibly even stronger than she was. It would be a terrible fight. But that was just the way this was going to have to go. Hopefully I would have more backup, if I was still alive. Hopefully there was someone out there in the world who knew how to deal with this kind of thing. Because I was just a rookie cop, far out of my league.

My innocent baby would be protected at all costs. Right or wrong. I sent a prayer up, asking for forgiveness. I couldn't even be specific, because I didn't know if my choice was right or wrong, but God would know the groaning of my heart. According to my father, He always knew.

"Now what?" I finally got the courage to ask. Things were feeling a little anticlimactic.

Ghira didn't have to answer. A booted foot stepped through the portal.

My heart thundered in my ears, stomach nearly heaving up the little breakfast I'd been able to force down as the figure that belonged to the boot emerged. He was tall, with long blond hair and features so sharp, skin so ashen, he looked chiseled from stone. A dark cloak was thrown around his shoulders. His pants were a material I'd never seen before, thick and silky. If he weren't so real and solid, if not for the absolute terror that rippled through me just at the sight of him, I'd mistake him for a statue in one of those pop-up Halloween stores. I had to assume that this was Kienthall. Ghira's husband was actually here. His piercing eyes swept the room before settling on Ghira.

"Not exactly the greeting I expected," he said. "Where is all this beauty in the world you keep going on about?"

The joy on Ghira's face disappeared, replaced by emptiness. "This place was best suited for creating a portal. With your ability, we will be anywhere you want in moments."

Kienthall didn't acknowledge her. He noticed me, and tipped his head, considering me. "Is this the one who delayed my arrival?"

Oh no. How did he know that? How did he know I'd destroyed the portal? Didn't it mean anything that I'd rebuilt it? Even though it had been under threat of death to my daughter. I itched to move, but didn't dare to with his eyes on me.

"Yes," Ghira answered shortly. She moved over close to him and rested her hand in the crook of his elbow. "Shall we go?"

"Go?" He laughed. "When there's much fun to be had here?" His gaze swept past me to the bodies littering the floor. "Several of these humans are still alive."

"It would be best not to remain," Ghira said. "Law Enforcement far outnumbers us, and they no doubt have their eye close on the situation. They will be here soon, when they don't hear from one of their own."

"So?" Kienthall threw up his hands, gesturing to the room. "Let them come. Look what you've done with the rest of them."

"I have lived in this world my entire life." Ghira ground out. "You have never been here. Trust me on this. I will not be able to stop what's coming on my own."

The two of them locked eyes, some battle going on between them. I backed away a step.

Kienthall scowled, clearly unhappy with Ghira questioning him. He grabbed her arm roughly. "I've been waiting decades for this moment. Don't presume to tell me what I should do now that it's finally here."

"As if I haven't also longed for this moment?" Ghira asked.

Longed for this moment? With this guy? Something was more wrong with her than I'd ever thought. They had been communicating somehow, so it wasn't like he'd changed a bunch since they'd been separated.

"Now show me somewhere useful. I tire of this dreary space." Kienthall's words drove the breath from me. If they left, who knew what damage they'd do elsewhere. If I could keep them here...

Ghira nodded, eyes downcast. Kienthall's eyes flashed pink. Apparently he could see something I couldn't, because he smiled, turning his head and looking around like someone wearing a VR set.

"Wane," I whispered. The flash of movement from my sword shrinking caught my attention. It had fallen fairly close to me, I just couldn't see it in the gloom of the warehouse.

Kienthall closed his eyes, and Ghira's attention stayed fixed on him. I scooted over and grabbed my earring, slipping it into my pocket.

"This will do," Kienthall said.

Before Ghira could respond, the air around us shimmered, and the world roiled. I tumbled to the floor of a posh penthouse suite, screeching across the marble tile of an immaculate kitchen. Kienthall already lounged on a sofa, snapping his fingers. "Fetch me wine. The journey has parched me. And something to eat."

Ghira, standing behind him, jerked her head toward the kitchen. "You heard him."

I moved to obey. Maybe if I played dumb long enough, they'd basically forget I was here. I was still a little woozy from the teleportation, or whatever that was. Somehow we'd been in a warehouse, and now we were in a condo or something. The place looked like it cost twenty thousand a month in rent. Polished hardwood floor stretched into the living room, with white leather sofas and a chandelier dripping with diamonds. I didn't even think it was weird anymore, taking this new development in stride.

Where was Wenslo? At this point, I didn't see help coming from any other direction. I'd despise the man a little less if he saved my life.

As I dug around in the fridge looking for wine, I eavesdropped on the two in the other room. She was trying to tell him things about Earth, but he kept interrupting her. He talked down to her, like she was a child. And she just always agreed with what he said. Did he always treat her like this? Like she was... less? I almost felt sorry for her. Almost.

After a moment of digging around, I found a bottle of what looked to be an expensive vintage. *Don't come home,* I whispered internally to whoever lived here. If they were even still alive. I didn't know, with the fae involved.

Uncorking the wine, I poured it into a crystal glass. I gripped the counter for a moment, giving myself just a second to take a deep breath. The other two still argued quietly in the other room.

I didn't want to give him any reason to get angry with me. I squared my shoulders and picked up the glass, moving toward the couch.

Walking hesitantly toward Kienthall, I offered the wine with a polite smile.

He took one look at the glass, then sniffed it delicately. His face contorted in a grimace of distaste. "What is this? I'm beginning to think this world is the most backward I've ever been to."

Most backward he'd ever been to? Did that mean there were other worlds than just Earth and Faerie? Wenslo had basically said that there were, but at this point, I didn't trust anything he'd told me.

Kienthall took a sip, grimaced, and threw the cup, dark, rich liquid splashing onto the exquisite rug. "Is this the best you can provide?" He stood and stretched. "Typical. I'm hungry," he told Ghira. "I haven't feasted properly in years."

"There was some ham in the fridge," I said. I didn't want to draw his attention to me, but at the same time, I had absolutely no hope that he'd forgotten I was here. All of my training said to make him see me as a person.

What was better than just a person? A helpful person, hopefully.

Kienthall snorted. "This human is absolutely ignorant. How did she best you?" He turned from Ghira to look at me. My skin crawled under his gaze. "This place bores me," he announced, standing from the luxury couch he'd made himself comfortable on. "We can come back when we're done. Take me somewhere more... fun."

Ghira nodded, but she didn't look happy that he didn't find the place she'd chosen for him perfect. Maybe I could use the tension between them to my advantage. I'd have to be patient, but maybe, just maybe...

Kienthall's eyes glowed pink. He smiled, a disgusting smile, and the world blurred.

CHAPTER FIFTEEN

The world blurred and spun around me as we teleported again. I squeezed my eyes shut against the dizzying sensation. The sugary scent of funnel cakes and popcorn filled the air, giving me an idea of where we were while my eyes were still closed. Excited screams rang around me. When I opened my eyes, I was standing in the middle of a crowded amusement park.

Kienthall let out a delighted laugh, his teeth glinting. "Yes, this is much more amusing." His gaze raked over the oblivious families milling around. "So many humans, ripe for the taking."

Dread clenched in my stomach. I scanned the park, looking for anything I could use as a weapon or means of escape. My hand went to my pocket, finding my shrunken sword earring still there. If I could get enough distance between us, I could potentially catch Kienthall off guard. But with this many bystanders, I couldn't risk it yet.

Ghira shifted uneasily beside me. "We should move on quickly," she muttered under her breath. "Too many prying eyes here. Humans aren't as weak as you seem to think they are."

Kienthall shot her a scathing look. "I don't take orders from you, wife. We will stay as long as I wish." His eyes gleamed, and he licked his lips. "I want to sample what this world has to offer."

He began to stride through the crowd, his movements predatory. As he passed people, they shivered and recoiled, though they didn't seem to know why. Kienthall drank in their unease.

Ahead of us, a toddler broke into tears as Kienthall approached. The child's mother swept him into her arms, glaring distrustfully at Kienthall.

"Get away from us," she hissed. Kienthall's mouth twisted into a cruel smile, staring her down without answering. The woman paled, stumbling back.

Maybe the situation would handle itself. Maybe people would know to stay away from him, just on instinct.

But the mother froze when Kienthall got closer. A murmur went out from the people around us. The crowd was starting to notice. Maybe someone would call 911.

And then what? Cops would arrive, and Ghira would force them to kill each other.

Kienthall stepped in close to the young woman with the kid, leaning down close to her face. Why didn't she move? Was she...

I noticed her eyes. Pink. I turned a glare on Ghira, but she didn't look back toward me, concentrating on her husband. Kienthall pulled a knife, and the crowd burst apart, running in panic, screams changing from excitement to terror.

That was enough. If I drew my sword, I had no doubt Ghira would throw that mom, or worse, her kid, in front of me. So I left it in place, darted forward, and grabbed Kienthall's arm, the one with the knife. It didn't budge. He was far stronger than I was. I wouldn't be able to stop him physically.

"Stop," I growled. "You want to go after someone? I'm right here. I'm the one who kept you trapped, remember?"

Kienthall rested his gaze on me. For a moment, an immense pressure squeezed my skull. I gritted my teeth, willing my mind to resist Ghira. This was the strongest Ghira had ever come at me. Heat flared in my side in response, and the pressure receded.

Kienthall's eyes widened, just a little. Before I could react, he grabbed me by the throat and slammed me against the side of a ring-toss game booth. My head cracked against the wood and stars burst across my vision. But not enough to hide the mother and son, darting away behind a tent.

Mission accomplished.

"You may be able to resist Ghira somehow, but make no mistake, human," Kienthall snarled, his hand tightening. "You are no match for me."

Black spots swam in my eyes as my air supply dwindled. The world tilted.

Just then, a balloon popped loudly right next to us, making Kienthall flinch. His grip loosened enough for me to suck in a desperate breath. I saw Ghira standing nearby, holding the tattered remnants of the balloon in her hand.

Kienthall's attention snapped to her. "Don't interfere, wife," he threatened.

Ghira's eyes blazed. "Enough games," she snapped. "The police will already be looking for us. We can't afford to waste time tormenting every human we see. Their guardian systems are good here, there may be responders in the next few minutes."

"And how is that a problem? You haven't convinced me." Kienthall's lip curled in a sneer. "You've gone soft after all these years trapped on this miserable planet." His hands clenched into fists. "If you won't indulge me here, then perhaps I'll pay a visit to the human's offspring instead."

Everything inside me went cold. "Don't you dare go near my daughter," I choked out through my bruised windpipe.

Kienthall smiled. "Ah, does that upset you?" He leaned in close. "For some reason I can't seem to feel your fear for her. That's fine. Imagine how delicious her fear will be when I appear in her bedroom tonight."

Rage boiled inside me, scalding away the chill. I slammed my forehead into Kienthall's nose. He reeled back with a muffled curse, blood streaming down his face.

Before he could recover, I tore away and sprinted into the crowd, people stupid enough to stay behind and see what happened. A man yelled indignantly as I shoved through them, but I didn't stop. I had to get distance and find a way to get to Kenzie first, when I didn't even know where she was.

Suddenly, something was shoved out in front of me. I crashed to the ground, the impact jarring through my bones. I got a look to the side at a man holding a cane. He looked just as surprised as I felt.

Ghira.

Kienthall stalked toward me. "You'll pay for that, whelp," he growled. He reached down and grabbed me by the ankle, pulling me along back toward Ghira. "No one bloodies me without consequence."

I clawed desperately for anything to hold onto on the pavement. My fingers closed around a chunk of rock. With the last of my strength, I rolled over, twisting my back, and hurled it at Kienthall's head.

It struck him squarely in the temple. He dropped my leg. I scrambled to my feet, swaying. My body felt like one massive bruise, but I couldn't stop. Sirens sounded in the distance, something I couldn't have been happier to hear. Once they got here they would be a problem, but for now they provided a great distraction. Hopefully even a point of contention for Ghira and Kienthall.

Suddenly, Ghira appeared at my side and gripped my arm. Before I could react, the park disappeared. The world tilted sickeningly, and we reappeared on an empty sidewalk. I barely had time to register the change before my legs buckled. I collapsed to my hands and knees, heaving.

Ghira stood over me, looking around warily as I vomited into the gutter. "Get up," she snapped.

Kienthall's face was livid. "You forced me to bring us here?" he screamed. "You don't force me to do anything!" He slapped Ghira across the face, hard enough she stumbled. I almost felt sorry for her. Almost.

"I had no choice!" Ghira yelled back, getting in his face. "You won't listen to me! The authorities here number in the hundreds, just in this area! In the tens of thousands in the larger city and suburbs, hundreds of thousands in the country! And they won't be bringing just guns. How will we fair against an attack chopper? Ballistic missiles? Don't underestimate how much they fear us, and the lengths they will go to if needed to stop us. We cannot stand against them. You can have your fun, but quietly!" Ghira nodded toward me. "Just get out of here. You are of no use to us."

I started to back away. She didn't have to tell me twice.

"No." Kienthall said. "I may not be able to use her fear, but she disrespected me. She must die." He lifted an eyebrow. "Slowly. Painfully."

"As you wish," Ghira said, dashing any hope I had of her pitying me. "But not here. I just picked an easy place to get away from the carnival. Let me take a moment and find a more appropriate site for what's to come." She closed her eyes. Seeing other places, or just thinking, I didn't know.

It didn't matter. I had to get away from them before she found somewhere else to go. If I didn't, I would never get away at all.

I inched backward while her eyes were closed. But Kienthall lifted an eyebrow, silently threatening me. I stopped, my training kicking in. *Don't ever let someone take you to a second location.* I tensed, getting ready to make a run for it, whatever the consequences.

The world tilted, making my stomach roil again even though there wasn't anything in it. Kienthall had teleported us again. When my vision cleared, I found myself in a dimly lit basement. The air was dank and frigid, with a metallic smell that raised the hairs on my arms.

I scanned the space warily. The rough concrete walls were covered in an array of terrible instruments. Knives, hooks, chains, a hatchet, and other everyday things that didn't look everyday here, in this place. Many had rust-colored stains that made my stomach turn. Whatever this place was, it wasn't good. And judging by the lack of dust and cobwebs, it was still in use.

"Where are we?" I asked. The place gave off serial killer vibes. I marked the only exit in my head, a strong looking metal door at the top of a flight of stairs. That basically confirmed we were in a basement.

"Somewhere more interesting," Kienthall said. He let go of Ghira and strode over to examine a particularly wicked looking curved blade. Kienthall let out a delighted laugh. Somehow it was even more creepy than when he was angry. "Oh yes, this will do nicely." He trailed his fingers almost lovingly over the curved blade, then moved on to a saw. "I can taste the exquisite agony these tools have wrought. The amount of fear soaked into the walls... I can practically taste it. Good job at last, wife." He glanced over his shoulder, pinning me with his piercing gaze. "Don't worry. You and I are going to become very well acquainted with each other soon. Just give me a few more moments, if you would."

I tensed, ready to defend myself if he came at me. But he seemed content to ignore me for the moment, moving on to inspect the rest of the tools hanging on the wall.

Ghira moved to Kienthall's side. "My love, I know you've been waiting for this for a long time. But taking a cop only puts us more at risk. We need to go somewhere no one can find us. We need to plan, to prepare. There are many places we could hide where no one will be looking. The desert, the mountains, jungle, plains, any type of world you can think of. I know you can only move us a short distance at a time, but we can do another jump now, and then-"

"Would you shut up about this? You've told me, repeatedly." Kienthall glared at her, the expression strong enough that it would have sent me packing if I was the one it was aimed at. "I've been trapped in Faerie with eyes on me at all times for far too long. I don't need someone looking after me here as well. Now that I'm free, I'll do as I please."

He turned his cold gaze on me. "Starting with killing this wretch for imprisoning me even longer than I had to be."

Ghira looked away, giving in to him. I almost wanted to cry. Who'd have thought I'd be rooting for Ghira at any point in time. If she could convince him that it wasn't safe here, that they needed to leave...

Then they'd just be more prepared when the time came for them to do whatever he was here to do. He seemed to have a plan past just killing some low-level cop.

Ghira wandered, inspecting the room, while Kienthall studied the tools on the wall. She moved over to stand with him. "I don't understand your fascination with such crude methods," she said, wrinkling her nose.

Kienthall let out a snort. "Of course you don't understand. You've never experienced the exquisite symphony of screams that accompany true artistry. You're almost human yourself, in some ways. A pity, but that will change eventually." He grabbed her face in his large hand, but it looked like he kept his grip gentle. "I will teach you. Be with you every step of the way."

Ghira's eyes lit up, and she smiled. The first real smile I'd ever seen on her face, with none of the usual crazy behind it. Maybe they really did love each other.

Going back to the wall, Kienthall reached out and caressed a set of pliers, his eyes distant. Strange how a normal tool that I'd used a hundred times in my life could make my body go cold. "The rush when warm blood splatters your face, the sweet pleas for mercy that gradually descend into incoherent whimpers..."

Frigid terror trickled down my spine, but I forced my expression to remain neutral. My hand crept slowly to my pocket, finding the reassuring shape of my shrunken sword. As long as I could keep them talking, give myself time to think, I might have a chance. I shuffled a little toward the stairs.

"Ahh, ah, ahhh," Ghira warned, not even looking in my direction.

I paused, mind whirling with options on how to stall and keep myself from being tortured.

"Why do you keep acting like you've been trapped in some other strange place forever?" I asked. "You're fae, right? Weren't you at home in Faerie?"

"There are those in Faerie who... disagree with how I enjoy living my life," Kienthall said. "It's made being there quite boring. Let alone those who wish me dead would have a much easier time of it in Faerie than here. Just finding me here would be a difficult task, unless they find someone to help. And they're much too busy with ruling Faerie to worry about Earth."

Those that wished him dead, in Faerie. Ah. It wasn't just humans that hated him. Or humans that would hate him, once more got to know him. I felt around in my pocket, keeping eye contact with Kienthall. "Have you been here before? It almost sounded like you've been here before."

He laughed. "You're a brave one, aren't you? You do know I'm about to kill you. In a horrible manner."

"I know." I found my phone and punched in 911. I didn't know where I was, or if I had any service, but I couldn't let this guy go out into the world. It was my fault he was here in the first place. "But that doesn't mean I'm not curious."

Thankfully I always kept my keypad tone off. My phone buzzed in my pocket, like it was trying to connect. The dispatcher would see my number. If the captain was still alive, she'd have it flagged in the entire country by now. Someone was coming. I had to believe that. Maybe to find my body, but so be it.

Kienthall turned to me, a predatory excitement smoldering in his eyes. "But why speak of hypotheticals when we have a guest to entertain?" He started toward me, hand outstretched. "Let's begin, shall we?"

"Wait," Ghira said, cocking her head. "Is that…"

"911, what's your emergency?" a tiny voice asked in my pocket.

"She called for help!" Ghira screeched, coming at me. Kienthall grabbed her midair.

This was it. If they weren't going to kill me before, they surely would now. But people would be here soon. People who could hopefully handle Ghira. Someone had to have survived the warehouse. There had to be another plan in the works by now.

Which meant I had to incapacitate Kienthall myself, before he teleported us away. It didn't do any good for me to call for help here if Kienthall just teleported the two of them, or worse, all three of us, somewhere else. I didn't know what it would take to keep him from using his ability, but surely death would put an end to it.

I yanked the earring from my pocket. "Gain!" The sword grew to full size in my grip. It still didn't feel like it belonged there, but it was becoming more natural. I took a swing at Kienthall, hoping to catch him by surprise.

He stumbled back, for once looking shocked. A short window of advantage was all I had.

I took it.

I jumped forward, sword straight in front of me.

Ghira hit me from the side, sending me smashing into the wall, hard. My phone crunched in my pocket. I rolled, jumping back to my feet and rushing forward again, trying to keep her off-balance.

I had no idea if her husband was as good with a sword as she was. If I let her press me, she was going to win. She'd proven that all the way back in Faerie, the first time I met her.

She pulled a sword out of nowhere and swung at me. I rolled again, avoiding her completely. If we went head-to-head, she would win. I dodged another blow.

"Let her come," Kienthall said, his voice ringing through the basement.

Ghira instantly stopped, stepping back.

That wasn't good. They both thought he could take me.

I didn't give him a chance to grab a weapon. I charged, sword tip at gut level. Kienthall disappeared at the last second. Something kicked me in the back of the knee, sending me sprawling again.

Of course. He could teleport. He didn't need a weapon to stop me.

Angry tears filled my eyes.

No. It would not end like this.

I got back up and took a swing, careful not to let myself lose my footing.

Kienthall blinked away just long enough for the sword to pass through where he'd been standing, then blinked back in the exact same place. He laughed.

"Humans are weak. The weakest of the races, I believe." He wandered toward the wall of torture instruments. "I almost feel bad for what will happen to this world in the next few months." He selected a chisel of some sort, taking it off the wall and studying it for a second. "Almost."

I lunged forward but was too slow yet again. "Ah!" I yelled in frustration, making Kienthall laugh behind me.

"This has been fun. But I'm growing bored. It's time to move on," he said.

I turned to face him, under no illusions that his comment meant anything but pain for me.

"Maybe I'll still go after your daughter next," he said, staring at me, waiting for a reaction. "It won't be as fun, since you won't be there to watch, but I'll just believe in my heart that wherever you are after death, you can feel your daughter's pain."

"My love," Ghira said. "Why waste time on a child? There are so-"

"Silence," Kienthall said. "I'm talking with the worm. Do you think your child will try to be brave, as you have? How long will she squirm before she cracks?"

Rage built inside me. Heat filled every cell, my face flushing. "Don't even mention Kenzie," I warned, my voice gritty, intense. He would not hurt my daughter. He wouldn't get the chance.

"I'll more than mention her," Kienthall said, smirking. "I'll tell her you sent me. She'll be calling for her mother as she dies, and her mother won't answer."

I raised the sword and screamed. The light in my wound flared so hot I felt the skin around the edges sizzle. I didn't care. I thrust my hand out and a bolt of light shot from it, slamming into Kienthall's chest.

He flew back against the wall with a crash, chest smoking.

I looked down at my hand in shock. Had I done that?

Ghira rushed over to Kienthall. He shook her off.

I bolted for the stairs while they were distracted, but Kienthall suddenly appeared in front of me. His eyes were wild, hair disheveled.

"What was that?" he asked, voice as crazed as his eyes. His gaze swung to Ghira. "You said humans don't have powers!"

"They don't," Ghira answered, sounding off. "I've fought this one before, she showed no signs of an ability in any of our other interactions, other than I can't control her."

"Fine then," Kienthall growled, no longer having fun. I could get some satisfaction from that, at least. Even if I died, I'd ruined his day. "We'll study her body after she's dead."

I adjusted my stance, keeping the point of my sword trained on Kienthall's chest. My emergency situation training took over, steadying my nerves. "Stay back," I warned. "I won't ask twice." If I could make him believe that I knew what I was doing, that I'd hurt him intentionally...

Searing pain erupted across my cheek. Kienthall reappeared across the room before I could even react. I staggered back, clapping a hand to my face. It came away wet with blood.

Kienthall held up the curved knife, its edge now stained red. I hadn't even seen him grab it. The brief glimmer of hope I'd had for a moment when I'd knocked him back flickered out. How was I supposed to stop someone I couldn't hit?

Kienthall lunged again, impossibly fast. I barely managed to dodge, his knife grazing my shoulder. I retreated toward the wall, holding my sword out defensively. Kienthall stalked after me, toying with me. He could have killed me already. Maybe he was trying to get me to do whatever I'd done last time again. I'd be glad to, if I knew how.

Ghira watched impassively from the side, making no move to intervene. Our eyes met briefly. Was that a flicker of sympathy in her gaze? Or was it just curiosity at what I was or how I'd done what I had a few moments ago?

Hopefully I lived long enough to ask those questions myself. But I had no time to analyze it. Kienthall struck again and again, each time just nicking me, drawing blood.

In a brief moment where he waited, I tried to force the light out of my hand again. I gritted my teeth, throwing my soul into it.

Nothing happened.

Still, I wasn't about to make this easy for him. The next time he lunged, I ducked under his arm and dealt a vicious slice to his side. I caught him by surprise, and he let out an irritated hiss as his shirt began blossoming red.

Before I could press my advantage, Kienthall's fist collided brutally with my jaw. An explosion of white-hot agony deafened my senses. The ground rushed up to meet me.

Through the ringing in my ears, I heard Kienthall's angry hiss. "You do show spirit, I'll give you that." The cold kiss of a blade caressed my throat. "But playtime is over now."

As the knife began to bite into my windpipe, something stirred deep within me. A frantic energy that caused the light in my abdomen to blaze even hotter than before. I thought of Kenzie. Of her growing up in a world controlled by a monster. Of her growing up without me, broken as I was, I was still her mommy. The heat built up inside me, painful at this point.

On pure instinct, I threw up my hands. A searing blast erupted from my palms, driving Kienthall back with a scream, body leaving a trail of smoke through the air. I blinked, stunned by how much stronger this time was than the last.

Kienthall recovered quickly, his expression murderous. His clothes still smoldered, and I could detect a slight limp, though he hid it well. Bits of his coat were charred, revealing burned skin underneath. There was caution now in his eyes as he circled me.

"What manner of creature are you?" he hissed. Somehow he ignored his smoking clothes and the burns that covered half his face. Could this thing even be brought down?

I stood slowly, watching him warily. I had no idea how I'd produced that blast of light, but it had to be the will-o-wisp. Not that I had the luxury of questioning all of that right now. I had to stop this monster and protect my daughter.

Kienthall's lip curled into a sneer. "No matter. I'll flay the flesh from your bones and find out for myself." He flourished his knife. "Let's see how long that unnatural light of yours can sustain you!"

He sprang, but this time I was ready. I thrust out my hands, willing the heat inside me out through my palms. Dazzling light leapt outward, scorching Kienthall's outstretched arm. He howled in agony, dropping his knife to clutch the charred and blistered limb.

Before he could recover, I pressed forward. Blast after blast erupted from my palms, driving Kienthall back step-by-step. The will-o-wisp flared hotly, sensing my desperation.

With one last massive burst, Kienthall flew across the room and slammed brutally into the wall. He slumped to the ground, wisps of smoke rising from his ravaged body. He wasn't moving.

Warily, I edged closer, my hands still outstretched and ready. But his eyes were open and blank, mouth stretched.

My knees wobbled with relief and delayed shock. I was alive.

It took me a second to realize the danger wasn't over. I whirled around, searching the room for Ghira. She stood close to the stairs, staring at the carnage. I tensed, waiting for her to make a move, but she merely stood silent, taking in her husband's corpse with an unreadable expression. After a long moment, she met my eyes.

"I won't underestimate you again," she said quietly. "You will pay for this. You took the only thing I loved from me. I'll take the only thing you love from you."

She turned and charged up the stairs. I tore off after her, but the door slammed in my face. A lock clicked on the other side. I threw myself against the door, hard.

It didn't budge.

This place had been made to keep people in. And now, it kept me from my daughter.

CHAPTER SIXTEEN

I fought down panic as it threatened to overwhelm me. I couldn't stay trapped down here while Ghira hunted my daughter. But pounding on the immovable door was wasting precious time and energy. I forced myself to take a deep breath, fighting for calm.

First thing first.

I moved over to Kienthall's body. My eyes watered at the stench of burned flesh. I nearly retched. This truly was one of the worst smells on the planet. I'd only ever had to be around it once before, at a house fire that three unfortunate souls hadn't made it out of.

I bent down close, holding my breath, and felt for a pulse. I kept my fingers against his neck far longer than I would for a human. Maybe fae had a different pulse rate, I didn't know. Maybe they didn't have a heartbeat. That would explain how terrible they were.

No. He was definitely dead. My stomach turned, and I stumbled back so I could breathe. He'd been a terrible... person? Which helped, but didn't stop the pain of the fact that I'd killed someone. It never did. I'd been on scene with other officers in the aftermath of a shooting, and every time it had been a broken person left holding the gun.

I'd deal with all that later. Right now, I had to get out of here.

I reached into up my pocket and pulled out what was left of my burner phone. Useless. It wouldn't even turn on. I tossed it on the floor and jogged back up the stairs. It was a pathetic attempt at a jog, really, but the best I could manage. The cuts and bruises up and down my body stung, slowing me down. I reached the top of the stairs and studied the door for a moment.

No. I hadn't missed anything. There was no way to open the door from this side. Not even a handle.

My heart pounded in my chest as I threw myself against the cold, unforgiving metal door. The force of the impact reverberated through my body, and I winced, cursing under my breath, my eyes darting around the dimly lit room.

"Think, think," I muttered to myself, fear in my voice. Could I blast it with light? Would it just bounce back and kill me? I moved forward and ran a finger down the door crack. It was tiny, not even letting in light. My mind raced through the possibilities, desperate for a solution. Images of Kenzie plagued my thoughts. What if Ghira hurt her? Worse, what if she took her away?

"Mommy's coming, baby," I whispered. I scanned the barren room, searching for anything I could use to break through the door. My gaze fell upon a rusted pipe, but it was securely bolted to the wall. I glanced at an old wooden chair. It looked like it would break with one blow.

Nothing in the room looked helpful. At all. Most likely by design.

Anger burned through me, only a slight relief from the fear. And with the anger, my wound heated up. Maybe I could melt through the door, like a lightsaber or something.

A swirl of hope started in the pit of my stomach. I laid my hand against the metal of the door, willing all of my fear and anger into it.

Nothing happened.

I imagined Kenzie, forcing myself to feel everything. My need to get to her. The chance that she would be hurt. My frustration at not being there for her.

A blast of light flew from my hand, hitting the door, and bouncing back to knock into me. I tumbled down the stairs, sprawling at the bottom.

Tears stung my eyes, but I forced myself up. I moved to climb the stairs yet again, my toe clunking against something at the base.

My sword, forgotten in the desperation to get free.

I bent down and picked it up, truly looking it over for the first time. The captain had said they'd run tests, and hadn't found anything unusual. But I knew different. If it could shrink and grow, what else could it do?

Worth a try.

I bounded up the stairs, hope giving me the extra bounce. With a deep breath, I raised the sword above my head and brought it down hard against the door like it was an axe. A shower of sparks erupted from the contact, illuminating the room for a brief moment. The blade sliced into the metal, shaving off a thin strip.

I hacked at the door with all my strength. Each strike left my arms trembling, but I refused to slow. *I'm coming for you, baby. I'm coming.*

Metal shards fell away, littering the floor around my feet. Sweat dripped down my forehead, stinging my eyes, but I didn't care. My daughter needed me. My hands burned, blisters forming on my palms.

With painstaking effort, a small hole formed in the door. I rammed the sword through, twisting it back and forth until the space looked large enough for my forearm. "Wane," I said, and stuck the sword through my earring hole so I didn't lose it. I reached my hand through the jagged hole, ignoring the sharp edges that nicked my skin.

I fumbled blindly, searching for the lock, and when I finally made contact, I almost sobbed in relief. The click of the latch echoed through the room, and I pushed the door open, revealing a perfectly normal household hallway.

The house was creepy, because it was completely normal. No lights were on up here. The sun must have started to set, because it was pretty dim. I stuck to the wall, looking for an exit. The last thing I needed right now was to run into whoever had outfitted the basement.

Was I still in California? It wasn't like basements were super common here.

I crept past the living room. There. The front door came into view. Almost out. I sprinted the last few feet, yanking on the door handle. The door flew open, surprising me enough that I nearly spilled onto the front porch.

I stumbled out onto the street, squinting at the closest road sign.

Wait. I knew this place. I wasn't far from the safehouse Mr. Abeyta had offered me.

The house next door looked normal. A basketball hoop out front said maybe kids. I ran up the sidewalk and pounded on the door.

No answer.

I pounded again.

It wasn't worth waiting. I ran for the next house, leaping over a short fence, muscles trembling after all I'd put them through today.

This time my pounding made someone yell for someone else just on the other side of a red door.

I swayed in place as footsteps moved closer, followed by the click of a lock working.

A teen opened the door a crack, then stared at me, her face giving me a good guess of how I looked at the moment.

"Hi," I said. Even my voice was rough. "I need to use your phone."

Her eyebrows went up, and she took a small step back into the house.

I shoved my booted toe into the crack of the door. "Please."

Her eyes widened. She didn't say anything, but stuck a cellphone through the crack in the door.

"Thank you." I took the phone and stepped away as I dialed. I didn't even really care if she overheard my call. She'd think I was crazy, but that didn't matter at the moment.

I finished punching Travis's number in and hit send. I didn't have to wait long. He answered on the second ring.

"Hello?" His voice sounded odd until I remembered that he wouldn't know the number on his caller ID.

"It's me," I answered. "Where's Kenzie?"

"Jayla!" His voice totally changed. "Where are you? Grayson called looking for you, are you okay?"

Grayson called. Grayson was alive. I bit my lip to keep from crying. I would have to ask about him later. Right now all that mattered was Kenzie. "Where's Kenzie?" I asked again.

Travis paused on the other end of the line.

"Where's Kenzie?" I shouted into the phone.

The door clicked closed, locking from the other side. The teen must have written off her phone.

"You told me not to tell you," Travis said.

"Things have changed," I ground out. "She's in trouble." My voice broke, and I couldn't go on.

"I'm on my way to her." Somehow his voice stayed strong. Hard. Though not hard at me, I still felt it. I'd never heard this tone from him before.

"Where is there?" I asked.

"I can't tell you, Jay," he said. "I'm sorry. Grayson called. He told me what that woman can do. Maybe she's controlling you right now."

"She can't control me at all!" I was back to shouting. "Just tell me where she is!"

Sirens sounded down the street. Not an unusual sound in LA, but when I glanced up from where I'd been staring at the ground, I caught a glimpse of how many of the neighbors had stepped out to watch the drama.

The sirens were for me. Again. And now I had to decide if to take the chance that they would believe me about what was going on, or that I'd get locked up somewhere, unable to go after Kenzie.

I didn't even know if the captain or Agent Bylilly were still alive. And even if they were, our group effort hadn't gone very well last time. I couldn't trust anyone to save Kenzie but me.

"Jay?" Travis asked on the other side of the phone. Of course he hadn't hung up. His car door slammed, and he started the engine. "I'll be to her in thirty minutes. Stay on the line if you want."

"I'll buy you a new phone later," I yelled toward the red door, then headed for the street. "Where are you now?" I asked Travis. "We can go together."

"I'm just leaving the house," he answered. "But I can't wait for you, sorry."

"Don't get near her," I whispered back to him. "The woman with pink eyes."

"What was that?" Travis asked.

I hit the end call button. He was leaving the house. Kenzie was within thirty minutes of where he was now. She was with Travis's stepsister, the one he never saw. They didn't get along. At all. I wouldn't have guessed if it wasn't for the distance clue. A genius place to leave our daughter.

I upped my pace. The stepsister only lived fifteen minutes from where I was right now. Fifteen minutes by vehicle.

Time to give the neighbors something serious to talk about.

My feet pounded the pavement as I sprinted down sidewalks and scrambled over fences, all too aware of curious eyes tracking my progress. No time for stealth or excuses. I'd explain myself to the authorities later. Reaching Kenzie first was all that mattered.

The wail of sirens faded behind me. Sweat trickled down my spine. My body was getting near its breaking point. Even in the Academy I hadn't been pushed this hard.

I could get a car at the safehouse. Hopefully. Last resort. It would be much better to find one along the way. The phone I stole kept spitting out directions to the intersection I'd told it to take me to close to the safehouse. I was afraid to put in the full address. It really was just paranoia. Cops couldn't track a phone that easily.

Yet.

But I was taking no chances.

I wasted time checking a couple cars for keys. This was LA. People didn't leave their cars parked, waiting to be stolen.

Still about a mile from the safehouse, I nearly jogged past a car sitting on the curb. I could hardly see straight at this point, and only noticed the smell of exhaust after I had reached the hood. Exhaust in LA? Normal. But when I stopped and the pounding in my ears went down a little, I could hear the engine idling. If I hadn't been puffing for air, I couldn't have missed it. The engine ran rough.

I bent down, leaning into the whole catching my breath thing as I checked the car over. Old and definitely worse for the wear, but no one inside. A little pizza delivery sign on top.

Good enough. I checked the house. A young guy was standing on the porch, looking like he was waiting to get paid. Hopefully he didn't lose his job over this. I quietly opened the driver's door and slipped in, holding the door open a crack. It didn't look like it would close without slamming it.

I put the car in drive and let it roll forward. It had a high idle, moving along pretty quickly.

"Hey!" A shout came from the house. "That's my car!"

The time for subtlety was over. I slammed the door and rammed down on the gas pedal. The car lurched forward awkwardly. Good thing I wasn't taking it far.

The suspension squealed in protest over the first speed bump. I looked in the rearview mirror. The poor kid was chasing me on foot. I was gaining ground, but slowly.

It took two blocks, but I finally left him behind.

I let up on the pedal a bit, just keeping pace with traffic. The last thing I needed was to draw attention. This car only had to get me a few miles. I'd ditch it and face the consequences after Kenzie was safe.

Scenarios played on repeat in my head. Kenzie snatched from her bed, crying and confused. Ghira dragging her from the house. Lifting her sword... I forced my thoughts away, focusing intently on the evening traffic. *I'm coming, baby. Hold on.*

The nice housing divisions changed in a block. Chain-link fence and dirt yards flew by as I broke way too many traffic laws to count.

There. The house. A small place, that used to be white. Weeds grew in the front yard, and a shutter was almost ready to fall off one of the windows. This was a place where I would have never left Kenzie. Under any other circumstance.

I braked hard beside Travis's familiar vehicle, gravel spewing. He must have drove like a mad man to beat me here. Doors slammed inside the house as I sprinted up the sidewalk. I pulled my earring and asked it to shift into a sword before slipping through the front door, not taking the time to knock.

Something was wrong. I could feel it. I crept down the small hallway/entrance, moving toward the living room. I'd only been in this place once before, and I scrambled to remember the rest of the layout.

Two bedrooms, a kitchen, a backdoor into a nasty backyard.

"No!" Travis yelled from somewhere toward the back door. I dashed in that direction, covering the short distance in a couple of strides.

I had to control myself. I had to get the jump on Ghira. If she saw me first, I didn't stand a chance fighting against her. I slid to a stop at the door, pulling up the stained curtain, just a bit, to get a look outside.

Something crashed into the other side of the door, sending me stumbling back.

The door burst open, spilling Travis and Kenzie into the kitchen. He hit the floor hard, twisting to make sure Kenzie landed on top of him. As soon as he saw me, he lifted Kenzie up toward me. "Take her! Go!" His voice was rough, in pain.

On instinct, I grabbed her and took off for the front door. She wailed, reaching back toward Travis. I glanced back to see if he was following, but he hadn't gotten up.

Bad. So bad. But I couldn't carry both of them, and he would choose Kenzie over himself. Every time.

I met his eyes. *I'm sorry,* I begged with my whole being. He nodded, and then shooed me away, pulling himself across the floor to block the door.

I only made it another step before something cracked against the back door. Someone was trying to bring it down. If it had been Ghira, her sword would come straight through. Which meant Ghira had another person here, under her control. And she could be anywhere.

We burst outside, Kenzie still wailing.

"Daddy!" she screamed, breaking my heart. I used my free hand to tuck her face into my shoulder.

A feminine voice, vaguely familiar, screamed behind us, and the door gave way with a loud slam. I got a glimpse of Travis's stepsister, holding a shovel, eyes pink. She moved to step over him, and he grabbed her ankle, spilling her on the floor beside him.

He rolled over, grappling with her on the floor. If I could lock Kenzie in the car...

I ran.

Travis, Travis, Travis, my heartbeats shouted as tears stung my eyes. Lose them both, or lose only one. Those were my options. I was nearly to the car when she walked out from behind a tree, face like a slab of marble, completely without emotion, sword held loosely in one hand.

"Finally," Ghira said. "It ends."

CHAPTER SEVENTEEN

Ghira's face didn't show a single emotion. No grief over her husband. No glee at catching up with me. Nothing. It was worse than the other faces she'd shown me. Far worse.

"This is it, human." Her voice sounded... tired. Like she didn't want to be here either. "I have your daughter now. As I promised, if you did not obey." She bowed her head for a second. "Why didn't you obey?"

The air hung heavy between us, charged with tension. The fading light cast long shadows on the sidewalk. Distant sounds from the city clashed with the quiet around us. Too much quiet, with this many houses around.

I slowly shifted Kenzie to my other hip, awkwardly making sure she didn't get anywhere close to the sword I still managed to have a hold on. She snuggled into my shoulder, sensing the gravity of the situation without understanding it. My wounded and exhausted body protested the movement, but it had also been protesting her weight on my other side, so there was no getting out of that.

"I warned you," Ghira said, taking a step toward us, the tip of her sword dragging along the sidewalk.

Kenzie clung to me tighter, her small body trembling against mine.

Every instinct screamed at me to shield her, to put myself between her and any danger. My muscles ached, my side throbbed, but I straightened up, putting on the best front I could.

"Why didn't you obey?" Ghira repeated, her voice a whisper of frustration.

"Because you were going to let a monster free on Earth," I said, my voice stronger than I felt. "Would Kenzie have been safe growing up here with Kienthall doing whatever he wanted, to whoever he wanted?"

A flicker of something passed over Ghira's face. Respect? Understanding? It vanished too quickly to be sure, leaving me to wonder about the emotions hidden behind her stoic exterior.

"How did you defeat him?" she asked. "How? Fae are far superior to humans. You shouldn't have been able to touch him. Where did the light come from?"

I shrugged.

Anger covered her face then. She thought I knew, but wasn't telling her. I did have an idea, thanks to Wenslo, but I didn't even know if he was right or not.

"You don't understand the plans you've destroyed," she said, her voice gaining strength. "This is bigger than you, bigger than me. Kienthall was supposed to start a great work. There are others who will be greatly displeased with you for what you have done. You will die for the choices you made."

"I don't care," I shot back. "All I care about is keeping my daughter safe."

Behind me, the scuffle in the house had grown quiet. Bile rose in my throat. Was Travis dead? He'd never hurt an innocent person, and though Natalie wasn't innocent in general, she didn't deserve this.

But Travis was protecting Kenzie. And he would do anything for Kenzie. Until I knew otherwise, I was going to believe he was alive.

I backed away from Ghira slowly, not daring to turn my back on the open doorway, unsure who would come out. And of the color of their eyes.

Ghira sighed, a sound that carried decades of weariness. "I once had a daughter," she said, soft enough I almost didn't catch it. "I failed to protect her. I see the same determination in your eyes that I once had in mine."

I hesitated, caught off guard. Was that genuine sorrow in her eyes? It was hard to tell, hard to see past everything she'd done to me in the last few days.

Before I could respond, the sound of approaching sirens shattered the tense silence. The neighbors must have called the cops. *No, no, no.* My heart raced, thoughts spinning out of control.

If they got here and she took control of one of them, it would be the warehouse all over again, only worse because the cops showing up here weren't expecting to go up against a fae murderer like the team I'd helped lead earlier.

I sat Kenzie down, feeling her eyes on me, filled with a terror no child should know. Her face, framed by the dimming light, would haunt me forever. She put her arms up, wanting me to take her back into mine.

"Honey," I said, my voice trembling despite my efforts to sound calm. "I need you to do something."

"What, Mama?" she sniffled, tears brimming her eyes.

"When I say so, I need you to run. As fast as you can. Find someone to help you, other than Daddy or Aunt Natalie, okay?"

"Why not Daddy?"

Ouch. "Daddy might be hurt. I need you to find someone else, okay? Someone your age." The thought made me sick. I'd seen far too many things happen to children, things that shouldn't happen to anyone. But the chance of something happening to her with someone else was much less than the fact of what was about to happen here. At least if she found someone her age, they would have a parent around. I could trust another parent. I had no choice.

Ghira had paused, staring us down, but not moving forward. She was letting me say goodbye.

I looked back down into Kenzie's watery eyes. Her lip had popped out, which meant she was about to refuse me. "None of that," I said, voice stern. I didn't want that tone to be the last thing my daughter remembered from me, but if she lived to remember, that would have to be enough. "Mommy loves you. Are you ready?"

She nodded slowly, her small form a silhouette against the twilight.

I spun her around, steadying her. "Go!" I yelled.

She ran, her small figure quickly swallowed by the shadows. Pride and terror battled inside me as I watched her for a second, then turned back to face Ghira.

"You've only delayed the inevitable," Ghira said, face toward the ground. "A fae cannot break their word. Your daughter must die by my hand."

I filed that bit of info to think about later, if there was a later. "I helped you with the portal," I answered, my hand trembling on the hilt of my sword. Would the will-o-wisp help me again, if it came to that? I didn't know. "I fulfilled my end of the bargain."

"You had a plan to stop me. You weren't truly cooperating. My hands are tied," she said, finally looking up. Her eyes met mine, cold and unyielding. "I'm almost sorry. Your daughter seems sweet. I can give you one last kindness. You won't be here to see it happen."

And then she lunged at me, sword raised.

I acted on instinct, dodging to the side. The blade nicked my arm, but I ignored the pain and shifted my stance. We faced each other, Ghira hesitating. This hadn't ended well for me in the past. But this time I might have help. If I could control the will-o-wisp.

"What?" I snarled. "Willing to attack me when I don't have any chance of winning? Willing to chase down an innocent child who can't defend herself? But scared of me now that you know I'm far more powerful than you'd ever guessed?"

Her face hardened again, and she rammed her sword forward.

Mine met hers, the metal clashing and ringing across the street, overpowering the sound of sirens.

This fight was different. She was the one on the defensive, even though she was still obviously much more of a swordsman than I was. I pushed, using her wariness to my advantage. I wouldn't use the will-o-wisp here, where anyone could see or film what happened, unless I had to. And if I had to, I'd deal with the consequences. I could spend my life being poked and prodded if it meant my daughter lived.

We continued to exchange blows, each of us looking for an easy opening. She was wearing me down. Not that it took much. My vision swam, muscles trembling. I jumped back, and Ghira paused, not pressing the advantage.

"Don't make me kill you," I got out. It sounded tough, but I didn't have anything left to follow through on the threat. I wasn't even angry anymore. Just tired. So tired. I poked at the will-o-wisp with all the feeling I had left, but it didn't respond. Had fighting Kienthall been too much for it? I hadn't felt its warmth since the serial killer's den.

"I'm beginning to think you can't," Ghira answered, not even winded. "I can't control you, or your daughter, but I'm beginning to see that you can't control yourself either."

Wait, she couldn't control Kenzie? Of course she couldn't, or she'd have just made her come back. Had the will-o-wisp protected my daughter as well as me?

A screen door creaked behind me.

"Ma'am?" a voice I didn't recognize asked. I glanced over to see a bent-over senior citizen, dressed in shorts and slippers. "Just hold on. The police'll be here any minute."

"Get back inside," I yelled at the kind old fellow. Not that he would be much of a threat if Ghira sent him against me, but I didn't want to hurt him.

I looked back at Ghira, and the side of her mouth turned up in a creepy smile.

Shuffling footsteps came at me from behind. I slid to the side, where I could see both Ghira and her new minion.

"Paul!" an old woman called from inside the house. "Get back in here! Paul!"

He just tottered forward, eyes glowing pink.

The front door of the house next to theirs opened, and a young Latino stuck his head out. "Mr. Tate. Get back inside, Mr. Tate. You can tell that woman is no good, just looking at her."

Another face joined his at the door, peeking out below her big brother. "Is it? Is it one of those fae?"

Mr. Tate ignored them, moving over to grab a rock out of his yard.

I turned back to Ghira. "Don't do this. Please. They aren't any threat to you."

"But you are," Ghira snarled back.

With a flick of her eyes, the door to the neighbor's house flew open, and the teenage boy stepped out with a baseball bat, the pink of his eyes standing out against his skin.

"Don't make me hurt them," I begged Ghira. If I could stall her, help would be here any minute.

"Make you hurt them?" Ghira's voice had gone sickly sweet. "Of course not."

The boy reached into the house and drug his little sister out by the hair. She screamed and flailed, crying as she fought back.

"Let's see if you care about other little girls as much as you care about your own." She lifted an eyebrow, and the teen lifted the bat.

"No!" I couldn't stop the shriek that went out of me. I ran for the siblings. A huge man burst out of a house across the street, nearly flying across the road and hitting both kids with a hard tackle. I drooped in relief. I would have never made it in time. Doors opened, up and down the street, people of all ages moving outside with makeshift weapons. Several went to help wrestle the teen to the ground, while others formed a wall between them and Ghira and me.

I teared up in relief at the moment of rest. The cop in me wanted to yell at everyone to get out of the area. To go back inside, and wait to see what happened. But I couldn't do this alone.

A small woman with bright red hair pushed through the others and came to stand by me. "Your daughter is safe," she said.

The words nearly sent me to the ground. I couldn't blame anyone for not stepping in to help me earlier. But if people weren't willing to help a three-year-old...

"Thank you," I whispered.

"This changes nothing!" Ghira screamed. "It just gives me more pawns to play with!"

The huge guy behind me had forced the bat away from the kid. But suddenly it was him charging in my direction, plowing through his neighbors to get at me, causing screams as people were thrown to the ground.

I sidestepped, letting him blow past me.

The only way I'd be able to stop a man of that size was with a weapon. Permanent damage, if not death. He turned back toward me, eyes scared behind the pink. I couldn't. He had family too, somewhere. He'd come out here to help. He'd very likely saved my life, or the life of the teen. If the will-o-wisp could protect me, and Kenzie... My side heated faintly, like I hadn't felt since I'd blasted the door. A strange mix of relief and fear hit me. It was still there.

Obviously fighting against himself, the big guy took a step toward me.

"That's enough," I said loudly. "The same power that protects me, now protects these people too. You can't control any of them."

Ghira's face screwed up, like she didn't believe me. I didn't know if I believed me. But light burst from my body, creating a dome over all of us, extremely bright now that the sun had completely set. Then the dome disintegrated into sparks that floated down from the sky like a firework with no heat or sound.

Everyone went quiet, looking up as the light drifted down.

I kept my gaze on the big guy. He blinked, his eyes flickering between pink and brown.

It was working. Somehow, it was working.

The first cop car skidded around a corner.

Ghira curled up a lip, nearly feral as she stared me down. "This isn't over. Watch your back." She spun and took off, disappearing into the growing dark.

I stood there for a moment, stunned, trying to process what had just happened. I was still alive. She'd run. Ghira had run. But there wasn't time to stand around thinking about that. Travis was still inside, possibly hurt, and Kenzie was... I looked around wildly for the woman who'd told me that she knew where Kenzie was earlier.

I scanned the chaotic scene while shrinking my sword and sticking it back in my ear, searching for the woman with bright red hair who had spoken of Kenzie. Panic knotted in my stomach. Where was she? Where was my daughter?

The street was a blur of motion and noise, neighbors talking in hushed, urgent tones, many looking in my direction, police officers securing the area. More people poured out of the houses lining the street. I pushed through the crowd, my eyes darting from face to face, desperately looking for that flash of red hair.

"Excuse me!" I called out, trying to catch anyone's attention. But everyone was too caught up in their conversations. "Excuse me!" People looked at me, but backed away. I wouldn't get any help from them, not after they'd seen me do something weird.

Finally I spotted the woman, standing a few feet away, talking to a police officer. I rushed over, my heart pounding.

"Where's Kenzie? You said she was safe," I blurted out, my voice sharper than it should have been.

The woman turned to me, her expression calm. She reached forward and squeezed my arm. "She's down with Saidie." She pointed to a house a few doors down. "My teenage daughter. Your girl is scared, but seems fine."

"There are people in there," I pointed toward Natalie's house. "They're hurt. I don't even know if they're still alive." I fought back tears, thinking of Travis, broken on the floor.

The cop nodded and reached for his radio. "We're going to need to ask you some questions," the officer said.

I didn't wait for another word. I sprinted toward the house she'd pointed out, my breaths coming in short, sharp gasps. Reaching the door, I knocked frantically, each thud of my fist echoing my racing heart. I tried the handle when I didn't get an immediate answer. Locked. I pounded on the door again.

The woman with red hair stepped up beside me. "It's okay. It's me," she yelled through the door.

The lock clicked on the other side. A teenage girl with chopped off hair, the bottom layer dyed black and top platinum blonde, threw open the door and jumped her mom. "I thought you were dead for sure!"

"Kenzie?" I asked, trying to peer past them into the house, impatiently waiting through their little reunion.

The woman tugged her daughter to the side, allowing me to enter. I rushed into the house.

There, in the living room, huddled on the couch with a stuffed animal clutched tightly in her arms, was Kenzie. Her eyes, wide and filled with tears, met mine. She flew off the couch and in an instant, she was in my arms, her small body trembling.

"Mommy!" she sobbed, burying her face in my neck.

I held her close, my own tears mingling with hers. "It's okay, baby. You're safe now. Mommy's here." I slumped down, nearly crushing her, needing to squeeze her more than I'd ever needed anything in the world.

After a few moments of clutching her tightly against me, I gently pulled back to look at her. "Are you hurt?" I searched for any sign of injury.

Kenzie shook her head, her grip on me never loosening. "I was scared," she whispered.

"I know, sweetheart. I know." I kissed her forehead, relief flooding through me now that she was in my arms. I gave her another squeeze.

"Daddy?" Kenzie asked.

My heart shattered. I didn't know. I didn't have an answer to her question. "Let's go find out." I stood, lifting her with me and staggering a bit.

"She can stay here," the red-haired woman offered. "Until you do what you gotta do."

I clutched Kenzie tighter. The woman meant no harm. But this girl wasn't leaving my sight. Not with Ghira out there somewhere. "Thank you for the offer. But no." I walked toward the door, Kenzie snuggled in close. Once out on the porch I paused, turning back. "But thank you. Thank you so much. I'll be grateful forever. If you ever need anything, go to any station, and ask for Officer Nofsky. They'll get a hold of me, and I'll do whatever I can for you."

Then, with Kenzie in my arms, I stepped back out into the street. The entire thing was now filled with police cars and curious onlookers.

More sirens were on the way.

Hopefully an ambulance.

I hiked Kenzie back up on my hip, pushing myself even harder. I had to find out about Travis. I had to know.

I worked myself between people over to Natalie's house. There were extra cops out in front, and the crowd was thicker. The neighborhood all knew something bad had happened here but didn't know what.

Pausing, I peered between two of Natalie's neighbors to get a look at the officer at the door. A cop I didn't know. Not unusual. There were way too many of us in the city for me to know every single one. The question was, would he recognize me.

Probably. Which would be fine, unless Ghira was actually still here, hiding in the shadows.

I shivered, looking around. But everyone had normal looking eyes. At least the ones close enough for me to see.

After a second of assessing, I filtered the rest of the way through the crowd to the front. The officer already had tape up. I moved to slip under it, but he stopped me.

"Hey. Hey there, stop," he stepped between me and the house. "We've got injured. Waiting on an ambulance."

An ambulance. Someone was still alive. "This is my sister-in-law's place. One of the injured people is my husband."

His face softened, and he lifted the tape. I ducked under. Good. So far I hadn't had to play the cop card.

"I can't let you in, but we'll see if we can get an update." He led the way up onto the porch and into the light. Kenzie kept quiet, snuggled in close.

I felt the officer stop, and looked over. He had his hand on his gun. I panicked, checking his eyes, but they were normal.

"You're the one that robbed the museum," the cop said.

"Yes, but I'm off the hook for that. Check with Captain Harlow at the Foothill Community Police Station. Tell her we need to talk." He eyed me for a second, but apparently with a toddler on my hip and me swaying with exhaustion, I didn't look like much of a flight-risk. "Do you know anything about what happened inside?" I nodded toward the house.

"No, ma'am. I'm sorry." He turned and popped his cell off the holster on his belt.

While he was distracted, I slipped past him toward the front door of the house. He didn't expect me to take off in that direction, apparently, because I went right by him. I tried putting Kenzie down, but she wouldn't have any of that, clinging to me like a barnacle.

I didn't want her to see what might be just inside. I turned her into my shoulder, and put a hand on the back of her head, just in case. "Travis?" I yelled through the door frame. Was he alive? Could he hear me? "Travis!" This time it came out frantic, pained. I held my breath, praying for an answer, too scared to go any farther and find out what had really happened.

CHAPTER EIGHTEEN

Exhaustion washed over me as the adrenaline started to fade. My arm throbbed where Ghira's blade had nicked it, and my side ached with a dull, persistent pain. I leaned heavily against the doorframe, closing my eyes.

He was dead. He wasn't answering. I couldn't take my daughter in there. Couldn't have her see... I didn't know what.

"Jayla?"

Travis's voice snapped me out of my haze. "Travis?" I yelled, shoving my way through the front door.

"Living room," he called back, voice hoarse.

I shoved past two officers in the hallway, rounding the wall that separated the hallway from the living room in a rush. Travis was there, in a folding chair against the wall.

"Daddy!" Kenzie yelled, wiggling to get free.

I set her down and we ran at Travis together. It wasn't until I was close that I noticed his hands, cuffed behind his back. I stopped beside him, and he looked up. His face was bruised, lip bloody. His eyes were rimmed in red, like he'd been crying.

"Are you hurt?" I asked. He would know I meant more than just his face.

"No," he whispered. "Natalie's dead."

No.

I dropped to my knees beside him, pulling his head down into my chest. His body shook with new tears. I wanted to ask how, but I didn't. I looked up at the closest officer for confirmation. I recognized him from shared training with another station. He nodded, making my heart shatter.

I didn't know Natalie. I hardly cared about Natalie. But she died helping our family. Had she known the danger when she'd agreed to keep Kenzie? She couldn't have. Even Travis hadn't truly known.

"I killed her," Travis got out, voice muffled.

I pulled him in tighter, not knowing what to say. There was nothing I could say.

"Daddy." Kenzie tugged on Travis's shirt.

"It's okay, baby," I wrapped an arm around Kenzie, pulling her into our hug. "Daddy is having a very bad day." I looked over her head to the officers watching us. "Can we get him out of these cuffs, please?"

The officers shared a look.

"Come on. This is stupid." I leaned back from Travis. He bumped me with the toe of his boot and gave me a little half smile, shaking his head.

He was right. Of course he was right. I couldn't be one of those family members that kept the police from doing their jobs. If they didn't know about Ghira, then this all looked bad for Travis. Really bad.

"Call my captain," I snapped. "Let me talk to her, she'll tell you." Fear tried to shove its way up into my heart. I shoved it back down. It wasn't as hard a shove as it should have been, my soul was emotionally exhausted. "Captain Harlow. She's... okay, right?" Had Ghira taken another person from me? Was Grayson okay? Agent Bylilly? A flood of bile started up my throat. Was anyone else dead because of my decisions?

"I'm okay."

I jerked toward the voice. Yes. It was her. The captain was here. This time a tear did break free. I wiped at my face with my shoulder, arms still holding my little family.

The captain walked into the room, another person behind her I didn't recognize. She looked absolutely exhausted. Probably almost as bad as I looked. And it wasn't the physical exhaustion that caused a soul to feel like this. She gestured toward the woman who'd entered with her. "This is Utica. She's our official liaison with... whatever agency the federal government is cooking up to deal with the fae."

Utica gave her a disapproving glare. She was exactly what I would expect an agent of some shadow organization to look like. Dark suit, hair up tight, grumpy expression on her face.

"The hold dropped as soon as that man took you and Ghira away from us," the captain continued. "Bylilly is going to be fine too." She looked at the floor. "We lost Grant and Havers."

Two more people to hate Ghira because of. Two more to feel guilty about. The team at the warehouse had been mostly federal agents, but two of our officers had been there just to guard the doors. They should have been safe. "How did you get here this fast?" I asked.

"As soon as I heard there were two women fighting in the street using swords, I knew it had to be you. I started this way. Just got here because of traffic."

LA was weird. But swordplay wasn't normal, even here. "Grayson?" I asked.

"He's in bad shape, Nofsky." She sighed and closed her eyes for a second. "They think he's going to live. But I doubt he'll ever serve again."

Alive. I could deal with anything else, help him get through anything else. He was alive.

"She escaped," I whispered. I didn't have to say who. She knew.

The captain jerked her head toward Travis, and one of the officers jumped forward to unlock his handcuffs. Once they snapped free, Travis rubbed his wrists for a second, then pulled Kenzie tight to him. Normally she would have wiggled away, but not today.

The captain waved over the officer who'd just freed Travis. She leaned in close, but I could still hear her. "Get those pictures from the body cams at the warehouse out in circulation now. Everyone needs to be on high alert."

"Are you sure you want to do that?" Utica said.

"I don't care what you want to tell regular people, mine will be prepared. If you aren't going to let me share the footage to prove what this fugitive can do, at the very least you can let me have a plan in place for finding the fae and getting you the information, then letting you take her down."

The two of them stood eye-to-eye for a moment, staring each other down. But the captain won.

"Okay," Utica relented. "If you give them orders not to engage."

"Trust me," the captain answered. "I don't want any more casualties. We know when we're outmatched. You'll get a call as soon as she pops up somewhere."

"Are we free to go?" I interrupted, barely able to string the words together. "It's been a really long day. We just want to go home."

Travis stood, his warm presence behind me making me feel safe. At least, safer. Kenzie shifted restlessly, and Travis picked her up.

Both the captain and Utica swung to stare me down. I liked it much better when they were glaring at each other. "Home? You really think it's safe for any of you to go home?" Utica asked.

She was right. Of course she was right. This wasn't over. But where would we go?

"We'll put you in witness protection," the captain said. "Just until this all gets straightened out."

"We'll need full access," Utica interrupted. "And we have better resources. We could get them out of the city."

Too much. This was too much right now, I couldn't handle it. I'd lost track of how many times I'd almost died over the last few days, let alone how many times I'd almost lost someone I cared about. I needed to get away from Ghira. But the place didn't need to be permanent right away.

"A safe house here provided by the captain until we can get rested up," I interrupted. "Two days max. And we'll use that time to figure out something for the future."

The captain and Utica eyed each other for a moment, then both nodded.

"Scratch that," I said. "We'll be given money and a phone, and I'll find us a safehouse. If Ghira gets to anyone who knows where we are, she can get it out of them.”

The captain grimaced, but she couldn't argue. She knew.

“Officer Nofsky, someone needs–”

“No,” the captain cut Utica off. “If I have to give her my own money, I'll do it. Nothing is coming from the department with strings attached. She knows more about this threat than anyone.”

“Which is exactly why we need to know where she is at all times,” Utica argued.

I left them to argue, looking back at Travis. “Are you sure you aren't hurt anywhere? Do we need to go to the hospital?”

“Hospital?” Kenzie repeated, looking over at me with her big eyes.

“No, I'm fine,” Travis said. “I just need a shower, and then a hot bath.” He waited until I looked at him, then held my gaze. “How long do you think you'll be in witness protection? Will we get to see you?”

Normally he caught onto things faster than I did. He really was in shock. The redness around his eyes had faded some, but the dullness… that wasn't Travis. At all. “It isn't just me going into witness protection, Trav,” I said gently. “You and Kenzie are going to have to be protected too. And there's no one on Earth that can guarantee your safety if you're somewhere she can find you.”

He blinked for a moment. “Right. I'll make a list of things I need from the house.” He popped out his phone, typing with one hand while holding Kenzie close with his other arm.

Of course he'd pull himself together. He'd always been the rock in our relationship. Every fight, every squabble we'd had that led to us being separated seemed petty now.

“They can find us different places to stay,” I offered, swallowing the statement that wanted to come out after that. “You know. If you don't want to be with me.” I held my breath, waiting for his answer. I'd never rest if they were in a different location than me.

“No,” he said. “We're in this together.” He went back to his phone, in-charge mode activated. It had bothered me before, when he took charge of a situation. But right in this moment, I didn't want to have to make another decision for a month.

I slid down into an old ratty recliner against the wall. From this angle, I could just see the top of Natalie's head down the hallway, lying on the bloody floor tile. I closed my eyes against the tears. I felt my side for my little parasite, but there wasn't any heat.

Had I killed it, asking so much of it in the last few hours? If I had, that was a good thing, right? Who wanted a parasite living inside them?

I did. If it protected my family from Ghira.

The sounds of arguing faded as I leaned back farther into the chair. We were safe, just for this moment. Ghira never had attacked this many people at once, that I knew of. She'd handled things in the warehouse, but she'd avoided larger conflict as much as she could, to the point she'd fought with Kienthall over it.

Somehow, we'd survived. My body went cold, and all of the blows she rained down on me earlier came rushing to the front of my consciousness. Every nick, every punch.

Good thing I was sitting down. The room spun. I tried to hold it together, but didn't last long before I gave up and passed out.

CHAPTER NINETEEN

Two days. My two days were up.

I'd spent the last forty-eight hours recovering. And checking on my daughter every thirty seconds. Travis and I had fallen back into an easy routine. Somewhere much better than how we'd left things, but nowhere close to how we'd been in the early days.

Just friends. And co-parents. But I couldn't help but see him in a different light.

My phone buzzed. I checked the screen as I walked. The text was from an unknown number.

'I am still owed. I will be in touch. Mr. A.'

Great. I did still owe a gangster. With everything that had happened since I'd met with him, him helping me had completely slipped my mind. It shouldn't matter at this point. I wasn't going to be around town much longer. But it did matter. I settled my debts.

I should be avoiding anywhere, anyone, or anything that Ghira might use to find me. But there was one stop I had to make before I left LA.

The steady beep of machines greeted me as I walked down the sterile hospital hallway. I scanned the room numbers until I found the one the nurse had given me. Taking a deep breath, I gently knocked on the door before easing it open.

"Grayson?" I called softly. I didn't even know if he wanted to see me or not. I'd almost gotten him killed. More than once. No one would tell me much about his condition, other than he wasn't going to die.

They were probably trying to keep me from doing anything stupid. Like visit him in the hospital.

My partner lay propped up in the hospital bed, covered in a thick layer of blankets. Depending on how he was feeling, that would be something to tease him about. He always pretended he wasn't cold, because it was only old people who were cold all of the time. His face was pale and drawn, dark circles under his closed eyes.

I moved over to the bed, pulling a chair in close.

The scraping of the chair legs made Grayson startle awake. His eyes were wide, panicked, for just a second before he figured out it was just me. Then he managed a weak smile. "Hey Jay. Wasn't sure I'd see you again. I hear you're supposed to be disappeared." He sounded like he was teasing, but I could tell it bothered him. He'd always been an overprotective partner. "I thought the warehouse might be where we said goodbye."

"You aren't getting rid of me that easy," I answered, my tone light. But we both knew it was fake. We sat there in silence for a second before I couldn't take it anymore. "I'm so sorry," I said, my voice monotone so I didn't start crying. "I didn't want to leave you there. But Kienthall-"

Grayson shook his head. "It wasn't like you had a choice. And then after you were free, going after Kenzie? If it was T.J., I'd have done the same thing. You are going to have to tell me the whole story someday though." He winced. "Maybe not today."

Just like that? He was going to forgive me that easily? Too bad it was much more difficult to forgive myself. An uneasy silence fell between us. The steady beep of the heart monitor filled the room.

"How is she? Kenzie?" Grayson asked.

"She's okay," I answered. "Partially thanks to you. Travis too. We're hiding out until the government can decide what to do with us."

Grayson's face clouded at the mention of Travis. There was no love lost between them. That was mostly my fault. All those hours sitting in a patrol car. Grayson had heard my side many, many times.

"For now we're all staying together. For Kenzie's sake," I added.

Grayson nodded, though his jaw was tight.

Time for a change in subject. "What have the doctors said? How are you healing up?"

At that, Grayson glanced away. "Not sure I'll ever be back on the beat," he said quietly. "The bullet did a lot of damage. Shattered my femur. Nerve damage. Doc says I'll walk again, but always with a limp."

My heart broke, and every part of the peace I'd found in the last few minutes dissolved. He'd wanted out, but not like this. All of the things he'd planned to do in retirement... "I'm so sorry," I whispered, squeezing his hand.

We sat in silence for a few minutes. The weight of Grayson's devastating prognosis hung over anything else I could come up with to talk about.

"Are you going after her?" Grayson finally asked. "I'm starting to think you're the only person who can."

No. I couldn't. The will-o-wisp hadn't lit up since two days ago, when it had saved me from Ghira, out in the street. It was strange how quickly the thing had started feeling normal to me. The little bursts of heat were gone as well. Without it, I was just as susceptible to Ghira as anyone else. "I think she's had enough," I told Grayson. "She probably went back to Faerie."

He lifted an eyebrow. "Without a portal?"

"She's really good at making things happen. Maybe she went to Indiana. It looks like there's a whole colony of fae there now." More of them. Hundreds, even. Were they all like the fae I'd met? Wenslo had been selfish, but hadn't felt like a murderer. But the others...

Grayson just shook his head, his eyes distant. He looked old. I'd teased him about his age before, but I'd never truly thought he would ever retire. Now... his injuries had taken a toll. His upbeat humor was gone, replaced by a bone-deep weariness.

I stood, shoving the chair back. I shouldn't have come. I shouldn't have risked it, shouldn't have dragged him back through such raw memories, barely starting to heal. I'd left the warehouse right away that day, I hadn't had a choice, with Kienthall flinging us all over the city, but Grayson had lain there in the middle of all of the dying agents, waiting for help.

"You just focus on getting better, okay?" I said.

Grayson attempted a smile that didn't reach his eyes. "Watch yourself out there, Jay. Don't do anything stupid."

I didn't answer as I stepped out of the room. The truth was, if I ever got the chance to take Ghira down, I was going to do whatever it took. She had threatened my family and destroyed my partner's life. She killed without remorse, burning to the ground anything in her way.

My new basic burner phone rang, startling me enough I almost fell off the curb outside the hospital. I still hadn't gotten over being jumpy. I checked the phone screen. The station.

"Hello," I said into the phone, not identifying myself. Just in case.

"Nofsky," the captain said. "We brought someone in. He's refusing to talk with anyone but you."

My heart dropped before my brain caught up and I registered that the person who wanted to talk was a he. Unless Kienthall had come back from the dead, I didn't have any real problems with any men right now. "Tell him it's too bad," I said. "I'm not coming in."

"He insists he has information that could help you." The captain's tone softened. "I know it's risky, but I think it may be worth it."

There wasn't anyone worth putting Kenzie in danger for. Without the will-o-wisp, even I could be forced to hurt her.

"He says he can help you with Ghira," the captain continued. "And I'm inclined to believe him. He's a friend of yours."

"A friend of mine?" I didn't have any friends. Well, I'd found out I had a few. But I didn't have any who could help me with a crazy fae woman who wanted me and my family dead.

"At least someone who's helped you before. It's the guy who robbed the museum."

The guy from the museum. Another fae, just using people to get what he wanted. Though at least he did seem to have a little respect for human life.

Wenslo.

CHAPTER TWENTY

Coming back to my normal was odd. Beyond odd, bizarre. The station was exactly the same as the last time I'd been here. I was the one who was different.

The captain met me at the back door, the one set up for prisoner transfer. She used her badge to open the locked door and held it open for me. I walked past her, inside.

"Have any idea what this guy wants with you?" the captain asked. She didn't go for any pleasantries. We'd been doing update phone calls every three hours anyway.

"No," I answered truthfully. I'd thought that I'd never see him again. We'd tried what he wanted to do, and failed. He should be half way back to Faerie right now. If he even lived there. "Does anyone else know I'm here?"

"No." The captain unlocked another door. This one led to the temporary holding cells we had to keep prisoners in until they could be transferred. "I made sure everyone was out of this area. Busy day, you know?"

Of course she'd taken care of it. But I still couldn't stop looking over my shoulder. This was the first time I'd been in public since the showdown on the street, not counting my quiet trip to the hospital right before this. Grocery delivery was an amazing thing.

The captain led me over to holding cell two, then stepped back, letting me move in close to the bars. On the other side, Wenslo rested casually against the concrete wall.

"I gotta say," I leaned in against the bars to get a better look at him. "I was surprised when the captain called and said you'd been brought in."

Wenslo opened his eyes and grinned, shoving off the wall and meandering over to the bars. "How else was I supposed to find you? You inconveniently went into hiding."

Of course. I should have known. I crossed my arms, staring him down through the bars. "What do you want?" He'd helped me a few times, but he'd disappeared when I'd needed him the most. And that whole thing with the bracelet? It hadn't been to help me at all. He'd just wanted to control Ghira.

He held up his hands in a placating gesture that looked completely out of place. "Just to talk. We need to figure out some things." He lifted an eyebrow, pointedly staring down the captain.

She checked with me, and I nodded. Wenslo had never shown any signs of wanting to do me harm.

The captain walked to the other side of the room.

"No, no, Captain," Wenslo said, in a sing-song. "You can go to your cameras, but if you want my help, you're going to have to get out of earshot."

The captain, not used to being told what to do, looked more frustrated than I'd ever seen her. But she obeyed, walking out of the room and closing the door behind her.

Wenslo grabbed the cell bars and leaned in close, coming down to my height. "She's still out there."

I gritted my teeth. "I'm well aware."

"I sided against her," he continued. "Neither of us is safe until she's handled. Permanently." He pulled a slip of paper from his pocket. "This is my new number. They are tracking my old one by now. Give me a day, and then get in touch."

Slowly, I reached forward, taking the paper.

After I'd taken it, he leaned in close again. "We have important work still to do, if you want to save your world." Then he stood up straight and held out his hand. The lock clicked, and he gave the door a slight push.

It popped open, and he walked out.

I stepped back, not really surprised, but also not knowing what to do.

He started for the row of lockers against the wall. "Your captain is probably at the video cameras by now. I'll take my leave."

My hand instinctively went to my side. "Wait," I said.

He paused.

"The will-o-wisp. It helped me against Kienthall, and then against Ghira. But I haven't felt it since then. And I haven't seen it glow."

He cocked his head, considering. "I don't know much of will-o-wisps. But I hypothesize that the amount of energy you channeled through it was beyond its capacity. You may have damaged or even killed it."

My breath caught. I was torn. To not have a strange parasite growing inside of me should only be a good thing. But in this case... "So the protection for Kenzie..."

"May be gone," he shrugged.

I sagged against the bars. If the wisp was gone, my daughter was vulnerable again. Vulnerable to a monster who wanted her dead. And there wasn't anything I could do about it.

"Is there any way to tell if it's still there? Still alive?" I hated the note of desperation in my voice. I scrubbed a hand down my face. The only way to shield my daughter, ripped away.

"I'm afraid fae knowledge of wisps is limited." Wenslo looked actually sorry. "They are...unpredictable creatures." He studied my face for a moment, then sighed. He took the last couple steps over to the lockers and held up his hand. The lock flashed, and he opened the locker marked cell two. He took stuff out and slipped it into his pockets, then turned and held something out to me. A small totem carved out of wood, but very old. It was possibly Native American, though I didn't know much about history. "This was the reason we were separated in the museum. I went and took this, to protect myself from Ghira. It shields the mind." He turned and started for the door again.

"What about you?" I asked.

"I'll find another. There has to be something else in this world that was made to combat the fae." He paused at the exit. "Don't let your friends find that. They'll take it from you. I wouldn't blame them. They need all the help they can get against Ghira, but it's not meant for them."

He was right. Bylilly would snatch it in a second. I slipped it into my pocket, running a finger down it.

He nodded toward the camera. "I think the captain is finding out right now that cameras don't always work well on the fae."

That was good. No video evidence that he'd given me something. I was already going to have to explain why Wenslo had wanted me here, and that would be fun enough.

A thought struck me. "Why didn't you just unlock the doors back in the museum then? Why did you make me go with you?"

Wenslo glanced over his shoulder, eyes laughing. "Where's the fun in that?" Then he vanished around the corner, leaving me standing there alone, lost.

I didn't feel like getting asked a bunch of questions right now. Especially when I didn't have answers to those questions. So I said a nearly silent apology to the captain, and took off for the exit before she got back.

The little white car I'd rented was there waiting for me. I wouldn't risk an Uber driver's life. Anyone close to me right now was at risk. I'd had a car delivered the same night we'd gotten into the safe house. Today was the first time I'd driven it. Kind of a waste to just pay for it to sit in the drive, but there was no way I was going to leave us without an escape plan.

I slid behind the wheel and peeled out, flying out of the parking lot and onto the road.

The streets of LA blurred past as I drove, my knuckles white on the steering wheel.

Seeing Wenslo had raised more questions than it had given answers. I still didn't know if I could trust him. But he could very well be the only thing that could stop Ghira. I reached into my pocket and clutched the totem for a second, reassuring myself that it was there. Ghira couldn't control me when I had it. I had to believe Wenslo on that, or I'd go crazy.

With a deep breath, I forced my fingers to relax. It would be dumb to get pulled over right now. I eased my foot off the pedal, just a little. I needed a distraction. And though I didn't really want to, I needed to check in on my dad. We hadn't spoken since I'd left the panicked voicemail warning him to get out of town. I pulled out my new burner phone and typed in his number. I didn't have any numbers saved in it, just in case.

"Hello?" My dad's familiar voice washed over me.

"Hey, Dad. It's me."

"Jayla!" He sounded relieved. "Are you alright? Where have you been?"

I grimaced. Our relationship hadn't been good since I'd left Travis. Really, it hadn't been that great ever, but it had taken a serious turn then. Right now though, he only sounded like he cared. "I'm okay. Just dealing with a difficult case right now. The perp threatened my family. I wanted to make sure you're safe."

"I'm fine. What about you? Travis, Kenzie?"

"We're all good. We might not be able to go back to normal life for awhile though. Things are going to be different until I get everything completely sorted out."

There was silence on the other side of the phone. "Are you going to be okay?"

"Yeah. Yeah, we'll be fine." I had to believe that. If I didn't, I'd live every moment in constant terror. Wenslo and I were going to find a way. We were going to be fine. I didn't say anything about Ghira still on the loose. As far as my dad needed to know, the danger had passed. Hopefully I could keep it that way. "Maybe stay where you're at for a bit. Just in case."

"I'm at home," Dad said, making me nearly grind my teeth in frustration. Why could he never listen? "My people need me. I couldn't stay away without knowing there was a good reason."

"My word isn't a good enough reason?" I ground out. Here he was, caring more about the people of his church than me. Like always.

"Jayla. Your word is everything. But I'm not afraid. Mrs. Peterson lost her husband. And Hailey and Yusef are getting married, they need counseling. What was I supposed to do?"

"You'll do what you think is best," I answered. I wouldn't leave this conversation on too bad a note. Right now, any conversation could be our last. There was no reason to waste my breath on trying to convince him to hide out somewhere until the coast was clear. He never listened to anything I said.

"I love you, Jay."

The anger melted out of me. He wasn't the kind of man that expressed his feelings very often. And he only called me Jay on special occasions. "Love you, too, Dad. Please be careful."

"Who needs to be careful when you've got Someone looking out for you?"

I sighed. We'd had this conversation multiple times. God may be on his side, but He also allowed free choice, which included evil. If Ghira decided to go after my dad, God might not step in. The whole thing was complicated. "Bye, Dad."

"Don't wait so long to call next time," he answered, then ended the call.

By the time I hung up, I was pulling into the nondescript neighborhood that held our safe house. It was just a rental, actually, because I didn't even want friends to know where we were and still hadn't accepted help from the captain or Agent Bylilly.

I eased the car into the driveway beside the SUV Travis was renting. Home. Or the closest thing we had to home right now.

My phone buzzed, and I flipped it open to a text from Bylilly. Time was up. They were going to relocate us soon. And she had a proposition for me, that she only wanted to talk about in person.

Wonderful.

The front door of the house banged open.

"Mommy!" Kenzie catapulted herself off the porch and flew down the walkway, her little arms outstretched.

I jumped out of the car and swept her up, breathing in her sweet scent. "Hi, baby. Were you good for Daddy today?"

She nodded, grinning.

I did a quick visual check of the perimeter while hustling toward the door. "You know you aren't supposed to be outside."

Her lip popped out, and she went into the initial stages of a pout. Outside was her favorite thing, and she hadn't been out since we'd moved in here.

Travis appeared in the doorway, smiling, though it didn't quite reach his eyes. He hadn't shaved yet today, and had a five o'clock shadow. That along with his messy hair, jeans, brand new t-shirt and bare feet? He'd never looked better to me. "Hey. Just in time. I just threw a pizza in the oven."

I blinked back tears. Happy tears, for once. Or maybe bittersweet. We still had a long road ahead of us, but whatever we went through, we could do it. Together.

I nuzzled Kenzie's soft cheek. "Come on, munchkin. Let's go relax and have some pizza with Daddy."

She cheered and wiggled to get down, stampeding into the house. Travis and I shared a real smile, and he held out an arm. I looped it over my shoulders, and we went inside together.

One last check out the door showed no movement. Travis paused while I flipped all the locks, and then we headed for the kitchen where Kenzie had started singing some silly song she'd learned from one of the shows she loved.

Later, I could worry about the future. About Ghira, and the difficult decisions ahead. But for now, I would simply enjoy these moments with the people who mattered most.

EPILOGUE

The bell on the door jangled as I walked into the diner. Now, after all I'd been through in the last week, the greasy smell of bacon and eggs was almost comforting. I spotted Agent Bylilly already seated in a cracked vinyl booth near the back, facing the door. Her eyes tracked me as I wound through the sparse late-night crowd and slid into the seat across from her.

"Thanks for meeting me here," I said.

She nodded, eyes flicking around the room. "Of course. This is as good a place as any."

She probably had no idea why I'd picked this diner. Where I'd been when it all began. Honestly, I didn't even really know. Other than I knew the place, and would notice if something was off.

A tired waitress came over and took our orders. I didn't recognize her. Grayson and I always came in the morning. He couldn't do biscuits and gravy after five o'clock. Acid reflux.

I just ordered a coffee. It would be more terrible than normal, probably having sat around half the day instead of being fresh and terrible, but I couldn't help myself. We were quiet as the waitress left.

The silence lingered a moment, until Bylilly leaned forward, folding her hands on the table. "I want you working for me full time. You've experienced firsthand what we're up against. Your skills would be invaluable."

My skills? We were at a week now, and the will-o-wisp still hadn't warmed at my touch or shown its presence in any way. "I'm not sure I would be much help. I've only dealt with a couple fae."

She leaned in, putting her elbow on the table to support her. "You have more experience than my entire agency combined. None of us know how to deal with the fae. Most of us have never even met one. We're like sitting ducks out there."

I leaned away from her intensity. "You know everything I know. We've had like ten debriefs."

"Knowledge is different than knowing." She tipped back away from me, like she'd just noticed how she was coming across. "You could help save so many people. There are things you'll notice that no one else will. Memories that will be jogged. Other than some of my team getting to know fae in Indiana, we are all in the dark."

The waitress came with my coffee and Bylilly's tea, sat them on the table and then left. I grabbed a packet of sugar and ripped it open, a little more forcefully than I needed to, not meeting her gaze. "I can't. You know I can't have people knowing where I am."

"I understand," she said. "I figured you'd say as much. So I have a proposition." She slid a thick folder across the table. "Cases we could use your help on. You'd be contracted, like a consultant. Work one at a time, on your own terms. Not only will you be helping us, but we'll be helping you. Paying you well enough you can move your family around with you. Protection."

"Your protection didn't do much last time," I said. But I pulled the file over and flipped through the pages, scanning the details. Missing persons, strange murders, suspected fae involvement.

"We don't even know that the fae are involved in any of these. We just need you to take a look, see if something stands out to you. It won't even be like field work. You'll never be in any danger. We're hoping maybe that fae contact of yours, Wenslo, would be willing to be called in as well, as needed."

Wenslo. That was probably a huge part of why they wanted me. I still hadn't called him. I still didn't know if I wanted to.

"You find somewhere safe for your family while you work," Bylilly continued. "We provide any resources you need. When the job's done, you move on. We'll keep an eye out for Ghira. You'll be the first to know if she resurfaces."

It was tempting. The idea of hunting down the fae who hurt people, of helping families find closure... And of finding a way to stop Ghira. To finish what we'd started, so I didn't have to worry about her anymore.

I stirred in a second sugar. The coffee was just as bad as I'd expected. "I'll do it," I finally said. "But my family comes first. If I ever feel they're unsafe, I walk away, no questions asked."

Bylilly nodded. "Of course."

"And I need you to listen to me. If I say no guns, that means no guns."

Bylilly cocked her head. "We will discuss things as they come up, but there is a chain of command for a reason."

As much as I hated the sound of that, it did make sense. After the warehouse, hopefully she'd listen to me in the future. And if she didn't, I'd leave. I tapped the file. "Give me the details on the first case. We'll leave for Fort Wayne soon. Just tell me who to contact when I get there."

A slow smile spread across Bylilly's face. She tossed an ID badge on the table, already made up with my picture and everything. "Welcome aboard, Agent Nofsky."

I grabbed the badge and stared down at it. This was it. A whole new life was about to begin.

ABOUT THE AUTHOR

Growing up, it was impossible to catch Cassie Greutman without a book in her hand, even at the most inappropriate times. Since then with the rise of ebooks, it's only gotten worse. With her full-time job of caring for over thirty horses, some of that has changed to audiobooks, but you can bet there is always some type of story rattling around in her brain. She has always loved stories in any format, whether that is in movie, video game, or book form, and hopes to tell stories that catch a person's imagination and interest like so many have done for her.

As a finalist in the Cinematic Book Competition with Screencraft of more than 1200 entries, five-star ratings with Reader's Favorite, and a win with The Indie Author Project, Cassie has been throwing all of the extra time she has into building worlds for everyone to enjoy. When she isn't stuck in a book, of course.

Follow Cassie on Facebook and TikTok for updates on new stories!

https://www.facebook.com/cassiegreutman/

https://www.tiktok.com/@cassiegreutman

Or join Cassie's newsletter for free short stories in your inbox by going to:

www.cassiegreutman.com

If you'd like early access to stories as I write them and behind the scenes posts, check out:

    https://reamstories.com/page/lh4u19l5l3